Liza Cody grew [...] painting at
the City and Guilds [...] Art School and the Royal
Academy School. She has worked as a painter, furniture-
maker, photographer and graphic designer. Her first
novel, *Dupe*, won the John Creasey Award for the best
first crime novel of 1980 and was nominated for an
Edgar Award in the USA. *Under Contract* was shortlisted
for the Gold Dagger Award and in 1992 *Bucket Nut*, her
most recent novel to date, won the Crime Writers'
Association Silver Dagger Award. Liza Cody now lives in
Somerset.

'Three cheers for a thriller-writer who's turning from
"promising" into "not to be missed".' *Mail on Sunday*

'Cody's always in control; the plots twist and turn . . . the
dialogue rattles like rain on a roof-top; the characters are
defined with a quiet assurance.'
MARIA LEXTON, *Time Out*

'One of out most inventive crime writers.'
CHRISTOPHER PYM, *Punch*

'Fresh, original and spellbinding. A winner'
Kirkus Reviews

'Reeks of authenticity from start to finish . . . Will have
you writhing and reaching for the TCP'
Liverpool Daily Post

'Poverty-stricken Ethiopia and its inhabitants are the
vivid setting for this provocative thriller that showcases
Cody's deft, sparse literary style' *Publishers Weekly*

By the same author

THE ANNA LEE MYSTERIES

Dupe
Bad Company
Stalker
Head Case
Under Contract
Backhand

NOVELS

Bucket Nut

RIFT

Liza Cody

ARROW

Published by Arrow Books in 1994

1 3 5 7 9 10 8 6 4 2

© Liza Cody 1988

First published in the United Kingdom by
William Collins Sons & Co. Ltd., 1988

This edition published by
Arrow Books Limited
20 Vauxhall Bridge Road, London SW1V 2SA

Random House Australia (Pty) Limited
20 Alfred Street, Milsons Point, Sydney,
New South Wales 2061, Australia

Random House New Zealand Limited
18 Poland Road, Glenfield
Auckland 10, New Zealand

Random House South Africa (Pty) Limited
PO Box 337, Bergvlei, South Africa

Random House UK Limited Reg. No. 954009

A CIP catalogue record for this book
is available from the British Library

ISBN 0 09 923121 2

Printed and bound in Great Britain by
Cox & Wyman Ltd, Reading, Berkshire

1

16 FEBRUARY 1974

If you want to drive from Kenya to Ethiopia, the most
direct road is north out of Nairobi, past Mount Kenya,
through Samburu, on beyond Marsabit. Eventually you
will arrive in Moyale. Moyale is a border town and you
must pass through it to get to Ethiopia.

Five small boys ran by the side of the car, and I opened
the window to ask the way to the crossing point.

One of them said, 'Go to the prison.' The rest hung
back.

'Prison?'

'Yes,' he said, holding on to the door handle. He was
bold and very curious. 'Where you going?'

'Ethiopia.'

'Why go there?' he asked, and spat into the dust. 'Is
bad place. Stay here. Are you Christian?'

I was so surprised I merely shook my head.

'Muslim? Jew?'

I shook my head again. I couldn't imagine why he
wanted to know, and having just driven through the desert
worrying all the time about the engine overheating, I was
in no mood to discuss religion.

'You are Pagan,' the boy announced decisively. He let
go of the door handle and spat again.

I drove on slowly. Orange dust swirled up from the
wheels and settled on the car, on my clothes, in my hair.
It smelled of pepper, and like pepper irritated the eyes
and lining of the nose.

Moyale perched on an outcrop of small reddish hills. It
looked as if it had been dropped there from a great height

and broken in two. The southern half was in Kenya, just an untidy collection of huts, houses, and dukkas.

The most solid part of town was around the prison compound, a dusty oblong surrounded by the prison, the warden's house, the police station and customs and immigration. It was deserted. Doors were locked, windows shut tight against the dust, shutters down to keep out the white, vertical sun.

I stopped in the middle of the two-acre yard and got out to stretch my legs. A scrawny, slow-moving dog appeared from nowhere and crawled under the car, where it lay as if dead in the meagre patch of shade.

The water in the plastic bottle was warm and tasted of chlorine tablets. I was too tired and overcooked to eat anything, so I lay across the two front seats and closed my eyes.

Bravado gets you into trouble. It leads to foolhardy actions. It can lead you to Moyale.

Two weeks ago, on the veranda behind Nairobi's YMCA, overlooking the swimming pool, it hadn't seemed such a bad idea. In fact it seemed fresh and exciting. But then it was about seven o'clock and the sun was doing its sudden vanishing act. Bats were making jagged lightning raids on the swimming pool, and crickets sang in the bushes. There was a cool breeze, I remember, and we were drinking beer with two guys who had recently fled Uganda. They were the latest émigrés who spoke wistfully of their homeland and the hardship they had suffered in the fight against tyranny. They both wore beautifully cut lightweight suits and cheerful collars of fat spilled over their identical white nylon shirts. I would like to have known more, but already one of them was eyeing me up in a predatory way, and I knew I had to ration my curiosity.

I moved a little closer to Charles and let him take over the conversation. It was a shift I hoped the Ugandans would notice and that Charles would not.

Charles had been in Kampala during the coup which

had brought Idi Amin to power, and what had been a catastrophe to the Ugandans sounded like an adventure coming from him. He was thirty-three, had been everywhere, and talked with nostalgia about a golden age when you could wander from country to country and barely needed a passport, let alone a visa. On the set he was called Wandering Chas. He was very good-looking.

'Where haven't you been, Chas?' I asked when the Ugandans had gone and we sat alone in the dark.

'Nowhere,' he said, stretching his arms out along the back of the bench. His arm grazed my shoulder and made it tingle. I wondered if it was intentional.

'No, I tell a lie,' he said lazily. 'I haven't been to Ethiopia. No one wants to make movies there for some reason. Ready to eat?'

We drove, in one of the unit cars, to a Chinese restaurant close to the Kenyan House of Parliament. In less than a week's time the car would be returned to the hire firm and the crew would fly back to England. The actors had already gone. All I had to do was help pack and label the costumes. My first feature film was nearly in the can, and in a few months my name would flash past on the credits: *Fay Jassahn, Wardrobe Assistant*. It was almost over but I didn't want to leave. I hadn't had enough of the brilliant sun and the huge domed sky.

'I don't want to leave,' I said, and picked at the chicken and almonds with the tips of my chopsticks. I successfully transferred some to my plate and felt cosmopolitan. A fan in the ceiling stirred the cool air and made the candles flicker. Romance, I thought, was just a step away.

'I'd like to explore the Rift Valley from here to Addis Ababa,' I said. I wanted to impress him, but he said, 'What for? Me, I wouldn't go anywhere I wasn't paid to.'

It's all very well to say things like that if your nickname is Wandering Chas and you are a lighting cameraman who is in demand all over the world. But wardrobe assistants are two a penny and I might not get the chance to come to Africa again.

3

'There's more to life than work,' I said. 'And there's more to Africa than what we saw from the window of an air-conditioned coach.'

'Yes,' he replied, 'and all of it's tough.'

'Beautiful, though.'

'You're a romantic,' he said lazily. In the candlelight I couldn't tell if his smile was complimentary or not, but I continued in the belief that it was.

'I could follow the Rift Valley north,' I sighed dreamily, remembering a bend in the road where we had come across it unexpectedly. The high ground disappeared, quite literally as if the bottom of the world had fallen out, and I had felt as you do when a lift drops suddenly – my stomach rose to my throat and I gasped for breath.

'I wonder if the Rift is the abyss part of Abyssinia,' I went on.

'Don't be daft,' Charles said. 'How would you get around: hitch like a hippy?'

'Of course not. I'd buy a car.' I had been told that a second-hand car doesn't lose its value in Kenya. You could buy a car, take a trip, and then, if you hadn't flattened it against an elephant, you could re-sell the car for what you'd paid. It was like keeping your money in a bank, I'd been told. I had the money. While the others stayed at the PanAfrica Hotel, I was putting up at a Quaker lodging-house for a quarter of the price. Freelance people often had to exchange comfort for hard cash if they are to survive the lean spells.

'You really are a romantic,' Charles said, and this time it was plain that his smile was amused and not at all complimentary.

'All adventurers are romantic,' I said, in a huff. 'Look at T. E. Lawrence.'

'All adventurers are adventurous,' he replied. 'Or daft. You aren't either. Put the idea out of your head. Anyway, what would Tony say if I told him you'd gone off jaunting?'

Tony. I was deflated. This explained the flattering

4

attention I'd received from someone who was quite a big wheel in the film crew. I do not normally attract much attention. And normally I don't want much. I like my position on the edge of big projects where I can play a part but do not have to carry a lot of responsibility. The rewards are not great, but then I don't want to be fabulously rich or a star. On the other hand, there's no doubt that I like to be part of the process that creates wealth and stardom.

'You like the excitement without the risk,' Tony said once, and there was enough truth in that to make me protest.

I protested now to Charles. I said, 'I don't need anyone to keep an eye on me. What on earth makes Tony think I do?'

'He's a good chap,' Charles told me unnecessarily. 'You don't have a lot of experience and he's just trying to be protective. Don't knock it.'

That was the end of the evening as far as I was concerned. We nibbled on some fresh lychees and afterwards Charles dropped me off at the Quaker house with a brotherly peck on the cheek. I don't know what else I had hoped for, but with the equatorial sky full of strange stars and crickets singing in the bushes and the air pulsing with the hot scent of Africa, I felt let down.

'Anyone got a copy of the *Standard*?' I asked when I got inside and found two of the other residents still up and drinking tea in the kitchen.

'Hello, Fay,' Rajib said. 'I didn't see you there.'

'She tiptoes around like a mouse,' Tom Okolo said. 'The *Standard*'s on the hall table.'

I took it to my room and turned to the used car column. There were two possibilities. I circled them and then went to see if Rajib was still in the kitchen.

Rajib was not a native Kenyan, but he had come in the first wave of refugees from Uganda when Asians were still grudgingly welcome in Kenya. There were several sets of distant relatives already in Nairobi who were helping to finance his law studies at the University. I liked him, and although sometimes he adopted an aloof, patrician attitude, he was not above bantering with me.

'Ah, Fay,' he would say as I scrambled to be on time for an early morning call, 'off to the illusion factory again? These big stars must be dressed and ironed and polished or they would not be beautiful. Hurry, Fay, the world needs beautiful people.'

Once when we were shooting in Nairobi I invited him to come and watch. He turned up his fine nose at the offer and sent instead two of his cousins, an exquisite pair of sisters, who intrigued the whole crew with their silent, fragile modesty. Actually they were a lot more modern than they let on in mixed company, as I discovered later, but at the time hardly a fingernail emerged from their blue and silver saris or a soft murmur passed their lips.

Because I had entertained Rajib's cousins a sort of bond had grown up between us. 'Obligations,' he sighed. 'My life consists entirely of obligations.' But really it was how he expected things to be. He truly believed that if I was a friend to Gita and Shanti he owed me advice when I asked for it.

I thrust the *Standard* under his nose and asked how to go about buying a car in Kenya.

'No, no, no,' he said after carefully reading the advertisements. 'Not these. See, this one belongs to someone up country. It will not be in good condition. And this one too. Why do you wish to buy a car, Fay? I thought you were going home.'

'I want to go to Ethiopia,' I told him, expecting to be applauded for my bravery.

'But you have a job,' he said. 'How can you afford to give it up?'

'The job is nearly over, and I want to see more of Africa before I go home.'

'Well, I don't think you will find work in Ethiopia.' The notion of travel for pleasure did not seem familiar to him.

'It sounds like a silly idea to me,' he said at length when

6

I had explained the plan in terms of an adventure. 'And I do not think your family will approve. But in the matter of a car, please let me check about prices or you will be cheated.'

That night I remember thinking how old-fashioned and cautious he was, and how smothered and protected Gita and Shanti seemed to be. I was glad I was free to wander without the dead weight of family approval around my neck.

2

He tapped politely on the bonnet of the car – a small man in an immaculate blue uniform and peaked cap. It was as if he were knocking at my front door. I sat up.

He coughed gently and said, 'You must wait till four o'clock for immigration.'

'Thank you for telling me.' I was inspired by his courtesy. I got stiffly out of the car and looked at my watch. It was stuck to my damp wrist and showed signs of corrosion. Two-fifteen.

'Perhaps you would take a cup of tea with me?' He made a vestigial bow and gestured towards the warder's house. 'I have many interesting artefacts on display.'

He led the way across the dusty oblong to his house. It was as neat and well-kept as his uniform. Even the rain barrel had a tidy wooden lid. I knocked it inadvertently with my bag as we passed and it gave a hollow sound.

'Daily we hope for rain,' he murmured as he opened the door. It sounded like an apology.

The warder had not anticipated refusal: everything was ready and waiting on a coffee table beside two 1972 copies of the *National Geographic*. The tea was very strong and made the Kenyan way with condensed milk. I hated it to begin with, but now I was quite addicted. As a pick-me-up it was second to none.

'You enjoy Kenyan tea?' he asked happily.

And not only your tea, I thought. I would have liked to lie down on his clean floor, shaded by his chintz curtains, and take a nap, but it was time for the real object of his invitation to be made plain. He wanted to show me his 'interesting artefacts', and if I really appreciated his hospitality I would buy one. This was a problem. The car might have been money in the bank but it did not leave much in the pocket.

However, I am white, I own a car, I travel, my clothes are good. How can I possibly be too broke to afford an artefact? I bought a fat little pot carved out of Kisii stone by one of the prisoners.

Sadly, I took it back to the car. Everyone here seems to want a patron. Everyone has something to sell, and whether it is an object, a service, or simply company, if you are not Kenyan, you are expected to buy. Clearly, it is not a matter of colour: Tom Okolo had problems as well. Like Rajib, he was from Uganda, although he was a refugee for political rather than racial reasons, and when he first arrived he had been depressed about the way everyone expected him to pay for the drinks. But Tom was a radical, and instead of drinks he treated his new friends to lectures about their post-colonial mentality. By the end of his first month in Nairobi his circle of acquaintances was much smaller. There was a dreadful simplicity about it: if you come from abroad you are rich, and unless you are very mean you will be a patron. There are no two ways about it.

As far as I am concerned, friendship is not based on patronage. It was beginning to dawn on me that I would not make many friends on this trip.

Take the prison warder. He was graduate of the University in Nairobi, he had a cool house, a bathroom with running water, a servant to make the tea. I hadn't seen his bedroom but I was sure he had clean sheets on his bed. He had, in fact, everything that I, at that moment, wanted most. Why was I supposed to be the privileged one who should patronize him?

The fat pot was of a browny pink colour with bluish veins and creamy patches. It looked strangely like human flesh. But it was cool to the touch and I held it to my cheek.

It was not like that between Gita, Shanti and me, although to begin with I had thought it might be. I was rather alarmed by their silent, passive company that first occasion when I showed them into the caravan I worked from. We were on location in a game park just outside Nairobi, and my main concern was that we would not have enough bush-shirts for one of the leading men who was sweating so much that he had to change after every couple of takes. They modestly averted their faces when he arrived, bare-chested, to complain about the sweat pads I had supplied for him. He was not normally famous for his forebearance – in fact, he had such a foul mouth that sometimes even the crew were shocked – but the sight of those two silk-covered heads and maidenly lowered eyelids inhibited him and I got away with only a few damns and bloodies.

Later, it turned out they were not at all interested in what he said, or how he looked, but they were absolutely fascinated by how much he earned. And although they were not well educated, their ability at mental arithmetic was impressive. From my rather vague guess at the size of his fee they quickly estimated what a day, an hour, even a minute of his time was worth. They concluded that his wife was a very lucky woman. When I told them that she considered herself very unlucky and was divorcing him for cruelty they stared at me, incredulous.

'Phah!' said Shanti, 'what nonsense. She should not be so feeble.'

By then, the day's shoot was over and we were eating ice-cream in a café near the centre of town. I was beginning to discover the difference between the flower-like impression they gave to strangers and the down-to-earth thoughts which they kept for each other.

'Those two,' Rajib said, when I reported the success of his cousins' excursion. 'Those two! Some man had better watch out.' There was a hint of admiration in his voice.

For a while I thought they were simply mercenary but that wasn't quite the case. It's true that they considered most questions in the light of financial security – to them the necessity for money was like the need for oxygen –

you would be a cretin to disregard it. But really what they dealt in was the currency of friendship: gossip, relationships, marriages, alliances. They very quickly found out about Tony. Under their delicate cross-examination I told them a slightly expurgated version of our relationship. I didn't think them quite modern enough for the truth, but I certainly told them that he wanted to marry me, and that I was not so keen.

'But what is his work?' they asked, and: 'Is his father rich? Does his mother like you?' Questions which in England I would have thought irrelevant. But I answered them as best I could and they were quite shocked to find out how little I knew about Tony's family.

It was interesting too the way they teased Rajib about girls they knew and whom he had scarcely met, but even though he and I lived under the same roof, the idea of a relationship between us never entered their heads. Although we were friends, I was not one of them, and therefore there was no possibility of a romantic connection between us. I was almost a sexless curiosity to them.

I felt I was less circumscribed by custom than they were, because I could certainly imagine a romance between Rajib and me: he was intelligent, good-looking, and gentle. Unfortunately, Rajib, like most of the men I met, treated me as if I was invisible. He was polite, even kind, when I called attention to myself, but as I am not someone who talks much it did not happen very often.

At a quarter past four two blue-uniformed officials strolled across the compound to the immigration building. I heaved the canvas bag out of the boot and followed them. The immigration desk was protected by an iron grille. I put my passport down and waited while the official filled his pockets with ballpoint pens and rearranged his rubber stamps. Sweat trickled down my neck and over my ribs making tracks, I was sure, in the dust.

'British?' he said brightly. I smiled and pushed the passport a little closer to him. He could find out all he

11

wanted from that. He studied the cover with a puzzled frown.

'Fay Jassahn?' he asked. 'Fay Jassahn, Miss?' The way he pronounced my name made it sound very foreign. He softened the J till it sounded like Y, and accented the second syllable. My family has been in England long enough for the name to be anglicized to the point that it is usually pronounced Jason.

'Fay Jason,' I said now, smiling and nodding.

'This is your father's name?' he asked, staring at me. 'You have not been married to a man named Jassahn?' I shook my head.

'You are perhaps Muslim,' he asked, frowning.

'Well no.' I looked around for clues as to what he would like me to be. There was only a framed colour photograph of Jomo Kenyatta.

'Perhaps a Jew?' he went on, frowning even more deeply.

'I'm English,' I said firmly.

'Ah! Church of England!' he announced, looking relieved. 'My cousin once visited Salisbury.'

At last he opened my passport and I began to understand the drift of his questions. He examined every stamp and asked, in depth, about every country I had been to in the past five years. His interest was in no way official, but his position gave him the chance to engage absolute strangers in long conversations. It was as simple as that, and I couldn't blame him: anyone would be bored in Moyale. All the same, I was glad that my passport was only five years old.

Like the perfect guest, I told him that nothing Europe has to offer could compare with the grandeur of Kenya.

'Then why do you wish to go to Ethiopia?' he asked with a triumphant look on his face. He had apparently caught me out in an act of extreme folly.

'I don't expect to stay long,' I said as if in agreement. I was beginning to get anxious. There was only about an hour of daylight left and I wanted to get across the border

12

while there was still enough to see by. 'In fact,' I added hopefully, 'I'll probably be back in a couple of weeks and we can renew this interesting conversation.'

But the conversation was not over, and I doubt if he would have released me in time to get through customs before they shut their office if another white hand had not slapped an Australian passport down on the desk beside mine.

The immigration officer's eyes lit up. He couldn't believe his luck: two diversions in one afternoon! He stamped my passport and waved me away.

The two customs men emptied my bag and together we gazed with great interest at my possessions. I had not brought much, a clean pair of jeans, a skirt, several changes of shirts and underwear. It looked pretty meagre to me but under their eyes even the English soap seemed exotic. Like the immigration man, they wanted to be entertained. Why for instance did I not do all my shopping at Harrods? – the only shop in England they knew about. Why was there no jewellery? Could the pills in the Paludrin bottle have been exchanged for dangerous drugs?

'And what is in this envelope?' one of them asked. It had the name Nastasia Beyer typed on it with the address of the American Express office in Addis, and was obviously a letter. But Kenya has very strict rules about exporting currency and he wanted to be sure.

'It's a letter I'm supposed to deliver in Addis Ababa,' I told him, hoping he wouldn't open it. Nastasia Beyer, whoever she was, might think I had opened it myself and read the contents. The letter was just one of the three commissions I'd accepted when word got around that I was driving north.

Things of any fragility or value, it seemed, were passed from hand to hand rather than entrusted to the mail service. It gave me a glimpse of the loose network of foreigners who kept in touch by unconventional means.

My first delivery was to a French engineer at one of the road camps in Marsabit. His wife had come to the Quaker house bearing half a crate of wine. The wine was part of a regular consignment of delicacies from France which she said made their life in Kenya 'supportable'. But the engineer was not due for leave in Nairobi for another month, and without the wine he would be too depressed to work efficiently.

Two days after the engineer's wife I met a Roman Catholic priest at the New Stanley Hotel and took possession of what looked like a well-wrapped shoe box which was addressed to Marsabit as well. I was convinced that it contained Holy Communion wafers, but by the time it was delivered the box smelled suspiciously of kippers.

I was disappointed by the kippers: holy wafers would have been much more poetic. But I knew the letter to Nastasia could not be less romantic because the writer had told me his story when we met at the YMCA the evening before I left. He had the look of boiled ham that fair-skinned people acquire in Nairobi instead of a tan, and his eyes were moist and anxious. It was his own fault, he said, that Nastasia had run off to Addis. 'I . . . er . . . misbehaved in Mombasa,' he said delicately, and the ham colour turned rosy. 'She told me two could play at that game and the very next day she packed up and left.'

She was driving north in a jeep with a Greek – out of Kenya and out of his life. He hoped the letter would make her change her mind, and I was to give it to her if I overtook her on the road, or failing that, I was to deliver it to the American Express office in Addis.

'I just wish she'd come back,' he said, fanning his hot face with the envelope. 'This isn't any place to play tit for tat. I'm worried about her – she's so impulsive, and besides I hear there's trouble in the north.'

This seems to me what everyone says: there is always trouble in the north. Of course, if you are in the north the trouble has moved south.

I didn't say anything about this. I just took the letter and zipped it into my bag.

14

'You won't lose it, will you?' he said, anxiously staring at the zip. 'I mean, things get stolen round here . . .'

'If you're that worried,' I said, 'why don't you post it?'

'As a matter of fact, I have.' He dabbed the beads of perspiration from his lip with his shirt sleeve. 'I mean, I've posted another one. I'm not taking any chances. But if you're driving you may see her before she gets there. Besides, who knows what the post is like north of the border. I'm just afraid if she leaves Africa I'll never see her again. Does that seem strange to you?'

'No,' I said, although it did. I wondered what it was like to be a wild, impulsive woman who had men fretting about her. I was trying to be adventurous myself but it wasn't really characteristic of me. Would Tony behave like this when he got my letter and realized I would not be home for another month? I thought not.

The customs man pinched the envelope and passed it to his colleague, who palpated it too. He was about to run his thumbnail under the flap when I was again saved by the Australian. He dumped his backpack on the table and said angrily, 'Hurry it up, can't you? It's getting late.'

This proved to be a bad mistake. When I left the immigration building, all his clothes were spread out on the floor and the two customs men were happily levering the soles off his shoes.

3

It was only about fifty yards to customs and immigration on the Ethiopian side of the border but it looked like a different country. The building was made of wood and had a rickety porch. It was manned by a single official in a khaki uniform with yards of white muslin draped about his head and shoulders. His office was decorated with a portrait of Haile Selassie.

This man also took his time. He examined every page of my passport and then disappeared with it into a back room. I waited as patiently as I could in the stifling heat and finally went to the door for a breath of air.

The immigration house faced south so that all I could see was the dusting of small lights springing up on the Kenyan side of town. I had the impression of an impenetrable darkness to the north, and this seemed, in a symbolic way, quite proper. Every time I cross a border, the arbitrary line which divides a continuous stretch of land, I have the frisson of stepping over it into the unknown. There is a possibility that a wonderfully different set of natural laws will now apply. That is part of the excitement of travel. It is also often part of the disappointment.

The fact that, in this case, the various officials made such a meal of my crossing, created a shabby ceremonial. And it was fitting that when at last the official returned my passport the new stamp in it was dated 9/6/1966. Not only was I well and truly in Ethiopia, I was also in Ethiopian time and had lost eight years.

I drove slowly up a dirt road looking this way and that for a place to stop.

Only one light shone. It was a sign advertising Fanta Orange. In such a dark town it seemed like a waste of electricity, but it was the only clue I had that strangers might be welcome so I stopped the car outside. It was a bar, deserted except for four men grouped around a table with a candle between them. They all turned to stare.

I said hello, suddenly very unsure of myself. They stared in silence. I stood first on one foot then on the other. After a while one of them shouted something and an old woman appeared from a doorway behind them. She wore a long black dress and a shapeless white turban.

I said hello again, and when that didn't work I tried, '*Jambo, habari?*' After all, we were barely fifteen yards from where everyone speaks Swahili. Obviously we were not close enough.

'*Masalkheri,*' I said a little desperately. I had, in two seconds, run through my entire stock of polite greetings without any response from her. 'I'm looking for a room for the night,' I went on in English. I mimed sleep. One of the men at the table burst out laughing.

'Good,' he said. 'Very funny.' He got up and came over, a tall, straight man in a khaki uniform. 'This woman has rooms. I tell her.'

The old woman did not respond to him either but shouted something towards the doorway and continued staring at me.

A fat girl in a dirty white dress came in and the old lady spoke to her without taking her eyes off me. The girl went away.

'Thank you for your help,' I said. The man beamed and came to attention. 'I am Chief of Police,' he said proudly. 'I help all in trouble. Where are your papers?'

He took my passport back to the table and discussed its contents at length with his three friends. The girl came back and beckoned. As I passed his table the Chief of Police waved my passport and said, 'Morning. I come morning. First I must study.'

I didn't like leaving it with him, but there wasn't much I could do. I followed the girl through the dark house and out into a compound behind it. It was too dark to see more than the outline of buildings on all four sides.

17

She opened a door and lit a candle stub, showing me an earth-floored cell just big enough to contain an iron cot. She put the candle down on a stool and turned to leave. I stopped her and mimed washing. She laughed and shook her head. I didn't know how to mime my other needs, but stood dumbly, my hand on her arm. She laughed again. I grabbed a torch out of my bag and followed her across the courtyard to another door.

The stench was overpowering and I held my breath to keep from gagging.

When I came out the girl was gone so I found my own way back and sat down, suddenly appalled. What on earth was I doing in this tiny, mud-walled room? The corrugated metal roof crackled as it cooled from the heat of the day – there was no air to breathe. Sinister rustling sounds came from the walls. I had left the water bottle in the car and I couldn't get it without passing through the bar again.

My courage had been eroded by the horror of that hole in the ground and I sat on the edge of the cot thinking about home. February is always miserable in London, and this year it would be even more miserable because of the miners' strike and the price of oil. But to come such a long way to this horrible room, lit by an inch of candle, in order to avoid the power cuts struck me as exceptionally stupid.

I have a room in a house just off Westbourne Road. There is a cubbyhole containing a basin, shower, and lavatory. Another compartment hides the stove, fridge, and sink. There is hot and cold running water. As long as I feed the meters, and providing there is no power cut, I can rely on gas and electricity. I may not be tidy, but I am clean. Dirt reminds me that things fall apart, bit by bit, and decay, and that nature in the form of mould, dust mites or bacteria is waiting to take over.

I complain about my room. For a chicken coop it's too expensive. There are people to the left and right of me, people above and below me. I feel hemmed in and sometimes I crave a wide sky and open country. In the new year, when sunrise is at eight o'clock and sunset is at half past four and the damp wind sneaks through the window frames, I long for heat and sunlight – especially light.

When the production company called and offered me the job in Kenya it was like the answer to a prayer. I even blessed the 'flu epidemic which gave me the opportunity. And from the minute we touched down at Nairobi airport I had been elated. The brilliant, sometimes cruel sun, the thin air, and the enormous sky made me feel literally on top of the world. I wondered why the axis of the globe did not run horizontally, allowing Africa to revolve in top place under the sun.

That night, however, I seemed to be underneath it all, amongst the mould and bacteria and the nameless things that crawled on the floor, up the walls, and in the straw mattress. I was unhappy and unsure and in the dark, alone among strangers, unable to face the effort of asking for water or something to eat.

There was no one to blame but myself. The most difficult thing to face is your own stupidity and I didn't face mine. I looked through my bag instead and was able to congratulate myself on having put in a torch, a packet of biscuits, and two books.

I pulled the cot away from the wall and opened the biscuits.

4

When I woke up there were insects running over me. They had disturbed me several times in the night, but now grey light seeped through the shutter and I thought there was someone singing. It had to be a dream. No one in Moyale could possibly be out there singing '*In Dublin's fair city . . .* ' I sat up, scratching frantically at my ribs. ' *. . . I first set my eyes on sweet Molly Malone . . .* ' I got up, itching everywhere, and pushed open the narrow wooden shutter. The world was dark grey. I looked at my watch: it was five-thirty. ' *. . . cockles and mussels, alive, alive-O . . .* ' A light tenor voice was singing pleasantly in the yard, echoing with reminders of bathroom doors and frosted glass.

I unbolted the door and went out. It was cool outside. I'd've done better to pitch my tent in the middle of the courtyard.

'*She died of a fever, And none could retrieve her . . .* ' came over the splash of water. Water. I picked my way across the compound and saw a slim man shaving in a bowl of water.

'Good morning,' he said, surprised. It was hardly even dawn. I said hello and looked covetously at the plastic bowl.

He said, 'Better wash before she turns off the mains.'

The old lady in the black dress lurked in the gloom of the porch guarding the water tap. She looked as if she hadn't been to bed.

The man sluiced his dirty water out of the bowl and handed it to me. I started to fill it trying to ignore the woman's hostile eyes. Water poured into the bowl but before it was half full she made an outraged hissing sound and jumped at the tap.

'Nice try,' the man said. 'I only got two inches out of her.'

I carefully carried the water back to my fetid lair.

You have to be scientific if you want to wash all over *and* do your hair in half a bowl of water. A lot can be achieved with a damp cloth and a cake of soap. But I have too much hair and strictly speaking it needs a thorough wash and a lot of rinsing. It is very greedy for water.

All I could say, after ministering to it, was that it was slightly less dirty than it had been. But I felt better. Deodorant, insect repellant, and clean clothes finished the job and I was ready to go out and find some breakfast.

But before that could happen the Chief of Police found me. He brought my passport and said, 'Greetings. You sleep well? Is good hostelry, no?'

'No,' I agreed. He beamed and said, 'Best in Moyale. I help you, no? Whose motorcar? Your motorcar? You have papers?'

I showed him the papers.

'Where you drive motorcar?'

'To Addis Ababa.'

He beamed again. 'Very fine city, Addis Ababa. You leave motorcar with me. Very safe in police yard.'

'Thank you,' I said. 'But I'm driving it to Addis.'

'Mmm,' he replied and went away with my certificates of ownership and insurance.

The tenor was in the gloomy little bar with breakfast of a sort on the table in front of him. He had thoughtfully prised an extra hard roll and a glass for the thick, evil coffee out of the old woman.

His name was Graham Fletcher and he was a teacher; or rather he had been a teacher. In North London he taught at a secondary modern for a while before coming out to Kenya on a year's contract. Teaching, he said, hardly came into it. He had become an administrator who fought with other more powerful administrators about money and allocations.

'I've spent a year in an office,' he said, 'and I haven't

21

seen Africa at all.' I nodded. That was how I felt too. Although we had been shooting on location at the coast and in one of the game reserves, we had been cushioned and cosseted, and the real Africa kept at a distance.

'How did you get this far?' I asked with what I hoped was the casual curiosity of one seasoned traveller about another's method of transport. Graham did not look like someone who hitched. He was neat in a clean blue shirt and denims, but most telling of all he wore white tennis shoes which were not too dust-stained.

'I was going to ask *you* that,' he said, pulling a rueful face. 'You see, I was told there was a decent road all the way to Addis so I bought a rather decrepit Land-Rover. But it's packed up. Yesterday, in fact.'

'Packed up?'

'Yes. If there is a decent road it doesn't start here.' He looked suddenly embarrassed. 'I did something a bit silly and the result is a broken axle.'

I stared at him, disconcerted. I too had been expecting if not a decent road at least one as driveable as the one from Nairobi to Moyale. The woman at the Ethiopian Embassy had said there was one, and the map showed a solid red line.

Graham dipped his hard bread into the coffee to soften it. 'The police officer has promised to try and get it towed back here today, but there's not much hope of getting spares this side of the border. I've been told there's a bus once a week to Mega, but the last one left two days ago.'

Now Mega is just up the road from Moyale. On the map it's barely an inch away. I looked at Graham carefully, and he seemed all right. He had light brown hair – the straight floppy sort I associate with intellectuals – and nice hazel eyes. But you have to be a bit cagey about who you offer a lift to here. I know, because the original plan, when I first decided to go to Addis, was to share the driving and expenses with someone else. What I discovered was that most of the people who wanted to travel there overland had no money. They couldn't share expenses. Some of them couldn't drive. Some of them didn't even brush their teeth. And all of them looked as if they'd crack up in an emergency.

At the time I was not expecting an emergency: the AA in Nairobi said there was a modern highway under construction all the way to the border. The Ethiopian Embassy said there was a modern highway under construction all the way from the border to Addis. But even with a modern highway promised, this is Africa, and I did not expect service stations, breakdown trucks, restrooms, or restaurants every twenty miles.

It was worse than I had expected. The AA had not exactly lied. There was indeed a modern highway under construction, and it was driveable, but only with great difficulty. They had got to the stage of laying down the hard core, a layer of small granite rocks, but no further. The traffic that used the road was mainly made up of huge trucks and construction vehicles, and these had worn ruts down to the bare earth, and built up crowns of rocks between them. None of these ruts and crowns suited a small car. A car could not straddle the crowns without tearing holes in its chassis.

The only way you could drive this surface was to steer with the wheels on one side in a rut and the other two wheels half way up the ridge. This put the car at a thirty degree list to port. It was especially wearing as you couldn't let your attention waver for a moment. The ruts and ridges kept changing and you had to select the best ones constantly. All the while you listened to the sound of stones being thrown up by the wheels and beating hell out of the undercarriage. It was like sitting in a foundry.

Another hazard was the stones thrown up by the trucks coming in the opposite direction. They roared towards you at ninety miles an hour in a cloud of dust and exhaust fumes and squirted rocks the size of golf balls at your windscreen. It was no accident, I supposed, that in the three days I took to drive to the border, I'd not seen one other privately owned car. Everyone else, it seemed, knew more about modern highways under construction than I did.

I had not expected much better in Ethiopia. But from what Graham said it was much worse. I took a deep breath and told him about the car.

'You drove here?' he asked with more incredulity than admiration. 'What in?'

'A DKW.'

'Jesus!' he said. 'Let's have a look.'

The car looked as if it was wearing deep tan make-up. It would have taken a lot of imagination to guess that it was really pale blue. But in spite of all the gingery dirt and in spite of a couple of punctures, it had reached Moyale unscathed.

'It was modified for the East African Rally a couple of years ago,' I told him proudly. Just as Mr Singh had told me. 'So it's not as frail as it looks.' I didn't mention that it had been unmodified in a lot of ways since, nor that frequently, especially on bumpy or corrugated surfaces, if flopped out of gear altogether. I was proud of my DKW. It had been, I thought then, a remarkably good buy.

'We finished,' Mr Singh told me. 'Fifteenth we finished. Look, I show you.' He took me into his steaming office, little more than a shack cobbled on to the edge of the dusty glaring yard, and showed me a colour photo of him and his identical twin brother Mr V. Singh standing in their racing overalls beside the gleaming DKW. In its rally trim it looked a little like a panda car – but sporty, definitely sporty.

The office smelled of motor oil and flypaper. There were two other pictures on the flimsy walls: one, inevitably, of Jomo Kenyatta, and the other, more puzzling, of the Aga Khan.

But I was not buying the car from him. I was buying it from Ralph Hendry, a colonial throwback if ever I saw one. He had brought it from Mr Singh after the rally, but Mr Singh still did all the repairs and servicing.

'You are returning to England after your trip?' Mr

Singh enquired politely. I told him I was. 'My brother now has a garage in Wolverhampton. You know it?'

I said I had been there and he smiled in relief. Perhaps he had been wondering if a place called Wolverhampton really existed. It was the sort of thing I wondered about too after a few weeks in Kenya.

'Come and see me before you go home,' he said. 'Maybe I can help you sell the car.'

'He probably wants you to help *him*,' the colonial type suggested as we drove back to the centre of town. 'If I know him, he wants to join his brother in the UK. They all do.'

'What on earth for?' I asked, looking at the bougain-villæa out of the window and remembering Wolver-hampton.'

'Africanization,' he said shortly. 'These Asians think they're having a tough time, so watch out. He'll probably come up with some illegal scheme for exporting money. They all do.'

'They all do.' If there's one thing I hate about the whites in Kenya it's this phrase. I finished my business with him as quickly as possible and drove back to the Quaker house.

The house at least was a microcosm of the world as I think it should be, and meeting-house isn't a bad name for it. The people who stayed there were mainly students: Tom Okolo, Rajib, a few Americans, a French boy, and me. We all shared one bathroom and a small kitchen. I won't say everything was harmonious because it wasn't. But at least we were on equal terms and nobody blamed the entire French nation when Paul forgot to clean the bath, or said all Americans were thieves when Caroline pinched Rajib's milk by mistake. No, Paul was a slob in his own right and Caroline had a rotten memory for who bought what. But then we all knew each other – not well, just enough to be sure that each of us was human.

I didn't feel quite human in Moyale. From the minute we walked out of the bar into the morning sun we were surrounded by a crowd of curious folk who looked at us as if we had escaped from a freak show.

Our audience was composed of men and boys. They mostly wore shabby Western clothes though some had shawls draped over their heads. They looked at us expectantly. I said, 'Good morning,' quite cheerfully. Graham said, '*Salaama*.'

A stir ran round the group but no one said anything till an old man with a long stick stepped forward and muttered something that sounded like, '*Tenasterling.*' Then they shuffled closer to the car and began to talk among themselves. We shook hands politely with the old man and he stepped back into the crowd.

'Er, well,' Graham began. 'Unaccustomed as I am to public speaking, and impressed though I am with the reception accorded to our humble presence, I have to express my doubts about this fine motorcar. I know I'm not the world's best driver, but a road that cracks up a Land-Rover may well be too rough for a DKW, and I haven't seen one single other vehicle coming in or out of this side of town.'

'Perhaps we'd better take a look,' I suggested. 'If we could get as far as Mega things might improve.' The crowd around the car parted.

5

Seen by daylight, the northern half of Moyale is a curious affair. The Kenyan half is by no means a modern metropolis but it is recognizably a town of this century with trucks and bicycles and some brick or concrete buildings. There was nothing like that here. The houses were made of mud and none of them had a second floor. A lot of them had a rough planked boardwalk sheltered by an overhanging porch which reminded me, oddly, of a frontier town in a Western film.

A little further on a huge spreading acacia tree grew out of the bare red earth between the houses. It seemed to be a meeting-place for the men because there was a small gathering there as well. They held their sticks across their shoulders, arms draped over the ends as if they had all been crucified, and pivoted to watch as we drove slowly past.

I drove slowly because of the dust, and therefore couldn't outstrip the army of small boys who ran beside us like outriders screaming, '*Ferenji, ferenji*, money!' It was not an inconspicuous procession.

The houses stopped, and the dirt road became a track that wound between tree-covered hills. It was cratered with large dry holes. When there were no holes the track was deeply rutted. I bit my lip.

After a long while, when we had crept only a couple of miles, Graham said, 'And if it rains?'

'Maybe the good road begins at Mega,' I suggested. But it was obvious, even to me, that the DKW wouldn't get us that short distance unless we were very lucky. This main road was like the very worst farm track and if we had been blessed with four-wheel drive it still would have been no simple matter.

I forced the shuddering car on a mile or so to where Graham's Land-Rover had foundered. It was a particularly bad stretch of track. There was a deep crater, almost a ditch, just before a steep incline. He should have engaged the four-wheel drive at the bottom, before the ditch, but he hadn't. On the second attempt he left the track because he thought he would get more purchase on the rougher earth. But he had hit a concealed rock and ended up with the Land-Rover hanging helplessly at an acute angle, undercarriage exposed.

It was like an illustration to a cautionary tale about what could happen to an inexperienced driver in Africa. I winced. Nearly all my savings were invested in the DKW, and I had risked the lot by driving this far.

'The lying cow!' I said mildly. It was too hot to lose my temper as spectacularly as I wanted. I got out.

'Who?' Graham asked, getting out too. The dust began to settle. He wiped the sweat off his forehead with a rusty stained handkerchief. Great black flies appeared from nowhere and swarmed around our faces.

'The woman at the Ethiopian Embassy,' I told him. 'She said the idea was to link Addis and Nairobi with a modern road, and that enormous amounts of money had been poured into it. She said the road reinforced the communications between Kenya and Ethiopia and symbolized the friendship between Kenyatta and Haile Selassie. I'm not such an idiot as to bring a car without some assurance there'd be a road to drive it on.'

'Of course not,' he said neutrally. He was more interested in brushing flies off his face. We both waved our arms about, and anyone watching from a hundred yards away might have thought we were talking in semaphore.

The car shimmered in the heat. Not only had it absorbed everything the sun had to offer, but we had been driving slowly in low gear and the engine was about to boil over. It was no better than a sweat box on four wheels.

We climbed slowly up the hill to the Land-Rover and stared at it as if it were a piece of sculpture. Certainly it was no use as a vehicle.

'What a mess,' Graham said gloomily. I got up from where I had crouched to examine the axle.

'Is it a write-off, do you think?' he went on. 'Maybe if I could get it towed back to Kenyan Moyale someone could cobble something together.'

It wasn't just the axle: as far as I could see he would need a new drive-shaft, and there was a leak of brake fluid too. I pointed this out and he looked at me in great surprise. Everyone is surprised at what I know about cars. But just then I was too hot to explain about my motor-mad brothers so I led the way back to the DKW.

Graham shook the sweat out of his hair and said, 'Well, I don't know. I can't hang about waiting for a tow-truck when there's no chance of repairing the damned thing. And I can't hang about waiting for a bus either.' He sounded irritable and petulant. Flies crawled around his eyes, and he swiped at them.

'Let's get back to Moyale,' I said soothingly and plucked at the drenched fabric of my shirt.

We climbed in and limped wearily back to Moyale. I couldn't even think about my own problems. The one thing on my mind was to get out of the heat and sleep. It was eleven o'clock.

The old woman had a few bottles of beer which she parted with most reluctantly for an exorbitant price. I took a mouthful and closed my eyes. I still saw the network of ruts, ridges, and craters. The warm bubbles burst against my palate. In the background I could hear Graham patiently negotiating with the old lady for something to eat.

He came back to the table and said, 'What're *you* going to do? Go back to Nairobi or wait for the bus?' I shook my head. Whatever I was going to do would have to wait for tomorrow. You can't start a long journey in Africa in the middle of the day, and besides the Chief of Police still had my papers.

The young girl in the white dress brought lunch. It was a sort of pancake which looked like a flat piece of foam rubber with a spoonful of sauce in the middle. '*Injera* and *wat*,' Graham told me. 'It's Lent here so there won't be any meat.' He tore off a piece of the foam rubber and moistened it in sauce. I copied. It wasn't too bad. The sauce was made of lentils and heavily spiced. We ate from the same dish and took it in turns to fan the flies away with a rolled-up map.

We had nearly finished when a commotion broke out in the street. There were shrieks of '*Ferenj*' and 'Money!' and a loud voice shouted, 'Take your dirty thieving hands off my bag!'

The Australian I'd last seen in Kenyan customs burst into the bar dragging his backpack. 'Jesus, what a bloody crew!' he exclaimed. 'Who's got the car? What's for tucker?' The scrum of small boys stopped in the doorway and stared, giggling wildly.

'They serve beer in this dump?' the Australian asked. He slapped the counter and the old woman materialized out of the gloom. She regarded him coldly. 'Beer,' he said loudly. 'And step on it.'

'*Yellem*,' the old lady said flatly.

'OK, I'll have some of that. As long as it's cold and wet.'

Graham got up. 'She said no,' he said. 'Shut up and mind your manners or she'll chuck us all out.'

'No?' the Australian said, visibly shaken. He looked parboiled; skin was peeling from his nose and forehead.

'Sit down,' I said, feeling rather sorry for him. 'You can finish mine.' He dropped on to a chair and grabbed my bottle. Graham soothed the old woman's ruffled feathers and eventually persuaded her to give the Australian a small bottle. I noticed, though, that he had to pay considerably more for it than we had.

'Is that your car?' he asked Graham. 'How about me bumming a ride to Addis?'

'It's Fay's,' Graham told him, 'and she won't be driving there. The road's not good enough.'

'I'll drive if you're not up to it. I'm used to this sort of thing.'

'It's the road,' I said. 'The *car's* not up to it.'

'Bollocks,' he sneered. 'You're too soft. This can't be worse than the outback.' Graham and I looked at each other and said nothing. In two short minutes he had succeeded in offending everyone within earshot.

'Just my luck,' he said. 'The only white men for a hundred miles and they have to be Poms. Well, I'm not festering in this dump with you lot. I'll thumb my way out.' He shouldered his backpack and marched out.

I retired to my cell with the water bottle and a can of flyspray.

6

I lay on the cot and sweated within a noxious cloud of insecticide. A lizard hunted on the wall by the roof. God knows what was lurking in the corners, but I didn't.

The thing I hate most about myself is my fear, and I will go a long way to hide it – even from myself. So when Charles said, 'Don't be such a romantic, Fay. You can't go to Addis on your own,' part of me knew he was right – I was just talking: the lure of the Rift Valley running north from the border was sheer romance. Another part of me, however, began making plans to prove us both wrong. I went about acting intrepid and before long I'd trapped myself. Charles tried to stop me, but in the end he gave up and the rest of the crew went home without me.

As soon as they had gone I started to make secret plans to sneak home myself. Looking back, it now seems as if I behaved quite perversely. I went to the airline and inquired about the availability of seats on a flight to London, while on the same day I arranged an Ethiopian visa.

You don't *have* to go if you don't really want to, I said to myself. But that is my mother's voice when my brothers egged me on to some adventure I was doubtful about. 'Scaredy cat!' said my brothers' voices. 'You're only a girl . . . a scared baby . . .'

My brothers are identical twins and they never needed my company. I was too young and the wrong sex. But I always wanted to join in, not for the sake of the activity, but because I hated to be alone. They had a wonderful game called Feet Off Ground which involved circling the house and garden by way of the garage roof, the garden wall, several trees, tightroping the front gate, and slithering along a neighbour's shed. The only rule was that at no time could your feet touch solid ground. It really was quite dangerous. The proof was that they only played it when my mother was out of the house.

I used to follow them round, plodding along below, watching with fear and envy. They leaped, balanced, and climbed. They whooped and laughed. I imagined the fall, the torn skin, the broken bones.

'Come on,' they shouted one day. 'You're big enough now. *We* did it when we were eight! Come on, it's great.'

So I climbed and balanced and slithered and jumped. But it was no fun at all because I was afraid of falling. It took me so long to get off the garage roof and down the drainpipe on to the next stretch of wall that the twins got fed up and went indoors. I completed the course by myself because I thought they'd be watching from a window and would never let me forget it if I failed.

But they weren't watching. When at last I went indoors myself, they were playing a game of Racing Demon. One of them looked up and said, 'Bet you put your feet down.'

'Didn't!'

'Did! You're only a baby girl.'

So of course I had to do it all again to prove I'd done it before.

Self-contempt is a great spur. And even if it weren't, there are any number of things I genuinely think are worth the risk. When I was thirteen, for instance, and first started collecting fossils, I found myself in all sorts of predicaments with cliff faces and tides but I dismissed them as necessary for the collection. I hoped the Rift and the Ethiopian lakes would be just as rewarding.

I must have slept because when I next opened my eyes the lizard had disappeared and the Australian had come back. I heard him talking to Graham in the courtyard. He said, 'Are you sure about that? She isn't just lead-swinging? You know what chicks're like when the going gets rough.'

Graham said, 'I'm telling you, Melvin, I was there too.

33

There isn't a hope in hell that car would make it. I want to get out of here as much as you do.'

'Well, maybe she doesn't. Thought about that, eh? It's all right for her, she can just tootle off back to the air-conditioned room in Nairobi. What's she want to go to Addis for anyway if all she's going to do is turn round and come back.'

'Keep your voice down, Melvin, or she'll hear you.'

'Well, why *is* she going?' Melvin asked more quietly. 'You don't see many chicks on the trail – not on their own, you don't. Is she meeting someone?'

'Ask her yourself,' Graham said, sounding impatient. I was beginning to approve of him. I sat up, making the bed clank noisily, and took a drink from the water bottle. It was nearly four o'clock. I wiped my face with a damp corner of towel and brushed my hair before sauntering out into the courtyard.

'Hello,' I said to Melvin, sounding quite surprised. 'No lift out, then? Bad luck.' I passed behind them and went on towards the bar. 'Well, I expect I'll see you later,' I said cheerily as I ducked into the dark back room.

On the street the sun glared blankly and the children gathered. '*Ferenj* – money!' they yelled, plucking at my shirt. '*Tenasterling,*' I said experimentally. They fell about laughing. It could have meant, Go away, white worm, for all I knew. 'Speak English?' I asked.

'Speak English,' a boy of about ten replied.

'Yes?'

'Yes,' he said, grinning from ear to ear. 'In school I speak English.'

'Very good.'

'Yes. Very good.'

'Where does the policeman live?' I asked.

'*Pleeseman?*' he gazed at me blankly.

'Yes. Police.' I drew myself up, shoulders back, and adjusted an imaginary cap. The crowd screamed with laughter.

'You come,' the boy said, grabbing my hand. 'I show.'

34

He dragged me off towards the border. The others followed, shouting and laughing. Every few paces one of them would step forward and touch me, and then double up shrieking with laughter. I hadn't the slightest idea where I was being led. Clouds of flies swarmed around us.

He led the way to a fairly solid-looking building with a porch. '*Pleeseman,*' he cried triumphantly.

The door was open, but I knocked anyway. 'Thank you,' I said to the boy. But he had no intention of going away. Nor had any of the others. They swarmed about, prodding me gently with the words '*ferenj*' and 'money' on their lips.

'Speak!' my guide urged. I knocked again and said, 'Hello, anyone at home?'

The boys reacted excitedly. 'More!' the guide commanded. 'You speak English good for me.'

' "Oh, what can ail thee, knight at arms," ' I said in desperation. ' "Alone and palely loitering. The sedge is withered from the lake and no birds sing." Humpty-Dumpty sat on a wall and if you lot don't shut up and go away you'll drive me round the twist.'

'*Roundytwist,*' he cried. 'Good. More!'

I knocked again and at last the Chief of Police appeared. I was very pleased to see him as my audience had become quite hysterical. The boys, however, retreated off the porch. He followed them down and picked up a stone, which he threw into the largest bunch. They scattered.

'Bad boys,' he said, dusting his hands.

'Oh no.' I was shocked.

'Bad boys,' he insisted grimly.

'Perhaps you're busy,' I said, with a placatory smile. 'I won't disturb you if you're busy.'

He smiled too with sudden charm. He looked as if he had just woken up. 'Always busy. But for you . . . you come for papers, I think. You leave car with me, I think? Very safe. I keep for you.'

35

'Well, yes,' I said awkwardly. 'Perhaps that would be best.'

'Is not good car, I think.'

'Not good enough,' I agreed sadly. It would have been impolite to criticize the road.

He sat down on the edge of the porch. 'Is very good bus,' he said consolingly.

I sat down beside him. Sun shone into my eyes and I wished I had put on dark glasses. A headache erupted from the back of my neck.

'What does *Tenasterling* mean?' I asked.

'You learn Amharic?' he said, delighted. '*Tenastilin* is good morning. Later you say *denada*.' He told me several more words and I wrote them down in the little book I had brought for my geological notes.

When I first began to plan this trip I went to the library in Nairobi and was surprised to find that apart from one book about Mussolini in Abyssinia, there was nothing about Ethiopia. Nor could I buy a phrasebook, and when I started asking questions I couldn't find anyone who had been there.

So, although I have a strong prejudice against anyone who throws stones at kids, I had to start somewhere, and I didn't know when I would next meet an English speaking Ethiopian.

7

On the way back from the police house I met a blond
newcomer weighed down by a kitbag and surrounded by
kids. He had just crossed the border and was carrying one
of the prison warder's little stone pots as if he had been
handed an unwanted drink at a cocktail party and didn't
know where to put it down. He looked shell-shocked and
his bright hair was plastered to the back of his neck with
sweat.

He gazed at me with a bewildered expression and said,
'You speak English?'

'Yes.' I pushed through the children. 'Where are you
from?'

'I'm Peter Kulker,' he said. 'Today I came from Marsabit, but first I come from Holland. What have I done?
What is *ferenj*?'

'I daren't ask but I hope it just means foreigner,' I told
him. 'You haven't done anything – we're just the local
freak show.'

'Ah.' He looked relieved. 'Is there somewhere to say?'

'*Ferenji* House is just up the road.' We started off in
that direction followed by the mob of excited children.
'The trouble is that there's only one bus a week and the
last one left two days ago.'

'Oh,' he said, jumping nervously as a small hand prodded him in the back. 'Well, maybe it's OK. Back there – '
he gestured with his thumb – 'are two Land-Rovers. They
will not cross today, perhaps. It is too slow. But tomorrow
I think they will come.'

'Great!' I said joyfully. I was tired already, having slept
badly on the insect-infested cot, but travelling means
moving on. There is very little to explore in Moyale and

besides it is difficult to be an observer when you yourself are being so continuously and intrusively observed.

I introduced Dutch Peter to Graham and Melvin who were sitting idly in the compound watching a thin, graceful woman stack charcoal and wood.

'Peter says there are two Land-Rovers coming over the border tonight or tomorrow,' I told them. Peter dropped his pack into the dust and squatted beside it.

'Good-oh,' Mel said. 'Think they'll give us a ride?'

'I think maybe.' Peter nodded. 'There are only two drivers.' He and Mel compared lifts that had brought them to Moyale and I stood listening for a few minutes. I did not intend to hitch all the way to Addis. What I wanted was a lift to somewhere with a regular bus service. To me, hitching was not an acceptable risk. But as I looked at the three of them – Graham, neat and respectable, Mel, thick-armed, and Peter, the youngest – I thought there would be safety in numbers. In a few days, Ethiopia would not seem so strange, and judging by the cheap price of the night's lodging, I would be able to afford a couple of weeks' travel by bus. If for some reason I couldn't cope, I would come straight back. It would be silly, having come this far, not to go a little further.

Graham had obviously come to the same conclusion. He looked up and caught my eye. 'Well,' he said. 'Two Land-Rovers. That solves my problem. Are you coming?'

'Aw, hell,' Mel groaned. 'Bloody sheilas. You're on your own, girl. Don't wait for me to carry your bags for you.'

'Wouldn't dream of it,' I said, offended. People think because I'm small I'm also helpless. I turned my back on them and went out to rifle the car. I had to make some choices between what I thought I would need and what I knew I could carry. But I started with a disadvantage: I had no backpack. It had never occurred to me that I would need one.

Packing a car is easy: there is always room for an extra roll of film, canned food, even a pillow. My water was in a gallon container – far too heavy to carry when full, but I was loath to part with it. If the old lady was anything to go by, I could expect future landladies to be extremely stingy with water too. And if all the beds I was yet to sleep in were half as horrible as hers I would certainly need my sleeping-bag. I wished I could take the camp bed but that was out of the question. So was the gas stove. But what about the binoculars? They were old and heavy, but they had wonderful lenses. I asked myself again why I wanted to take this trip.

What I had imagined at the rosy planning stage was a leisurely journey to Addis via the east side of the lakes. I would restock at Addis and come back on the west side. At the time I had no cause to doubt the map and it showed a passable network of red, yellow, and white lines designed for cars.

I had a hazy picture of myself camped by one of the lakes. The car was parked under a eucalyptus, the ground-sheet was attached to the roof of the car and stretched like a lean-to over the camp bed. Something nameless but delicious was bubbling on the stove while I, at the water's edge, watched the sun set over the Rift. In this hazy picture I made notes on rock formations and watched flamingoes and fish eagles through the binoculars. Sometimes I took photographs of gazelles and birds which would later be published in *Audubon* magazine.

I am not a particularly good photographer but I'm constantly optimistic. I had already used several rolls of film for what I was sure would be a spectacular series on water buffalo. More had gone the same way in my excitement about reticulated giraffes.

What it came to, though, was that if I could not indulge my enthusiasm for geology and natural history there was no point in making the trip at all, so I firmly put binoculars and camera on the pile of things I meant to take. A carton of cigarettes are a sort of international currency out here, especially American ones. Nobody seems to like them much but everyone wants to be seen smoking them.

Sweets are good value too – the more highly coloured the better – so I added a few packets of Life Savers. If you don't share a language with people it seems only polite to have some means to show that your intentions are friendly. The big smile isn't always enough here – or anywhere else for that matter.

I lugged the bundle through to the compound where Dutch Peter was telling the others the latest Nairobi gossip: the European community, apparently, were having one of their periodic flutters of anxiety. A white man had been found robbed and badly hacked on the outskirts of Snake Park, so badly cut about, in fact, that at first the police failed to notice the bullet hole in his chest. No one could understand why anyone would hack up a man who was already dead.

'Obviously a grudge,' Melvin said.

'Who was he?' Graham asked. But Peter had forgotten. He had the vague harmless expression of someone who gets through life without asking too many questions or expending a lot of energy. 'A local tour operator, I think,' he said sleepily.

'Who?' Graham asked again. 'Did they identify him?'

'I can't remember. Everyone said he should know better than to be in Snake Park at night.'

'Obviously,' Melvin retorted. 'Everyone knows that.'

I didn't so I kept my mouth shut. It was the first I'd heard of Snake Park, but it was only one of many places people warned you not to go to at night. It seemed to me that if you listened to everyone's warnings the only safe place would be the New Stanley Hotel. It wasn't that I ignored the advice. I didn't. I always listened. Local people have local knowledge, and their advice is usually very good, especially when it is snakes or the midday sun they're talking about. But I prefer to make up my own mind about people.

I can't afford to be prejudiced about anyone because my own family is such a mixture. If they were alive today, most of my father's ancestors would now be at war with each other: the Muslims on one side and the Jews on the other.

In the last few months, whenever I've been tired or depressed, I could almost take the Yom Kippur war as a personal tragedy, a fatal illness in my own body. It seems to threaten my existence, and I wonder, with all the hatred and prejudice in the Middle East, how a man like my father ever came to be conceived at all.

'People shouldn't take chances like that,' Melvin said, looking at me. 'You've got to know how to take care of number one out here. Nobody should expect anyone to look out for anyone else.'

'Isn't it the opposite?' Peter asked. 'Small communities who feel themselves under attack from outside, it is in their interest to help each other.'

Again I said nothing, but I opened a packet of biscuits and passed it round.

'I don't know,' Graham put in. 'In my experience, it's the way people band together to form exclusive little groups that makes outsiders resent them. Take the Kenyan Asians, for instance . . .'

'You take them,' Melvin interrupted, his mouth full of cream cracker. 'They're money-mad.'

'They're looking out for themselves – you should approve, Mel,' Graham said.

'I do. But they're still greedy buggers. They say down south they're leeching the country bloodless.'

I wondered what they'd done to him. My only contacts with Kenyan Asians were with Rajib's family and Mr Singh. Rajib was a student who wanted eventually to go to the London School of Economics and you could hardly say he was bleeding the country dry because he didn't even have a grant. He was supported by his family.

Mr Singh didn't bleed anyone either. In fact, as he explained it to me, his problem was that after Africanization he had been forced to take on mechanics who he didn't need and who he considered to be unqualified. He was philosophical about it. It was, he said, a form of tax

41

he would willingly pay as long as he could afford to if only the government would leave him alone.

But it was true too, as the colonial type had warned me, that he was beginning to consider joining his brother in Wolverhampton. I didn't like to think about this because on the one side there were punishing restrictions which prevented the export of money from Kenya, and on the other side were the harsh realities of British immigration. Since 1972 not a week had gone by without some story appearing in the papers about immigrants from East Africa being discovered cooped up in a truck or freezing in a trawler in the North Sea while trying to creep unobserved into Britain.

I hated to think of Mr Singh being squeezed in this way. He was small-boned and neat, even after work his shirt was immaculately white, he never seemed to sweat, and he was polite. The memory of him was in fact something of a reproach to the four of us and Mel in particular. We were all dirty, but Mel looked by far the worst. His blue and white check shirt was open to the waist and stiff with dust and sweat. Three-day stubble decorated a long muscular jaw and his hair looked as if it had been marinated in burnt fat.

'What else you got in there?' he asked. He had just finished the last of the biscuits and now he reached for my canvas bag. I removed it hurriedly and zipped it up. One thing was certain: Mel was an opportunist. I glanced at him with interest because of the four of us he looked most like a traveller.

Most of us travel: but only in conditions that reflect our normal way of life. We try to reproduce, in strange places, something of our own standards of comfort or hygiene or diet, and we often judge the success or failure of a trip by how similar conditions are to the ones we are used to. We aren't travellers – we're tourists.

With Mel I got the impression that, while he would grab ruthlessly at anything that was going, he didn't really care about comfort. As long as he was on the move everything was all right. You could tell by his boots: they looked like the hide of a very old rhinoceros and had come a long way. He'd walk rather than wait too long for a lift.

'How long did you spend in Nairobi?' I asked him curiously.

'Two weeks. I got sick.' Resentment creased his face. 'Waste of time.'

But long enough to become an expert on Snake Park, I thought. He turned to Dutch Peter and changed the subject. 'This guy with the Land-Rovers,' he began. 'Who is he? Where's he going?'

'Just a guy.' Peter was almost asleep, leaning back against the dirt wall. 'He is called Gabriel, I think.'

'Gabriel!' Mel hooted. 'What sort of name is that? Not another Pommy poofter, is he?'

'Ethiopian.' Peter closed his eyes again.

'They're very religious,' Graham told me. 'I'm told it's a very old sort of Orthodox Christianity.'

Mel said, 'Well, I hope he's angel enough to get me out of this dump.'

8

Later, after I had packed and repacked my bag several times without any great satisfaction, the three men came to my cell for a drink of water. The old woman had taken such a dislike to Mel that she refused all of them even a cupful. This was bad news. I had been hoping for some to wash with before bed. Now it looked as if I mightn't even be able to keep enough in the bottle to dampen my towel. I watched anxiously as they took turns at the bottle, and wondered if I could be losing my team spirit so early in the trip.

I didn't mind sharing my water, but I did object to giving it all to Mel. He rested the gallon bottle on his forearm, head thrown back, hairy throat working in great gulps as water poured down his gullet, but I couldn't bring myself to say anything.

Team spirit is important to me. If you work in the theatre or on movies, it has to be. And I think that is one of the things I most enjoy about my work: everyone buzzing like bees to bring a common project to its deadline. There is a sense of shared responsibility as well as shared purpose, and I like that too.

'Hold hard!' Graham protested at last. 'Leave some for the lady.'

'Berloody yell.' Mel wiped his mouth on his wrist. 'What you put in there? It tastes like a fucking swimming pool.'

'You are reading *Seven Pillars of Wisdom*?' Peter asked. It was on the cot along with a book about East African wildlife. He picked it up and the letter to Nastasia Beyer, which I had tucked into the cover for safety, fluttered to the floor. Mel squinted through the binoculars and said, 'You're never going to tote this lot, are you?' He upset

44

my sponge-bag and Graham and I bumped heads bending down to pick everything up.

'Strewth,' Mel said as he opened the first aid kit, 'you're a walking bloody pharmacy. Look, fellas, she's brought bleeding salt tablets!'

I blushed and snatched them back, but by then he'd found the cigarettes.

'Glad to see you've brought something useful,' he announced. 'Can I bum a smoke?'

'Be my guest.' I hoped he would hear the sarcasm. He didn't and he didn't seem in any hurry to leave either. The little room was stifling.

'For Christ's sake go outside if you want to smoke,' I said, manners deserting me. 'I can't breathe with you lot in here.' They left off examining my possessions and shambled out, leaving me sweating and alone in the verminous cave – minus a pack of cigarettes. One less thing to carry, I thought, gazing desperately at the unwieldy pile. At that moment all I was interested in was flyspray, insect repellent, and antihistamine cream. The bites I had collected during the night had erupted into scores of burning, itching hillocks, and I thought wistfully about what my mother did when I developed chicken-pox at the age of fourteen. When the urge to scratch became unbearable she would fill a bath with tepid water and add a couple spoonfuls of bicarbonate of soda. She put the radio by the bathroom door with the volume turned up high and I lay, mind blanked out by music, body soothed by bicarb. It was an eccentric solution but it worked.

Mother is an eccentric woman. Her mother came from Cuba, her father from Argentina, and she was born in Miami. By rights she should be an extremely unsettled person, but she isn't. She absorbed Englishness from the mythology of school playgrounds, the stories of older women, and Radio Four.

'England has made me English,' she say happily, while throwing green chillies into a bubbling pot of something wholly un-English. She always throws food. A pinch of salt, a handful of basil, garlic, carrots, all sail through the air and land approximately where she wants them to.

And as if her hybrid cooking were not enough to single her out, she wears the vivid colours which look so strident in grey northern light.

Yet, in an odd way, she is right. In emergencies she falls back on English remedies: *sang froid*, cups of tea, custard for tonsillitis, dry toast for nausea, witch hazel for bruises. But even these no-nonsense panaceas are applied with a flourish and murmurs of comfort which sound almost like native incantation.

Everyone who meets my mother is charmed by her. When they speak of her they do so with a broad grin. I am sometimes afraid that the grin is a little patronizing, but there is no doubt that she is well liked.

I like her myself, and it is puzzling that I should feel the need to get so far away from her.

9

We left Moyale before dawn the next morning. Peter and I bounced uncomfortably in the second of the two Land-Rovers like the last couple of matches in a box. Unwashed, unbrushed, short of sleep and temper, I gripped the overhead bar while the rough canvas hood rasped my knuckles.

Peter groaned as we hit a rut. 'Coffee,' he pleaded. 'Breakfast, Oh God. What are we doing? I think I will be sick.'

I wished I had been left in Moyale to die. But we were going to Dilla, scarcely two inches north on the map – two days, Gabriel assured us, on the road. What road? I asked myself as the Land-Rover lurched over a ridge and thudded down on the other side. Moaning, Peter tried to cushion his buttocks from the metal bench with his backpack. A sackful of farm implements landed with a loud clank on my ankle.

We couldn't see where we were going, and if Peter had spent the night in the company of as many hungry insects as I had, he would be itching all over too. We were a miserable pair.

Gabriel, driving the lead vehicle with Mel and Graham in the back, had turned out to be a stocky, energetic man. He seemed to have expected to pick up travellers waiting in Moyale, and disposed of us, without fuss or question, wherever he had space. As far as I could tell, he had crossed the border in the middle of the night, though how was a mystery. It must have been an official crossing, because it was the police officer who banged on my door at about three-thirty and told me there was a lift north if I wanted it. Gabriel, looking square and fresh in a neatly pressed bush-jacket, had barely time for questions or

47

greetings. We were bundled into the backs of his Land-Rovers before our gummy eyes had opened properly.

All we were told was that Dilla was on the way to Addis. No one had the opportunity to consult a map so we had to take that on faith.

'If I telephoned my father from Nairobi,' Peter said when we came to a short rest from the pounding, 'he would have sent me the air fare.'

'Why didn't you?' I asked.

'He would have been too happy.' He changed his grip on the roll bar and swivelled to face me. 'He thinks I am a . . . bum, is it? That I cannot live without him and his money. I wish to show him there is another way.' We could just see each other now in the gloomy dawn light.

'That's the price of pride,' I said, as the Land-Rover pitched and tossed us up to the canvas and down again on our raw spines.

'Do you think it is pride?' Peter asked. 'I thought it was independence.' He closed his eyes and that ended the conversation for a while.

The plastic window at the back was opaque with dust, but through the windscreen, past the burly silhouette of the driver I could just see that we were climbing through thinly wooded foothills. The windscreen was speckled with dead insects and smeared with their blood. I should have been more interested in my first view of strange countryside but I couldn't even raise the mildest curiosity. I was car-sick and far too uncomfortable.

By mid-morning, heat was added to the sum of our miseries. The swirling dust turned to mud on our sweating faces and the spare fuel cans stank. We were passing through some of the strangest landscape I have ever seen. It was a plain filled with termite mounds. They rose on every side, orange, red, yellow, and grey: some like blasted tree-trunks, some like columns, some like wasted Giacometti figures, some like stalagmites: a vast hallucinatory sculpture garden.

I wish now that we had stopped, that I could have taken

some pictures, because in retrospect it seems like a fever dream. I didn't even look at it properly, and when I returned some weeks later I didn't see it at all. It might never have existed.

Peter missed it completely. His eyes were shut, he rested his head against his raised arm as he was rushed and jolted, semi-comatose, through a great metropolis built and populated by insects. How long had it taken to build and how long it might survive were questions I resolved to ask later. I would find a book about termites and read all about it some time when I wasn't so sore, tired or queasy.

When at last we stopped it was not for rest or shade or even lunch: the lead Land-Rover had broken down. We crawled stiffly out into a wasteland of scrub and sand. I grabbed for the water bottle and then passed it on to Peter and our driver. Graham, Mel, and Gabriel were peering gloomily into their engine. Peter and the driver went over to them. Nobody asked for my advice so I disappeared behind some thorn bushes.

When I came back I felt a lot better. The ground had stopped rocking under my feet, and I sat down in the sparse shade. After a while Graham joined me. 'They're cleaning the spark plugs,' he told me.

'What happened?' I asked.

'No power,' he said. 'The engine started missing. Gabriel says it's dirt in the spark plugs. Want to take a look?' He was grey with dust and fatigue too. 'Jesus,' he went on, 'I don't want to be stranded here.'

There was nothing but short and withered thorn bushes for miles around. In the distance some low hills rose out of the heat haze; there was no sign of life, either animal or human. Insects were a different matter. They had found us as soon as we stopped.

'Have a look,' Graham urged. 'You know about motors. I don't think Gabriel does, and Mel's full of bullshit. The way they're carrying on, we could be here all night.'

'In a hurry, are you?' I said sarcastically, but relented when I saw the anxiety in his face.

'It's more likely to be dirt in the fuel line.' I didn't want to get up. I shaded my eyes with my hand and squinted towards the group around the other Land-Rover. They did not look at all happy and I knew that under this sun the metal would be too hot to touch.

'If cleaning the sparks doesn't work,' I said at length, 'get them to check the fuel filter. It's probably bunged up with dead flies.'

'Where is it?'

'I don't know,' I said irritably. 'I haven't looked. It should be next to the pump – a sort of glass bulb with the fuel line running in and out. Ask Mel.' I added nastily, 'This is just like the outback.'

When I opened my eyes Graham was back with the men. He was arguing with Mel, and Gabriel was staring over at me. I must have gone to sleep then because the next thing I heard was Mel saying, 'I told you it was the filter. It happens all the time in the outback.'

The sun had moved round and the shadows lengthened. Both Land-Rovers ticked over sweetly. Graham looked at me and shrugged. I was about to climb back in when he came over and said, 'Gabriel thinks you might be more comfortable with us.' Apparently, a place in the lead vehicle was considered something of an honour. Mel and I walked past each other like a pair of spies being exchanged. He gave me a sour look. I barely had the energy to raise my eyebrows.

Gabriel's Land-Rover boasted a square of foam rubber to place between coccyx and metal. Otherwise it contained even more oddly-shaped sacks than the other one. Gabriel, it seemed, had been shopping in Kenya. The long blue-black barrel of a rifle protruded from the neck of one of the sacks.

'What's the gun for?' I asked as I settled as comfortably as I could on the foam cushion.

'Crocodiles,' Gabriel said shortly. Then he softened and

went on, 'Dilla is at Lake Abaya. Many crocodiles.' He put the Land-Rover in gear and the lurching, bruising journey began again. Gabriel laughed suddenly; it was a laugh of pure joy. He banged the steering-wheel with both hands and turned in his seat to look at me. 'Made in England!' he cried. A huge grin split his face in two. 'You should export to Ethiopia. Then I could buy here. Not go to Nairobi to buy. Why not sell in Ethiopia?'

It turned out to be a good question. If ever there was a market for Land-Rovers it was Ethiopia, but the ones we travelled in between Moyale and Dilla were the first and last we ever saw.

I was looking forward to Dilla. There would be water. I could have a bath and wash my hair. Also, Lake Abaya was part of the African Rift, and perhaps my trip would really start there.

I had only read about rifting in books but it seems to be a spectacular geological event. They say that a rift is formed when movement by the continental plates forces the earth's crust upwards and outwards along a certain line. The valley is like the fallen keystone in a damaged arch. And when a rift is active, as the African one is said to be, there is volcanic and earthquake activity as well. The great slabs of earth's crust continue to move, so that eventually the African Plate will split, and the Red Sea will come pouring in to form a new ocean.

I was thinking, somewhat fuzzily, about this as we bounced and swayed into night. Would there be two Africas? What would they call the second one? Where would it stop? I wondered. And when will we stop? I asked myself miserably. But the journey went on and on and soon I couldn't even think about the Rift. I simply hung on.

'Yabello!' Gabriel cried suddenly. 'We sleep here.'

I remembered Yabello from the map. It was one town north from Mega, and, like Mega, the legend under the place name read 'good water'. I had not seen any good water at Mega, or anywhere else for that matter. Truth to tell, I had not even seen Mega. Perhaps we had bypassed it. Perhaps I had had my eyes shut, or perhaps it no longer existed. I never knew.

Nor was I to see Yabello that time. We arrived after dark and left before morning.

10

The night's rest, which had reduced me further towards itching exhaustion, had done something completely different to Gabriel. He looked like an advertisement for a tropical outfitter in his khaki bush suit and his well-brushed desert boots.

'Where on earth did he sleep?' I whispered to Graham as we bowled along in the weakening darkness. Gabriel was starched, perky, and bursting with energy. He regaled us with predictions of how envious his brother would be when we got to Dilla, and he showed all the cheeriness of a man on the last stretch before home. He made me feel downright inadequate.

We had not been given any candles that night, and what with fatigue and disorientation, I couldn't find my torch and so I can only describe the place I slept in by sound, smell and touch. It was tiny, dirty, and infested with things that rustled, whirred, and whined.

My mother always claimed that during the war she went to bed every night with her shoes on in case the house was bombed. Just what difference her shoes would have made was something she never explained. But following her example, I kept my shoes on that night. I felt that if I had my feet in them there would be less room for poisonous spiders to nest while I had my eyes shut.

Graham might have been thinking along similar lines because at that moment he asked if I had anything for insect bites in my bag. I passed him the tube of antihistamine cream, which started Gabriel off on a description of the malaria eradication programme in his area. Apparently the shallows of Lake Abaya were the breeding ground for mosquitoes. The reeds and weeds were infested with their larvae and only huge and regular doses of DDT could keep them down.

Gabriel was a chemist, he told us. I still don't know whether that meant he was a pharmacist or something grander. We never found a pharmacy in Dilla, but he certainly showed a great interest in the fact that we were both taking Paludrin every night.

And Dilla? – which he said was the most beautiful place in the world. Well, we arrived there in the afternoon and the lake was a sheet of hot steel, and in the distance, far away on the other side, cloud hung heavy over raw bare hills. This was indeed the Rift and it reminded me of what, on old maps, had been called the Mountains of the Moon. The mapmakers had them running east to west, north of and parallel to the equator. But at that time no one had explored much of inland Africa; they were guessing at the source of the Nile, and filling in with the ancient map of Ptolemy.

Gabriel dropped us on the main street and roared away in clouds of dust. We wandered around helplessly for a few minutes, with our bags hanging heavily in our hands, looking for a place to stay. We must have been a ridiculous sight – four tired and dirty strangers, swatting uselessly at flies and surrounded by a baying pack of children. Mel wanted a cold beer. Peter wanted a hot shower. Those heroic explorers, Burton and Speake, would have been ashamed of us. Which of us cared that this was the land of the Queen of Sheba or the legendary Prester John? Did I really care about plate tectonics or sea floor expansion? I did not. What I cared about was washing my filthy hair and finding a clean bed. I cared about filling my rumbling stomach and locating a proper, private water closet.

But I was not too uncomfortable to realize that I was missing something important, and as I dragged my aching body up the dusty street, I thought about T. E. Lawrence riding to Akaba. T. E. Lawrence notices things: even when he has fever and boils, and all the camels are suffering with mange, he can describe in detail a cinder crater, the sand, broken basalt and yellow water courses. There is a wealth of geological description in *Seven Pillars of Wisdom*, and when I was reading it in Nairobi I thought: how exciting it must be to see such things from the back of a camel. But when I was whisked through desert, scrub, and an extraordinary city built by insects, in the relative comfort of a Land-Rover, I was too tired and sore to notice anything. The details I can describe are all on my own body: the insect bites, the bruised backside, the grazed knuckles, and the irritation of sweat trickling down my face.

I was, I felt, a shamefully superficial person. All the things that excited me were second-hand, taken from books or films or TV programmes: things I could absorb without discomfort or effort. Now that I was actually walking through the Rift Valley it meant less to me than the search for somewhere to stay.

There was something approaching a proper hotel in Dilla: a room with plaster walls and a tiled floor. We even persuaded the management to turn on the water in the bathroom for half an hour.

'There's a bloody lake over there,' Mel grumbled, 'so why're they acting like water's bloody gold dust? Why don't we trek over for a swim instead?'

'Crocodiles,' Graham and I said together.

'Bilharzia,' said Peter.

'Balls,' said Mel, and strode purposefully away. The rest of us, scrupulously fair, took ten minutes each with the precious running water. Then we went out to explore the town and inquire about buses north. The crowd of children we attracted knew nothing about buses, but eagerly led and pushed us towards the market. It was held once a week in a field on the edge of town. People milled around: men with sturdy staves and white shawls, women in white calf-length dresses, men in ragged western garb, women wrapped almost to the eyes in coloured cloth, children clothed in anything and nothing. Some were selling strings of poor moth-eaten donkeys and mules. Some had just a few leaves on the ground with little piles of chillies or grain. But everywhere we went business stopped dead. We were not there as spectators: we were the show. People gathered round us to poke or prod or simply to stare.

It was very embarrassing for me because they obviously did not know if I was a man or a woman. In spite of my mop of long hair and coloured scarf, I was wearing jeans, and that caused confusion. One woman even tried to unbutton my shirt to see if the shape of my chest was real. I was soon limp with exhaustion and strain.

It was not as if the people were unfriendly exactly, more that they treated us as if we were not quite human – like a crowd of children when they see their first elephant: 'What is it? – Doesn't it look funny? – What does it eat? – Let's have a feel – ooh!'

In the end, I slipped away. Well, that's the wrong word for it. You can't slip away with a platoon of screaming, cat-calling children on your heels. But away I went, Fay Jassahn, the famous dancing bear, or talking monkey, or hermaphrodite, or whatever it was they thought.

This curiosity was something I never understood. Gabriel came from Dilla and he treated us as human beings. And we surely weren't the first Europeans ever to have stayed in this town. Nastasia Beyer and her Greek friend must have come this way only a week ago, because as far as I could see from the map there is no other way. It did not seem reasonable that the people who live on the main road between the border and the capital should be so excited by the sight of strangers.

Alone in my room I made a horrible discovery: somewhere in the market I had picked up two black and bloated ticks. One was fastened to my groin and the other had buried itself in the hollow of my shoulder.

My mother would probably have done something clever and painless with the juice of a lemon. I tackled the problem with a lighted cigarette and a pair of tweezers, and by the end of the operation I was shaking with sub-dued hysteria. Two ticks, that's all. Just think what T. E. Lawrence had to put up with.

I lay on the small bed with tears in my eyes and resolved to go home tomorrow.

11

But I slept better that night, and in the morning when the four of us gathered for coffee to discuss the next move, I was influenced by the others' wish to push north for at least a couple more days. Peter had been out and discovered a bus already picking up passengers for Shashamane.

'We can be there by the afternoon,' he said eagerly.

'Fine,' Graham agreed. 'From there it's only a day to Addis. We're nearly home and dry.'

What a beautiful name, I thought. And it stood to reason that the nearer the capital we went, the more comfortable the towns would be. Wasn't Dilla an improvement on Moyale and Yabello?

The bus was yellow and ran on four bald tyres. Its roof was piled with boxes, bundles, and cases. Some of the bundles heaved and squawked. There was poultry inside the bus too, and only the people fell silent as we climbed on board and found a couple of empty seats.

'What is it about these people?' Mel asked loudly. 'You'd think we all had two heads or something.' We squeezed our luggage in around us and sat down, Graham and I behind Mel and Peter. Mel turned round. 'Tell you what,' he began, 'I can't wait to get to Addis or some place I don't stand out like a sore thumb.' He twisted his hips to a more comfortable position. Peter was pushed towards the aisle. Like a fool, he had not fought for the window seat. Neither had I.

'And another thing,' Mel went on, 'when I get to Pom I'm not budging another step till I've made enough to fly home.'

'You might be around a long time,' I said. 'When I left

it seemed the whole country was strikebound. It looks as if the bright lights are out for a while.'

'No swinging London?' Peter asked, disappointed.

'London was dangling when I left.'

Graham laughed. 'OPEC and the miners,' he said. 'Don't worry, it can't last forever.'

'Bit of strife never worries me, mate. I'll manage. It's you Poms ought to worry. You've had it soft for too long. Look at Fay here. She was about ready to peg out last night.' He had caught me at a bad moment when coming to scrounge cigarettes. It was too soon after the episode with the ticks for me to be my usual unruffled self.

'What are you here for Fay?' Mel pursued. 'You didn't have to come. You aren't going anywhere.'

'She has friends in Addis,' Peter said.

'No, I don't,' I said surprised.

'I saw in Moyale, a letter you carry.'

I would have explained about Nastasia but the bus driver started to honk his horn and there was a last minute furore among the passengers and their relatives outside. People leaned out of the windows and exchanged farewells, bundles were secured more tightly, poultry screamed. The loaded bus began to wallow out of town, honking all the way.

Peter and Mel faced front again and I closed my eyes. I was beginning to feel sick already. I don't know what it is about travel sickness. I never feel queasy when I'm driving myself. It became a real handicap when my brothers took up rallying. But I suppose I should thank them, because that was when I began to learn about motors. They soon discovered I was useless as a co-driver, so I was demoted to driving the support vehicle which suited me better. As I said before, I'm good in a team, but I'm no good as a front-liner. Especially if I have to read a map at eighty miles an hour while throwing up in a helmet. The idea that I should become the lead driver never entered the twins' heads. And quite right too – I'm not competitive enough, and I don't like taking risks.

After a while Graham said, 'Do you want to sit by the window?'

'It's all right,' I muttered, gamely but weakly.

'Change over,' he ordered. We changed places.

'Sucker,' Mel said, turning again. 'You wouldn't catch me falling for that woebegone look.'

'What're you picking on her for?' Graham asked. 'She hasn't done anything to you.'

'Too right! But first sign of trouble who's going to hold us up? Women should stay home where they belong. I mean, why's she here at all? I bet she's had some ruck with her boyfriend.'

Graham said, 'There's no question of anyone holding anyone else up.'

'Yes.' Peter turned round and joined in. 'It is only by chance we know each other. No one is *with* anyone else. There is no responsibility.'

'That's what you think,' Mel said. 'Look at the way she's latched on to Graham. Why's he acting so soft – giving up the window seat, getting her a place in Gabriel's Land-Rover? And who had to move out to accommodate her ladyship, I ask you?'

'Perhaps he is a gentleman,' Peter suggested.

'So that's it,' Graham said. 'Well, let me tell you. That was Gabriel's own idea, because she knew what was wrong with the fuel line.'

'Balls.'

'And while we're on the subject – who begs for cigarettes, eats her supplies, and drinks her water?'

'Well, we all do,' Peter said.

'That's right. *All* of us, Mel.'

'That's what sheilas do,' Mel said, exasperated. 'They hold out little creature comforts so that when the going gets tough, some mug'll carry that ridiculous bag and water bottle. Some mug'll think he owes her.'

I kept my eyes shut and wished I had stayed behind in Dilla. I didn't feel connected to any of the others. Peter was right. It was only chance that had brought us all together. A week earlier or a week later and it would have been completely different.

But Mel in his abrasive way was right too. One of the reasons I wanted to stay away from England for a while was to loosen ties with Tony, my boyfriend, who showed distinct signs of wanting to become my fiancé. It was no fault of Tony's, but I didn't want to get engaged yet. Tony was older than I and he seemed to think that I needed looking after. I had only been living on my own for about eighteen months, and it is true that I'd made mistakes. But on the whole I was enjoying myself. I was making my own decisions, eating when and what I liked, and I didn't have to creep around when I came home from the theatre at one in the morning. I hadn't prised myself out of my mother's colourful nest to become Tony's fiancée. If I had wanted to be looked after, I would have stayed at home.

I know I find it difficult to make decisions, because they imply making a change, but that does not mean I want anyone else to make them for me. I'm slow, not indecisive. People are always making that mistake. They can't see that what I need is lots of time to get used to new ideas.

It drives my family wild, sometimes. They can sit round the dining table for hours discussing what college I should go to or what job would suit me best, while I appear to be doing nothing. Just like now, in fact. I should have been defending myself against Mel but I couldn't think where to begin, and besides, I was trying to think about what I really wanted to do.

Dithering is best done quietly, so I kept my mouth shut and thought.

What I wanted was a comfortable place to stop and look round. The further we got from Dilla, the more I felt it had been a mistake to leave. It might have been better to abandon Addis as a goal. I could have stayed a few days in Dilla, and perhaps hired a boat to explore the lake. The children would get used to me and leave me alone, and perhaps I could find Gabriel again and ask for

61

something more potent to deal with the insects. If I went on as I was now, in a couple of days I would be in Addis, travel-sick and tired, having seen nothing.

On the other hand, I was increasingly unsettled about the way we attracted attention. In Moyale it had been a nuisance, but funny. In Dilla it had been more than a nuisance: the attention had seemed almost threatening, and I hadn't been able to cope with it on my own. In the market, I had to admit, I had used Graham and Peter as shields, keeping close to them instead of exploring on my own. Graham in particular had been protective: he had put himself between me and the most aggressively curious men. He was a nice, ordinary Englishman, and I quite liked him, but he seemed in a hurry to get to Addis. I did not want to find myself in Addis just because I was staying close to a protective man. I had one of those at home.

Could I do without protection? There was no question about it in London. I sometimes needed help, but that is a different matter: people in an equal relationship help each other. Protection, though is one-sided. Parents protect their children: children are powerless and cannot protect anyone.

When I gave Graham antihistamine cream I was helping him: but when he pushed a curious hand away from my hair he was protecting me. Or was he? And was I, as Mel suggested, buying protection with water and biscuits?

In the theatre, we are a team. Everyone helps. I remember one of my first jobs was as a dresser in a production of *A Midsummer Night's Dream*. There were times when I didn't have much to do because a lot of the cast went on stage naked except for hairy codpieces and a lick of luminous paint. But the girl in charge of wigs and make-up was often rushed off her feet. So I would give her a hand, but always in the sure knowledge that if I got behind with the ironing she'd help me out too.

Things are different in Ethiopia. One contribution does not seem to be fair exchange for another. I might not have thought about it if Mel hadn't pointed it out, but now he had I couldn't ignore him.

In the stifling heat of the rattling bus I resented Mel almost as much as he seemed to resent me. I wanted to get away from him. You can't relax when someone keeps drawing attention to your weaknesses.

12

'There is something in it,' Graham said very quietly. 'You really shouldn't be here on your own. You do have friends in Addis, don't you?' I shook my head. The midday sun beat down on the tin roof like rods of fire. We had picked up and put down dozens of passengers and everyone sprawled on their seats in a heat-induced languor. Even the hens had given up protesting.

'What about this letter, then?'

'Why is everyone so interested in my affairs?' I asked wearily. 'I haven't poked my nose into yours, or Peter's, or Mel's.'

'I suppose it's unusual, that's all. Peter and Mel have been on the road for some time. Maybe they haven't come across anyone like you before. You don't look like a hippy or a traveller.'

'I should think not,' I said. My thoughts had tired me and made me feel contrary. 'You don't look much like a hippy or a traveller either.'

'I've only just begun,' he said gloomily. 'Who knows how I'll end up. But listen, if you want to turn back I'll contact your friends for you.'

I sighed. 'I haven't got any friends in Addis and I never said anything about turning back. What's the matter with you all? I came to see the Rift Valley, that's all.'

'You don't have to impress me.' He touched my arm gently. 'I can see how hard it is for you. If you feel you can't make it, I'll deliver your letter.'

He was offering protection again. I folded my arms and stubbornly ignored him. Why should he think it was any harder for me than it was for him?

It became hard for us all in Shashamane. To begin with,

while we were still on the bus, I was rather pleased. We were on a proper paved road and the road ran straight through town. But when we climbed out of the bus on to the large dirt square which acted as a terminus I began to see what had happened when a village became big enough to be called a town. From all sides came the usual army of boys, and with them came the beggars. Not just beggars. Some of them were lepers, hideously deformed. A few, without legs, propelled themselves over the square on their hands alone, or crawled at frightening speed towards us.

The Ethiopians who got off the bus pushed or kicked their way through the throng but we, who had no idea where to go next, were stuck in the middle of it. Blind and noseless faces were pressing against us. Stumps of hands, withered arms and legs were exhibited.

'For fucksake, move!' Mel shouted furiously. He swung his backpack violently and forced a channel through the crowd. 'If any one of you – ' he turned his fury on the rest of us – 'if any one of you so much as gives out a bloody farthing – I'll kill you.'

It is a terrible thing to walk past such horrible distress, such mutilation. It was the sheer number that unnerved me. I could not stop. How could I pick out one or two from the mob? I was afraid of being mauled. I was afraid of being touched by a leper. I was simply afraid. I put my head down and ran after Mel. We outstripped the beggars, but not the boys. A hand reached out to grab my bag. I yanked it back.

'No, stop,' a voice said. We slowed down. A little fellow in clean white rags danced ahead of us, white teeth gleaming in a broad grin. 'Stop,' he said. 'Come, I find good hotel for you.' He reached for my bag again.

'Don't let the bugger take your bag!' Mel snapped.

'It's okay,' I said, trembling and breathless. 'I can carry it myself.'

'Okay, but come,' the imp said. 'I show.'

'All right, but *not* that way.' Graham pointed back to the bus station.

'No, no. Come.' He trotted off and we followed helplessly behind. 'American?' he asked over his shoulder.

'English. Where are you taking us?'

'Good hotel. I help you.'

'Oh yeah?' Mel snarled under his breath. 'How much will that cost, I wonder.'

The good hotel turned out to be another bar with a compound behind it, almost identical to the one in Moyale. But nobody argued. Nobody suggested looking for a better place. We put our bags in the tiny rooms which surrounded the compound without protest. Guiltily, I gave the boy a little money and a packet of Life Savers.

'What a bloody fool you are,' Mel said contemptuously. 'He'll get his cut anyway.' I slammed my door and collapsed on the verminous mattress.

My mother can never walk by a collecting box, a pavement artist, or a busker without parting with a few coins. 'Share your luck,' she says. And I do. It's like touching wood, a superstitious insurance against future penury. Now I feel as if there is a clamouring mob of beggars weighing down the scales against me. I have upset the balance and things will go badly for me.

An illogical fear of poverty haunts me. It is illogical because the family is comfortably off and lives in secure middle-class circumstances, and they would always back me up if I couldn't get a job or ran out of savings. The fear, though, may be inherited from my father.

Dad would like to be an English gentleman. He wears old tweeds and goes to the golf club every Saturday. He has a sensible portfolio of investments like all his friends. But, unknown to them, he also hoards gold. His safe is sunk into the cement of the garage floor under a workbench and neither Mother, the twins, nor I know quite what he puts away. I imagine it to be a gipsy collection of jewellery and Krugerrands but I've never seen it.

I don't know what it means to him, because whenever he talks about world events it is in that reasonable, objective tone of voice they all use at the golf club. But when any shortage or world crisis hits the headlines he spends a lot of time in the garage. Understandably, we didn't see much of him when the Yom Kippur war broke out.

Dad is one of the reasons why I have so much sympathy for Kenyan Asians like Mr Singh. They are resented, encouraged to leave Kenya, but restrictions on the export of wealth mean that they cannot go except as poor men. Mr J. Singh would like to join his brother in Wolverhampton. But the family and, I suppose, the family fortune is in Nairobi. So he stays behind working, trying to find a way to export their savings. Meanwhile brother V. Singh works till his back breaks in Wolverhampton to build a secure base in case the family should be thrown out of Kenya without a penny. The trouble is that if some people had their way Mr V. Singh would be thrown out of England without a penny too.

My father is lucky. He is a British citizen now, and no one can throw him out of England, but none the less he sees his security in the sort of wealth he can carry in his pockets. I often wonder what he thinks he is hoarding for. Is he afraid a change of luck could leave him a beggar in a dirty bus station?

I certainly was that day. If my bag had been stolen or if my pockets had been picked I would have had no option but to beg, borrow, or steal enough money to get to the nearest consulate. And who would give me anything in Shashamane – where there is so much real poverty on display – when I, in my good shoes and western clothes, hadn't given so much as a penny to a man with no legs?

3

That evening we shared a plateful of *injera* and *wat* and afterwards I sat by myself in the compound and smoked a cigarette. I felt tired and jumpy, but when the imp and two of his friends arrived I was prepared to be sociable. They asked my name and whether or not I was a Christian. Then the biggest one glared at me coldly and said, 'Only whores smoke.'

I glared at him equally coldly and said, 'Rubbish,'

He said, 'You see women in there?' He pointed with his thumb at the bar. I had seen several women, all in white dresses with embroidered borders. 'They smoke,' he went on. 'They are all whores. Whores live here.' He stared pointedly at my cigarette. 'Only whores smoke.'

I stood up and ground the cigarette out with my heel. 'You've a lot to learn, sonny,' I said loftily and stalked back into the bar with all the dignity I could muster.

Graham was in conversation with two local teachers so I sat down with Peter and Mel. I said, 'There's a little know-it-all out there who says all the women here are whores.'

Peter looked mildly surprised and said, 'Didn't you know? These so-called hotels have several functions.'

'Oh,' I said, confidence oozing away. 'He also said "only whores smoke." '

'Yes,' Peter said. 'In Ethiopia smoking is . . . a sin . . . disgusting . . .'

'Immoral,' Mel supplied, grinning nastily. 'If I were you, Fay, I'd give the rest of your cigarettes to me. And lock your door. If word gets round you've been seen smoking they'll be queueing up in the streets.'

'Why didn't you tell me?' I asked Peter reproachfully.

He looked puzzled and said, 'I did not know you did not know.'

'We all thought you were a prossie,' Mel said. 'But we're saving our money for Addis.' I stormed away to bed and made sure my door was bolted.

What else didn't I know? Usually a traveller is overwhelmed by instructions before setting out. There is always someone to tell you to cover your head when entering Italian churches, or that women aren't allowed into mosques, or that it's unwise to wear shorts on the street in India. Normally a traveller will mind her manners and normally local customs and morals are pretty obvious. If you look into a bar and there are no other women in there, you hesitate to go in without finding out whether or not they are prohibited. Here, I had felt comfortable in bars because they seemed to be run by women. I should have asked myself what sort of women.

For a woman alone in a strange land it is wise always to appear respectable, and I'm sure that staying in brothels is not the best way to go about it.

But what was the alternative? I pride myself on being able to find a cheap substitute for the pretentious hotels a film crew seem to favour. The Quaker house in Nairobi was a good example. I may have to share a kitchen and bathroom, but it is pretty clean and comfortable. So far in Ethiopia I have not been given the choice. Gabriel had chosen the place in Yabello. But maybe, like the people in the market, Gabriel did not know I was a woman. I wore jeans and I knew where the fuel line in his Land-Rover was. Maybe to Gabriel those are both such masculine characteristics that he looks no further. Maybe he sees my size and shape as deformities in a man, rather than seeing my dress and knowledge as unusual in a woman.

But then how did the boy in the compound know I was a woman when he said 'only whores smoke'? Perhaps he didn't, I thought suddenly. Perhaps the insult was even more deadly than I thought, and he was trying to pick a fight. If that was so, my behaviour was appropriate for neither a boy nor a girl. I had failed on all counts.

I nearly cried I was so hot and confused. Both door and shutter were bolted tight. Mosquitoes whined about my ears and bugs crept up through the mattress to feast on my blood. Sweat trickled down to water them. What Boots sold as insect repellent in England was not up to the job in Ethiopia. I got up and opened the door.

It was late. No light shone from the bar and not a breath of air stirred in the compound. Shashamane was built in a basin which collected hot, foul air the way a cesspit collects waste. I could hear a low, constant rustling and thought it must be rats.

The place on my shoulder where the tick had been was sore. I lathered it with antiseptic. I doused my sleeping-bag with killer spray and laid it on the dirt floor by the open door. The fetid air clung like wool to my oozing skin. I tried to sleep. A dog howled.

14

Long before dawn the cocks began to crow and I heard people moving back and forth. I couldn't see what they were doing but they made a lot of noise.

I dressed and persuaded one of the women to let me have a little water. In the bar I asked for *dabo* and *buna*. There was no bread, but the woman brought a small glass of sweet black coffee. She was vastly amused with my attempts at Amharic. Like the boy in Moyale, she wanted to hear me speak. She gave me words to repeat and laughed uproariously at my efforts. She rewarded me like a good parrot by stroking my hair.

When Graham, Peter, and Mel stumbled in I held up four fingers and repeated the word *buna*. '*Arat*,' she said sternly. '*Arat*.'

'All right then, *arat buna*,' I said hopefully. She doubled up with laughter, but brought four glasses of coffee. No one spoke while we drank. The men looked awful. They had dark circles under bloodshot eyes, stubbly chins, and matted hair. It had not been a good night for any of us.

'Let's get the fuck out of here,' Mel said eventually. It was light enough now to see our way so we collected our belongings and paid the madam. As if he had been called, the white-shirted imp arrived to escort us to the bus station.

'Go away,' Mel said sharply. But he snatched the water container out of my hand and stayed with us. I didn't mind. I was tired, and besides it wasn't he who had called me a whore last night. That had been his friend and, of course, Mel.

'*Ferenji! Ferenji!*' cried the children, massing round us, from doorways and alleys. '*Ferenji*, money!'

'No money,' the imp said to me.

'Okay, no money,' I said, and he grinned.

But as we approached the bus station he began to look uneasy. We passed groups of men huddled together. As we went by they turned to watch us. Some of them raised their sticks.

'What's going on?' Graham asked, dropping back. The imp shrugged and seemed even more anxious. The children fell silent and some of them slipped away into the alleys between the huts. Mel squared his shoulders and marched on.

The bus station was crowded. Buses standing in the dirty square were surrounded by groups of young men and teenage boys who held their long sticks like lances. The beggars, who yesterday had seemed so threatening, now huddled at the outer edges looking intimidated. There were no women.

As we came closer we heard the hoarse sound of shouted speech. A barrel-chested man in western garb stood on the platform of a bus and harangued the mob below him. Another cluster of men tried to shout him down.

The largest, most aggressive group were trying to overturn a bus, while the younger ones at the back threw stones. Glass shattered. The bus rocked wildly.

'Fay,' Graham said quietly, 'stay close to me. Don't get separated.'

We were seen almost immediately. Some stopped their arguing and shouting; others ran forward. It was not menace I saw in their eyes but excitement. They wanted something to happen. They wanted something to focus on. People were better than buses.

I was more afraid of Mel than I was of the crowd. He was the one, I felt instantly, who would turn the excitement to violence.

He dropped his backpack and stood, feet apart, fists bunched, shoulders braced.

The men raced towards us, their sticks up. Graham pushed me behind him. Reluctantly, he and Peter lined up with Mel.

There were a couple of seconds, as we came face to face, when nobody knew what to do. A couple of seconds while everyone waited for someone else to start it. A boy picked up a stone. My stomach clenched. I thought: I can't throw up now. And giggled. I couldn't help it. It's nerves – the sort of thing that drives your headmistress wild with anger. In that tense hiatus, sticks raised, fists closed around stones, I giggled.

It drew attention towards me and then *I* had to do something. I couldn't just stand there giggling. I slid between Mel and Peter and stood in front.

'*Tenastilin,*' I said. '*Salaama.* Good morning.'

'Oh shit,' Mel said in a whisper.

I focused on the face closest to mine. I can't cope with a crowd. So I picked just one face. A handsome face with a high-bridged nose that reminded me of Haile Selassie.

'*Tenastilin,*' I said again.

'American?' he asked aggressively. His stick was ready.

'No,' I said. 'Definitely not American.' A hoarse murmur ran through the crowd. Men pushed forward to see better. It was a good thing not to be American. Why? Would British be any better?

'American!' he said again. He was accusing us.

'No, no,' I insisted. 'Irish.' I don't know why I said that, but I was looking for the name of a small country without the taint of imperialism.

'Irish?' he looked puzzled and almost disappointed.

'Yes. You know. Ireland, a little green island in the . . . the Atlantic.'

He had never heard of it. He turned to the men closest to him and spoke. Everyone started talking at once. They jostled each other. More men shoved in from the back. I was edged to one side. My legs felt weak and I wanted to sit down.

A small hand plucked my sleeve. The imp, still carrying the water bottle, gazed frantically up at me. 'You go now,' he said urgently. I looked round for Graham. I couldn't see him any more. Only Peter's blond head was visible.

'Peter!' I said. He didn't hear me. I was afraid to shout. The imp pulled at my arm.

'Come,' he whispered. 'A bus. I show you.'

I backed slowly out of the mêlée. It wasn't too difficult with everyone else pushing forward.

When we were clear the imp began to run. I stopped him. 'Walk,' I said. 'Walk slowly.' I was short of breath.

We walked. Some of the men followed. I thought: if we don't run, they won't chase. My legs were wobbly.

'A bus,' the imp repeated. 'Hurry.'

'I want to go back to Dilla,' I said stupidly.

'Yes, yes. Come.' He took my hand and urged me on.

Just outside the square, half hidden by a row of shacks, was a green bus.

'Give me money!' the imp pleaded, driven to despair by my slowness. I gave him some money and he dashed away. To my surprise he ran to the bus. He was only just in time. The bus was already moving. He stopped it by dancing frantically in front. He opened the door.

'Come!' he screeched. At last I could run. I sprinted to the open door and jumped in. The boy had already paid the driver. He thrust the change into my hand. I thrust it back. I didn't have time to thank him or say goodbye. The bus lurched and the imp leaped back into the road. We roared away in clouds of dust.

Only then did the men who had been following start to give chase. They were too late. A few stones bounced harmlessly off the metal roof and the watching passengers began talking and laughing and thumping the floor with their sticks. One man, who had his white shawl draped round his neck like a college scarf, hung out of a window and shot his rifle in the air.

The bus was packed to the roof. Perhaps it would be the only one to leave Shashamane that day. Some country people at the back rearranged their bundles and made room for me. They tried to talk to me, to ask questions, but when they found I didn't understand they left me alone. Nobody seemed to know what had happened. I

74

watched and listened as the excited questions flew back and forth.

I tried not to think about Graham, Peter and Mel and about how I had called to Peter so softly that he couldn't hear. And how I had not shared this escape. Instead I watched a woman swathed in coloured shawls as she suckled a child who looked old enough to go to school. I concentrated on her as if one day, in some production, I would have to reproduce her costume for an actress. A yellow shawl with red kidney shapes hung from her head. The folds were hitched up on her shoulder. One end hid her breast and the child's mouth while the other was thrown carelessly round her neck. She wore bangles of beaten brass.

The shining blond hair which curled on Peter's sun-reddened neck had not yet darkened with sweat. He had a rather fragile boyish neck. If someone hit him with a stick . . .

The woman twitched her long skirt more comfortably over her knees. It too was red and yellow in thin stripes. I might have a hard job convincing a designer that someone would wear stripes and kidney shapes together. The reds and yellows didn't match either.

Mel would be all right: stones would simply bounce off him. I could tell Graham was frightened even when he pushed me behind him. I could have grabbed his sleeve the way the imp had grabbed mine. I could have drawn him backwards out of the crowd. He could be with me on the bus.

It was simple really: just three large squares of coloured fabric. One was a shawl, one a blouse, and the largest one was a skirt. The difficulty would be in draping them correctly and making them hang in those loose graceful folds.

15

After an hour I could kid myself no longer. We were not travelling south towards Dilla. The sun was almost always behind us, and we were facing west. I could not reach under the seat for the map without disturbing my neighbours who were both fast asleep. So I sat very still and panicked.

There was a lot more to knowing where you are than being able to tell yourself, 'Well, you are in a bus. The bus is on an all-weather road. You are forty miles from Shashamane, heading west.'

I was sent to boarding-school when I was eleven, and I remember clearly how I felt waking up there on the first morning. I didn't know where I was. I knew I was in a small dormitory with five other girls in Wellington House at Lady Vera Soames School in Surrey, but I couldn't remember how I had got there. I don't mean that I had blanked out the journey with Mum and Dad, but more precisely, I couldn't retrace accurately the route from home. I felt that if I could retrace the route and then reverse it, travel it backwards in my mind so to speak, I would still be attached to home. But I couldn't, so I felt as if a string had been cut and I was whirling, adrift from everything that was familiar to me. It was a physical sensation, a sort of vertigo.

When the rising bell went I couldn't even find the slippers I had placed so carefully under my chair before lights out. And when I found them I was not at all sure they were mine. They looked different: the red seemed paler and the crisscross pattern looked blurred. It didn't occur to me that I was seeing them for the first time with tears in my eyes – I was sure they weren't my slippers.

The sense of unreality was strengthened further when

the register was taken before assembly. The teacher called Fay Jas*sahn* and it sounded so unlike the Jason I was used to that I failed to answer. It wasn't my name and I looked round the classroom with the rest of the girls to see who the stranger was. That was how I acquired my reputation for extreme stupidity among the girls as well as the teachers. So on top of the stigma of sounding foreign – 'Fay's father's a wog,' some of them said – they also whispered to each other, 'Fay's so thick she doesn't even know her own name.'

In the playground I was asked why I didn't go to school in my own country. By that time I was quite prepared to believe that Gerrards Cross was indeed on the other side of the world so I answered the question quite seriously – which didn't do my reputation much good either.

Treated like a feeble-minded foreigner, it was difficult to hold on to my previous identity of an average English girl. I was placed in the lowest division for all subjects, and after a while I began to deserve my position at the bottom of the class. If, by some lucky chance, I answered a question correctly the teacher would say, 'Very *good*, Fay,' in that surprised tone of voice so insulting to people who are bright enough to know they are not clever. But by then I was delighted with any compliment, however insulting.

I remember Dad's face when he read my first term report. 'Tries hard,' he said, brow furrowed in puzzlement as he scanned the comments. 'Tries hard? Makes a great effort to keep up? Should be congratulated on her attempts to join in class work? And what's this? Fay has been slow to assimilate . . . assimilate? What is the bloody woman talking about? Fay's always had lots of friends. She's the most gregarious . . .'

My mother interrupted. 'What happened, darling?' she asked.

'I got everything all wrong,' I blubbered like a five-year-old. 'They don't like me because I'm the only one who . . . comes from Gerrards Cross.' Well, I couldn't tell Dad I was the only one with a wog for a father, could I?

Mum and Dad exchanged a long look which excluded me completely.

Mum said, 'Well, the twins are tough, and redheaded like me. And anyway, they've got each other.'

'Maybe it was a mistake,' Dad murmured sadly. 'I thought a good private school . . .'

'You only have one childhood,' Mum answered. 'It's a pity to spoil it.' No more was said then, or at any other time. Dad finished his breakfast and went off to the laboratory. I went to my room. I hadn't the heart to join the twins at the cycle track.

At the beginning of the next term I found myself at a local day school with a lot of my old friends from primary school, and resumed my average English childhood in the middle of the Second Division. I forgot about the Lady Vera Soames School for Girls.

16

There was no glass in the bus windows. I turned my face into the gritty wind and watched the small farming settlements as we rattled past. Little round houses, untidily thatched, sat in the shade of eucalyptus trees. Thick-billed ravens with white patches on the napes of their necks fluttered between roofs and branches and pecked at piles of dung. Looking like prophets from Bible stories, men rode their mules alongside the road. There was plenty to see but physical discomfort came down like a curtain between me and the view. I was too tired, too dirty, too itchy, and too thirsty to escape myself. Above all, I was plagued by anxiety and guilt.

When I think about it physical sensation has always been able to override my mind. I remember when I first met Tony McKitterick we were walking next to the theatre workshop building at college and he was explaining something about Brecht. When he put his hand on my shoulder to steer me round a corner, the muscles of my arm and shoulder began to twang and vibrate. They sang and hummed, and Brecht completely disappeared. I had to look him up in the encyclopædia when I got home that night in case Tony thought I hadn't been listening.

Now I tried to make the sore place on my shoulder come between me and the nasty scene in Shashamane bus station. Later, when I dreamed about it, I always called loudly to Peter. 'Peter,' I shouted. 'This way.' And the crowd parted to let Peter, Mel, and Graham float through.

But my subconscious had not yet invented this happy alternative. Instead, I imagined the worst: hands that held the sticks descended murderously; stones flew through the air and split skin and skull; Mel's furious eye squashed like a grape under a hundred angry feet. I remembered

Peter's description of the dead man in Snake Park whose body was so badly mutilated that for days nobody knew he had been shot, and I saw the mangled assembly of human parts that had once been Graham, Mel and Peter. I dug a fingernail into the tick bite. The pain was a relief.

The bus stopped at Soddo just as the light was fading. It was the end of the line. I stood in the dust and was at once claimed by another boy in a white shirt who grabbed my bag and said, 'Come.' Who were these snowy-clad urchins? And why could they speak a few words of English when it seemed that no one else could? Sometimes I imagined that they were all the same boy, hopping from town to town ahead of me, pausing only to wash the tattered shirt so that it would be clean for the next stop.

I came to welcome the sight of them. But somehow they were always too quick for me. I never had a chance to take my bearings or find somewhere to stay for myself. I would leave the bus, stiff, tired, and hungry, and immediately have to chase after my bag and its small porter to another bar, another mud-built compound.

Who knows? There might have been a decent hotel in Soddo with running water and a flush toilet. But by the time I thought about it I was already installed in a foul and crawling cell. The trouble is that a traveller who doesn't speak the language of the country will be forced to act without eighty per cent of whatever intelligence she was born with. She will be like a child dependent on only the limited number of things she understands. And believe me, in a country like Ethiopia, the things you understand are few and far between.

I was sick of my own ignorance. What I needed was a good local informant, and later on that evening when I met Yohannes Mariam, I thought I had found one. He approached while I was eating a lonely plateful of *injera* and *wat* in the bar. The white-dressed women watched rather crossly as he carried a small carafe of pale-yellow liquid over to my table.

'May I sit with you?' he asked politely.

'Please do,' I said formally. He sat. I offered him food. He offered me drink. He took a token mouthful of *injera* and I sipped a token drop of the wine.

'*T'etch*,' he told me. It was rather nice and tasted of honey.

'American?' he asked.

'No,' I said cautiously. 'English.'

'Ah.' He looked disappointed. He introduced himself. He was from Gondar in the north and he was doing his first year's teaching at a Soddo secondary school. He was unhappy with the appointment because he thought the people in the south were an uncouth, primitive lot. He wanted a post in Addis or his hometown.

'But,' he said, 'I must go where the Emperor sends me.'

'The *Emperor* sent you here?' I asked.

'He is the father of all the people,' he said piously. 'we must obey him.' He didn't know anything at all about Soddo except that he despised it, so I asked him about what had happened in Shashamane that morning. He didn't know. Shashamane might have been on another planet instead of a day's journey away. 'But,' he added vaguely, 'the students are on strike. The students at the University are always giving trouble.'

'But why should they attack the buses? Why were they angry with Americans?'

He shrugged. He did not care. 'They are all Communists,' he said dismissively. 'The Emperor owns all the buses. But myself, I like Americans. America is powerful, very rich. Americans come here, you know.'

'Here?' I looked around the dingy bar, with its earth floor, rough wooden tables, and inadequate candlelight.

'There were two of them. We had most interesting conversations. They will send me books when they return to America.'

'Where were they going?' I asked. I have certain preconceptions about Americans too, and one of them is that they are fastidious about bathrooms. I wanted to find a town fit for Americans where I could wash my hair.

'One of them is a teacher too,' he said, straightening in his chair and smoothing his white nylon shirt. 'He owns a Jeep, a very fine vehicle.'

I thought immediately of Nastasia Beyer, who was said to be driving a Jeep. But she was with a Greek, and anyway her destination was Addis. I would have to post her letter if I ever found a post office.

'Peace Corps,' Yohannes went on. 'A very fine teacher for Peace Corps.'

'But where were they going?' I asked again, dizzy with visions of tiles and stinging showers. It felt like weeks since I had been clean.

Yohannes seemed incapable of answering a direct question. It was not a reassuring characteristic, especially in a teacher. 'I told him,' he said, 'the Americans should build a factory here. They need a modern factory. The people are too backward.'

'What would they manufacture?

'Progress must be brought to these people.'

'But what would be made in the factory?'

'They are like peasants, these people. All they will think about is their land.'

'But . . .' I was suddenly too embarrassed to press him further. 'Roads,' I said instead. 'Progress and money always follow a road.' I thought about my little blue DKW abandoned in the police yard at Moyale.

'You are right,' he said, giving me all his attention. 'It is the only way to bring civilization to these peasants. They must construct a modern highway.'

'A factory would be useless without a road to transport the goods,' I said, nodding like a lunatic.

He beamed at me. From his point of view, we were at last having an interesting conversation. I stared at the back of my hand and saw how pale and wasted it looked. There were plenty of deep hollows between the tendons. It had not been like that a week ago. Yohannes's hands held his glass with delicate strength. 'Economic improvement. Industrialization!' he bellowed. 'We will catch up and then we will surpass.' I did not contradict him, or ask him about last year's famine in the north. He poured me another glass of *t'etch* and reality slipped even further away.

17

Next morning, before dawn, the boy tapped on my door and told me that a bus was leaving for Arba Mintch. During the night I had resolved that I must leave Ethiopia as soon as possible. I must always travel south towards the Kenyan border. I must not go back to Shashamane but take the western route round the lakes. I must not be rushed into making any more mistakes, and, most important, I must double-check all information about the destination of buses.

With these simple rules in mind I dressed hurriedly and went out to find the bus. It was there all right, a yellow ramshackle affair which, even unladen, tipped to one side. But there was no driver and no other passengers. It would not be going anywhere for a while.

The rabble of children who had followed me to the main square followed me back to the bar. I found a woman and asked for *buna* and *dabo*. Surprisingly, she brought both. This, I thought, was going to be a good day, and I would try to remain clear-headed throughout. No more rushing around in a panic or blindly following someone else who claimed to know where he was going. I was on my own now, and I would make my own decisions.

With the map spread out on the table I considered the options. There weren't any. The road south went to Arba Mintch and that was that. If I stayed on the road – and I had no intention of leaving it – I must go to Arba Mintch. From there a road wound between Lake Chamo and Laka Abaya and eventually back to Dilla. The frustrating thing was that I was really quite close to Dilla now – as the crow flies. But between Soddo and Dilla lay a river, mountains, and a narrow stretch of desert, all part of the Rift, and no road crossed it.

I calculated: a day's journey to Arba Mintch, another day to Dilla, two days to Moyale. If I was lucky and didn't have to wait for transport I could be back in Kenya in only four days' time. I dipped the hard bread into the coffee and smiled. Only four more days.

The small boy sidled up to me. 'Arba Mintch?' I asked.

'Arba Mintch,' he assured me. I gave him half my roll and he grinned, displaying beautiful healthy teeth. I was struck by how clean and shiny he was. What was his secret? Had he slept in a filthy cot as I had? I scratched the latest crop of bites under my arm and wondered at him.

'Americans?' I inquired. 'Did some Americans come here?'

'American,' he said, nodding. 'Yes.'

'Where did they go? Arba Mintch? Shashamane?'

'Arba Mintch,' he said, with an even wider smile. 'Come.' I went. for once I felt I knew where I was going.

'Arba Mintch,' the driver confirmed when I paid him.

'Arba Mintch.' The passengers nodded and smiled as I squeezed in beside two fat women. The bus rolled out of Soddo, grinding its gears and sending up a fog of orange dust. The women covered their heads and mouths with shawls, chickens squawked, the goat under the back seat bleated. We crawled, swaying and lurching, up into the hills – hills grazed back to bare earth, where herds of goats or scrawny cattle pecked like birds, and small boys lay on rocks to watch them.

I sat wedged between two coloured shawls and listened to the explosive, staccato sound of Amharic as the women talked across me.

The bus trundled down into gullies where even the road had been washed away. Keeping a road in place is a job for engineers. But keeping topsoil in place is the job of ordinary farming folk and their animals. And it is a much trickier problem altogether, especially in a place that is subject to droughts followed by sudden, heavy rainfall. A farmer should be much better educated than an engineer. But he rarely is.

From what I could see from the window rain would be almost useless in those hills. Rain in fact would wash away what little topsoil was left. Overgrazed land doesn't have plants to tie the topsoil down and hold the water. When it rains, not only does the water run away but it takes the topsoil with it. You can't plant in what's left. It's barren and useless dust, without the humus and rotting things that produce nitrogen.

The fat woman on my left nudged me and offered half a bottle of a cloudy yellowish liquid. It looked suspiciously like a specimen bottle but she indicated I should drink. It turned out to be a rough, weak sort of beer. Everyone in the bus watched expectantly.

'*Egzerstilin*,' I said. Someone, the policeman in Moyale I think, told me it meant thank-you. They all burst out laughing. They encouraged me to drink some more. So I did. It was very welcome. The dust that hung like fog in the bus had made my throat dry and sore.

'*Talla*,' the woman said, tapping the bottle. '*Talla*.

'*Talla*,' I parroted. Everyone laughed.

A man wanted to know what was in my bottle. 'Water,' I said. '*Wooha*.' That broke them up. He unscrewed the cap, tasted it, and then passed it round. From the overhead rack, from under the seats, from shapeless bundles held on laps, other bottles emerged. Everyone, it seemed, brewed their own *talla*. The bouncing, swaying bus trip turned into a *talla*-tasting party.

I took a drink from every bottle held out to me. The man leaned over and slapped my knee – I was a good chap, I did not get drunk and fall on the floor. They laughed. I smiled to show I was cheerful and friendly, but I couldn't laugh because I didn't know what they were laughing at.

This, I thought, is what being a foreigner is really all about. It is not wandering through a strange country seeing unfamiliar people: it's when all the unfamiliar

86

people stare at *you*, and find *you* strange: when you can't fit anonymously into a crowd: when your passing is an uncommon event. It's when you don't understand the joke, and the joke may very well be you.

They were kind to me, the people on the bus, but kind in the way you are to an animal once you reassure yourself it doesn't bite. They insisted on playing with their pet long after the pet was tired and wanted to be left alone. They wanted it to parrot words which it did not understand and which they could not explain. They wanted to see how much *talla* it would take to make it drunk.

Luckily for me, *talla* is a weak beer. I don't have a very strong head for drink: some of the silliest things I've said and done have been under its influence. I became attached to Tony McKitterick at a rather sozzled student party. Not that becoming attached to Tony was silly, but the way in which it happened was, and it became the basis for a lot of the mistakes in our relationship.

It was an end of year party organized by the girls who had finished the Theatre Wardrobe course and were about to launch themselves at the real world. I was still a first year student but we were invited too, and we all helped with the preparations.

There were no men on the course. While there are plenty of men who design costume, it tends to be women who translate the designs into workable patterns and who make them up, and when they are made up, maintain them. It was a wonderful course, which took in everything from the history of corsetry to how to construct a space suit. We learned how to make calico look like velvet, how to knit and spray string so that it would pass for chain mail, and how to fashion precious stones from epoxy resin. But we didn't meet many boys.

For those of us without boyfriends, the least embarrassing way around the problem was to throw the party open to the rest of the college and invite people from Stage Management, Design, and of course the weirdos studying fine art.

87

Sewing looks like a very refined occupation. You can be the wildest maverick in the world, but if you are sewing, especially by hand, you can't help looking refined. Which was why the Theatre Wardrobe department was known in the College as the Ladies or, more rudely, the Virgins' Retreat. We resented this, so when the Organizing Committee began to discuss possible themes for the party it came down to two choices – tarts or nuns. A spirit of irony was alive in the department and nuns won.

It was a mistake, because our rowdy guests took the wimpled, habited hostesses as something of a challenge and went all out to render us drunk and undignified – not a difficult task at an art college party.

My own downfall happened when, very stupidly, I accepted a five pound bet to drink a tumblerful of gin and stand on my head. I wouldn't have accepted if I had not already been given a lot of spiked drinks. But I wasn't too drunk to realize the object of the challenge was to make me show my legs and anything else that would be revealed if a nun stood on her head. So I solemnly hobbled my long habit round my ankles with a belt before attempting the balancing act. Up went my legs, firmly tied together – stupid but decent. Down came another nun who was dancing topless on a table and having trouble with her dangling sleeves. Decency and indecency crashed in total disarray on to the floor and it seemed as if the whole of the Fine Art Department, whooping and hollering, fell on top of us.

If I hadn't tied my legs together, I would have escaped with a few bruises. As it was, I couldn't escape at all, and when Tony fished me out from the bottom of the heap, mopped me off, and drove me to Casualty I was suffering from a couple of cracked ribs and mild concussion. He has never revised the opinion he acquired that night, which is that I cannot take care of myself.

18

Talla is nowhere as strong as neat gin, but all the same the brown, reedy expanse of Lake Abaya went by in a blur, and when we arrived at Arba Mintch I wasn't half as clear-headed as I had promised myself I would be.

We were set down at a crossroads opposite a bar. But I was not going to be rushed this time, so I hung on to my bag and the now empty water bottle and waited till the other passengers had sorted out their luggage and drifted away. I considered the bar opposite. It was low, tin-roofed and built of messily whitewashed mud. It looked like all the other bars I had stayed in, but this time I wanted a place fit for Americans. So I ignored the boy who had claimed me for his own and was trying to shepherd me over to it. I started off down the hill to the busier part of town where I supposed there would be more choice. The boy sighed gustily but came too, and all the other children, to whom the arrival of the bus had been the main entertainment of the day, fell in behind.

Later I was to discover that Arba Mintch was the capital of Gemu-Gofa, the province I was in, but just then it seemed like an ordinary small town, dirty, dry, jerry-built of tin, mud, and cardboard. It had a bustling quality that I would like to have watched if I hadn't been pushed along by the stream of followers and the shouts of '*ferenj*' that warned everyone of my coming.

In fact, I was being warned myself. The first clue I had that I was going in the wrong direction was the dead mule. It was lying in the middle of the street where people had to step around it. It was so bloated with gas that it looked as if it would soon explode, and its legs stuck stiffly out like the legs of an overturned table. The eyes and muzzle were covered with a blanket of fat black flies.

Also, the further we went downhill the hotter and smellier it became, and I was uneasy about the men rolling rusty barrels of water along the street. If they were selling water by the barrel it meant there was none running. The bus had forded a nearly dry river bed on the outskirts of town and I wondered if these men made a living selling water from the stagnant pools.

Thoughts of polio and bilharzia brought me to an uncertain halt. Immediately the children gathered round and asked for money. To avoid them, I turned sideways into a shop. It was little more than a three-sided market stall but it gave me some protection. The proprietor rushed forward and shooed the children away with his stick. He didn't actually hit anyone but only because the children moved too quickly. The boy stayed close by my side. His attitude told everyone, including me, that I was his personal *ferenj*.

The shopkeeper, by a fractional movement of his facial muscles, transformed his ferocious snarl into a threatening smile and I knew I had to buy something. The only thing I really wanted was fly spray – or some poison powerful enough to deal with Ethiopian insects. To his consternation I acted out a small mime for him. I pressed the button of an imaginary aerosol can and killed an imaginary fly.

'Buzz-buzz,' I went. 'Tsst-tsst-dead.'

His mouth fell open. In desperation I imitated a predatory mosquito. His face cleared, and he rumaged under a pile of coarse fabric. With a smile of complete understanding he offered me a Cellophane packet of assorted fish hooks.

I suddenly felt very tired and depressed. I looked round. Behind him on a single bowed shelf were a few stained and dented cans. The writing on the labels was in Chinese but the pictures showed pineapple chunks. I bought one and the shopkeeper reluctantly let me go.

There were several bars on the other side of the street. Tacked to the wall of one of them was an enamelled sign that read Fanta Orange. I was overcome, not only with desire for a cool drink but also with a sort of nostalgia brought about by seeing, among the Amharic hieroglyphics, something I understood. We crossed the road.

A raised length of boardwalk ran along that side of the street. Just as we were climbing on to it brakes screeched and a klaxon screamed. People fled in all directions, and within a couple of seconds the street was empty. An armoured personnel carrier drew up in a billowing cloud of orange dust and half a dozen armed men jumped out. They leaped up on to the boardwalk and piled into the bar, stiff-arming me and the boy out of the way.

The boy fell heavily into the dust and tried to scuttle out of sight under the boardwalk. I stood stock still and wished I could make myself invisible. The last man out of the vehicle stopped in front of me. He gazed at me with expressionless eyes and said flatly, 'What you doing?'

'Tourist,' I quavered. 'Good evening.'

'Go away,' he replied, still without any special emphasis. 'And be careful.' He marched on.

I picked up my bag. The boy picked up the empty water bottle. He gave me a watery smile and said very softly, 'Good hotel. You come now?'

We walked quickly and quietly back up the hill, past the dead mule.

I said, 'What's going on?'

He was frightened. He kept looking over his shoulder and urging me to walk faster.

'What's happening?' I asked again.

He shrugged. 'Trouble,' he said, 'much trouble.'

'I can see that,' I panted, 'but what sort?'

'Big trouble.' He began to run, but I was hampered by my bag so he slowed down again. Nothing chased us except the flies.

Meekly I allowed him to usher me into the bar of his choice. It was growing dark and my attempt at independence had failed. He handed me over to a white-dressed woman and, confidence restored, grinned broadly. 'Good night,' he said cheerfully. 'I come tomorrow.'

'*Denada*,' I said. 'Can you find out if there is a bus to Dilla?'

'Dilla?' he asked, cheerfulness faltering.

'Dilla,' I said firmly. We stared at each other. 'A bus to Dilla,' I repeated slowly.

'Bus, yes,' he said brightly, and disappeared. The woman, heavy-hipped and shuffling barefoot in the dust, showed me through to the compound. She pointed out the tap and the foul pit which she called the *shintabite*.

It was in the *shinabite* that I found the remains of an airmail copy of *Time* magazine. It was hanging from a nail on the door and most of the pages had been ripped out and used for toilet paper, so the article about the plane spotters on trial for spying in Sarajevo was only partly there and the war in Cambodia had been torn in half too. I didn't mind. This was a December issue and most of the stories had been news before I left England. What interested me most was that quite by accident I had found the hotel fit for Americans.

19

'Soldiers are very bad fellows,' said Mr Latybalu. He speared a pineapple chunk with long thin fingers. 'We must be careful with them. They are given very much money. So much more than the poor teachers. We must all bow to the soldiers.'

This was in reply to my question about what had happened in downtown Arba Mintch. The short answer would have been that he didn't know. But Mr Latybalu didn't go in for short answers. He was another teacher, from Manze in the north, and he was on strike. At least he thought he was probably on strike because he had heard something to that effect on the bar's radio. The only news service he could listen to came from Germany but it was broadcast in Amharic.

I was worried because he also told me that the buses were on strike too, and I wondered if this was the cause of the violence in Shashamane.

'If there are no buses, how shall I get to Dilla?' I asked.

'Where is Dilla?'

I showed him on the map. He shrugged. 'Anyway, there is a flood,' he said, without conviction. 'Maybe there will be a boat.' He took another pineapple chunk. 'In England, how much do you give teachers?'

'About forty pounds,' I guessed.

'A year?' he asked, looking impressed.

'A week.'

He stared at me aghast.

'There are no strikes in England,' he stated emphatically. I laughed sourly and told him about the miners, the go-slow on the railways, the engineers, the firemen, and the meat porters.

'In England, there are many Communists?' he asked tactfully.

'It's a democracy,' I explained. 'You can be what you like, up to a point.'

'The soldiers permit striking, in England?' Obviously he didn't believe me, because when I said that what action the unions took had nothing to do with the military, he quickly changed the subject.

'In America everyone is rich,' he said. 'In America every teacher is given a car and a radio. My friend Mr Victor is a rich man. He has a Jeep and a radio.'

'Peace Corps?' I asked, becoming interested again.

'He is a very fine fellow,' Mr Latybalu said, looking sad. 'He will send me books when he returns to America. In America they understand the importance of education. Here there is too much ignorance.'

'Where is Mr Victor now?' I asked.

'The boys he teaches are very lucky fellows to have such a man. At my school where I work are very ignorant sons of peasants.'

'What about girls?' I asked with a fatalistic sigh. 'Surely it's as important to educate girls as boys?'

'Girls will be married.' He spread his graceful hands and looked hopeful.

'But do you think it right for children to be brought up by women with no education?'

'Ah,' he began, his eyes brightening. 'The education of women, yes, you are right, there is a theory . . .'

What, I wondered miserably, was I doing wrong? Was it impolite to ask direct questions? I imagined myself shaking Mr Latybalu by the collar of his impeccable white shirt and screaming, 'How do I get to Dilla, dammit? Is there or isn't there a boat? Where is Mr Victor? Answers on a postcard, please.' But I also imagined him drawing back in disgust and saying, 'Only whores ask direct questions,' so I held my tongue and listened to his theory.

When he had finished I said cunningly, 'In America,

94

all the women can read. Mr Victor must have a very clever wife. Such a rich man must have a very fine house too.'

'All the houses in Chencha are very fine,' he said, looking sad again. 'Not like here. What they need here is a building programme.'

'And roads,' I prompted, while glancing surreptitiously at the map.

'Ah yes, a modern highway . . .' He spoke at length about the benefits of a modern highway. It was a subject I did not have to listen to so I looked attentive and let my mind wander.

Of course there was no modern highway running to Chencha. It is in the hills due north of Arba Mintch, about 4,000 feet above sea level, and I had already passed by it on another road. And, as it was not between me and the Kenyan border, I would not be going there.

If Mr Latybalu was right and the road between the lakes was flooded, I would have to take a southern route around Lake Chamo. North was entirely the wrong direction for someone who wanted to get back to Kenya as much as I did.

Later that night, tormented by lice and bedbugs, I relit the candle and made a new plan which avoided the supposed flood. To tell the truth, I didn't really believe in the flood; there had not been even a spot of rain and the earth was as cracked and dry as an old biscuit. However, I traced an uncertain white path on the map – Arba Mintch, Gardulla, Gidole, and Conso. Then a sharp turn southeast to meet the Moyale road at Yabello.

White roads on a map are generally the dodgy ones and this one plunged across what looked like desert. If you couldn't get enough water on the shores of a lake, what would happen in a desert? We had passed through part of it between Moyale and Yabello on the first day's journey north and Gabriel's Land-Rover had broken down. I wasn't looking forward to doing it again. But beggars can't be choosers and the Gardulla, Gidole, and Conso road became Plan B.

The candle spat and went out with a hiss of singed wax, leaving me in the dark with the rustling walls.

20

Both Plan A and Plan B fell apart in the morning.

To begin with, there was no breakfast. I waited hopefully in the bar but neither coffee nor bread appeared. Chlorine-flavoured water was the only substitute.

The boy arrived with his cheerful smile and no sympathy.

'No bread,' I grumbled after we had said good morning.

'Yes,' he agreed as if this were normal – and for him it probably was. 'You want a bus. Come, I show you.'

But outside, in the early morning sun, there weren't any buses either. Instead, a battered, rust-pocked Toyota Landcruiser with four bald tyres and no exhaust pipe stood as if waiting for a not too fussy wrecker. Already there were eight people and a calf in the back.

'Hurry,' the boy said. 'Very good bus.'

'Hold on,' I protested. 'Where's it going?' But instead of answering he threw my bag on top of the calf.

'Wait a minute. Where-is-this-bus-going-to?'

'Where you want to go?'

'Dilla.'

Again the puzzled silence. A big man sauntered over and, to my consternation, hauled out a rifle from under the front seat and strapped it to the windscreen. The boy conferred with him at some length before coming back to me.

'He say much water, Dilla. No road.'

That took care of Plan A. I said again. 'But where is the bus going?' and he repeated, 'Where you want to go?'

'Gidole?' I suggested. Perhaps the Toyota was more a taxi than a bus. The boy and the driver conferred again.

'Gidole!' The boy beamed and threw the water bottle

at the unfortunate calf. The woman who owned the animal cursed us roundly.

Still I hesitated. He had been too quick to agree that the Toyota would go to Gidole. How did I know it wasn't going back to Soddo? – or even worse, Shashamane? – or somewhere I'd never heard of in the west? And then there was the gun, and the four unsafe tyres, and the fact that already it was dangerously overloaded.

The boy said, 'One week, no more bus.' He held up two fingers for me to count. 'One week. Hurry.'

What was that supposed to mean? But I weighed another week in Arba Mintch with its soldiers and dead mule against the Toyota. I climbed in. Three more passengers followed. We were all more or less sitting on each other's laps, and because of the calf there was nowhere to put our feet. And I very soon noticed that the calf was incontinent. It was not going to be a pleasant trip.

The driver raced his motor and honked his horn. The crowd of observers stirred expectantly. And then another horn blared, and another Toyota roared up alongside and stopped. At first I thought it was another load of soldiers, but when the dust settled I saw a dumpy middle-aged white woman wearing a nurse's cap. She exchanged a few words in Amharic with the driver, and everyone leaned closer to listen. Then they all turned and stared at me. One of my neighbours gave me a little push to encourage me to get out.

'Hey!' I protested weakly, but already everybody was rearranging themselves to let me pass.

The nurse beckoned authoritatively.

'Please wait,' I entreated the driver. He nodded and I clambered out over the tailgate. As I went to meet the nurse the driver hooted and pulled away, and my bag and water bottle were dropped over the side.

'Wait!' I shouted. But no one heard. The nurse got down from her Landcruiser and said, 'So sorry.'

'Now I'll have to stay another week in this bloody town!' I was suddenly close to tears. The Kenyan border retreated like the mirage of an oasis in the desert. I was too upset to remark on what a bizarre meeting it was. All I could think of was the Toyota racing towards home without me.

'So sorry,' the nurse said again. She didn't look sorry, though. She had the look of a woman carrying out her duty never mind whose feelings she hurt in the process. 'You are American. Yes?'

'Can't anyone get anything right?' I exploded. 'I'm English.'

'Oh dear.' She looked a shade less confident. 'They tell me you are American.'

'They tell you wrong. Why didn't you ask before . . .'

'Well, never mind,' she interrupted. 'Please to come with me.'

'All I want to do is go home.' Disappointment made me childish. I had thought I was only three days from the border. A week and three days seemed quite unbearable.

'I see you are sad to stay,' she said without any sympathy at all. 'But we have with us a girl who is very sick. I think you want to help. No?'

I might have told her that I was running out of the energy and money to help myself, but I just stood and looked at her. She must have read my mind because she said, 'Oh, you hippies, you think everywhere is Amsterdam where you can come and go with nothing and everyone will give. You are so foolish to come here on your own.'

'I'm not a hippy!' I burst out, although no one who saw my dirty hair or clothes could know what I was.

'Well, never mind.' She set her jaw. 'I am Sister Ingrid. Please to come with me. We go to Hospital of Norwegian Mission.'

As I followed her to her car I began to see for the first time the dark patches of sweat under her arms and along her backbone, and to notice how yellow the plump face was, and how dull the grey hair. She wore white canvas shoes and her bare legs were veined and lumpy. Her eyes

99

were deeply embedded in fat, but the pouches were brown-stained. Helping people in a place like this took its toll.

The boy had remained with the circle of other children and now he stepped forward to help with my bag. They had watched the whole exchange with hungry fascination, but for once they had not come too close. Maybe Sister Ingrid had a reputation.

I could only wonder at myself. I would have expected to be overjoyed at meeting a resident European – someone who could explain what was happening, or perhaps suggest an alternative way to get out other than following my own ignorant nose. It made me realize how exhausted and desperate I was becoming. I am not normally so unwilling to help when asked.

So I said, 'What can I do to help?' And meekly got in beside her instead of asking if she could bring me back and when was the next bus out.

'It is a pity you are not American,' she said as she started the motor. 'But you must speak to the doctor who knows more.'

21

The hospital was built around a courtyard very much like the bar compounds: all the doors and windows faced into the yard. It looked more like a well-run racing stable than a hospital. But it was made of concrete and it did have glass windowpanes. It seemed as if each patient was accompanied by his entire family, so all the rooms were crowded with men, women, and children. Some families appeared to have made camps in the courtyard and others sat in groups along the covered porch.

I was supposed to wait for the doctor in the compound, but, taking shameless advantage of such a modern building, I asked Sister Ingrid for the toilets. She knew exactly what I had in mind because she said, 'You may wash your face and hands. But do not waste water on clothes or hair. We have not enough for sick people.'

It was terribly frustrating. There I was faced with the first enamel basin I had seen for ages and conscience would not let me put it to proper use. And in case conscience was not strong enough, Sister Ingrid waited like a guard outside the door. All the same, half a basin of clean water was more than I was used to and I managed to do a fairly complete job in the five minutes she allowed me.

How did *she* manage, I wondered. Her uniform, even though it was sweat-stained now, looked as if it had been put on clean. But she was not a lost tourist. She was doing a job, helping people. She needed to be clean to do her job. My needs were frivolous by comparison. I was someone who would waste hospital resources.

The doctor made the same point in a different way. He was stooped and thin. His faded sandy hair was the same colour as his skin and his steel-rimmed spectacles seemed to grow out of his bony nose as if he never had time to remove them.

'We are awaiting supplies,' he said in that curt, irritable manner born of weariness. He showed me into a little office. The window was open but the blind was drawn and the room was dark and airless. He sat behind a metal desk and waved a tired hand towards a chair. I sat too.

'There is some trouble in the north,' he went on, 'and the supplies have not come. This is bad. In Arba Mintch is the only hospital for all the people of Gemu-Gofa. They have no other.

'But as well as a doctor I am also a priest, so I will not turn away people who come. However, this American girl who is here can get help and money from outside.'

'I'm not American,' I said quickly. 'And I don't have much money, but how can I help?'

He shook his head, dismissing my objections. 'We have need to contact her next of kin,' he said, 'perhaps they can send help. But this is difficult. The telephone does not work. It has not worked for many days. I would otherwise telephone to her embassy in Addis.'

I absorbed the implications of 'next of kin' and asked, rather fearfully, what was wrong with her.

'It is rickettsiosis, what you may call typhus. It is common here.' He looked up sharply. 'You are vaccinated. Yes?'

'Yes.'

'She was not so wise. She has also dysentery, which too is common and maybe she cannot avoid. But, you see, in Arba Mintch is epidemic and we have not yet our supplies.' He spread his bony hands.

'I see,' I said slowly. 'So you want me to get a message to her family or her embassy. Is that it?' I was not surprised that there was an epidemic in Arba Mintch but the news made me even more sorry that I had been prevented from leaving.

'That is not all,' the doctor said ominously. 'The man who brought her here, brought only her. We do not have her luggage or her papers, so although we know her name we do know who else to contact. She is now delirious. This man must be informed. He must bring her papers.'

'But I am not going to Addis,' I told him. 'I was half way there but there was some sort of riot at Shashamane. Now I'm trying to get back to Kenya.' I wanted to say that I needed help too, but shame stopped me.

'Trouble in Shashamane?' he asked and looked very thoughtful. 'It is spreading. We heard it was only in Addis with the students and teachers. Perhaps this is the explanation of the telephones. You are wise to avoid trouble. Wiser still you would not be here. But you are here, and we must make use of you. This man is in Chencha. He is Peace Corps worker.'

'Mr Victor?'

'Victor Bartholomew – you know him?' He stared at me suspiciously.

'I heard about him yesterday.'

The doctor's face twitched with a spasm of resentment. 'It is very irregular,' he muttered. 'This man brings her to me, sick and injured, and drives away. We have sent two messages to Chencha but we have heard nothing.'

'Injured?'

'Superficial,' he said, shrugging. 'But I must ask you please to go to Mr Bartholomew and persuade him to come. Or if he cannot, please to bring her luggage yourself.'

I didn't know what to say. In England I would not have hesitated, but now, when I wanted so badly to go home, I was hindered by visions of epidemics, spreading trouble, bad roads, and the fear of being stuck without money in an isolated place even further from Kenya than I was now.

As if sensing my doubts the doctor added, 'There is a healthier climate in the hills.'

'How do I get there?' I asked. I did not want to commit myself.

'You must ask in the town,' he said vaguely. 'They will tell you. And now – ' he looked at his watch – 'I must go.' He stood up. I stood up. He seemed to assume I had agreed.

'Wait a minute,' I said. 'What is the American girl's name? And how will I find Victor Bartholomew when I get to Chencha?'

'Everyone in Chencha will know.' He had his hand on the doorknob. 'The American girl is Nastasia Beyer. And now you must excuse me.'

He left me standing with my mouth open. Nastasia Beyer, who had left an English boyfriend in Nairobi to go to Addis with a Greek, had turned up in Arba Mintch with an American. And I, who should have gone to Addis alone in a car but actually got as far as Shashamane in a bus with three companions, was now only a few yards away from her. Neither of us should be here. If everything had gone to plan we wouldn't be. I would have dropped her letter at the American Express office and that would have been that.

But, from the moment I saw the date, 9.6.66, which the immigration man had written in my passport, everything had been played by Ethiopian rules – rules I knew nothing about. I wondered if anyone here ever achieved what they set out to do.

I supposed that in a place like this where there are so few white people, the ones you do come across, even if only by word of mouth, you will come across time and time again. And if there are only a few driveable roads you will find yourselves driving the same ones. But even so, standing in the doctor's shabby little office, I felt as if someone was playing tricks.

Nastasia and I were already connected by a letter which was in the bag I carried. I could not refuse to help. I wanted to help, or rather, I would have if helping had not been so difficult.

Certainly I wanted to see her. But when I made my way out into the compound I could not find Sister Ingrid. In the end, a turbaned man, thin but as far as I could see perfectly healthy, pointed with his stick towards an open door. Another man was squatting in the doorway, and past him I saw a small room with two beds. In one of them a woman lay propped up on pillows. Under it were two children, stretched out and fast asleep. I could not see who lay in the other bed because whoever it was had curled up facing the wall and covered her head with a sheet. The woman I could see smiled wanly. I gestured towards the other bed and she replied with a stream of Amharic. The man came in and stood beside her. The children woke up and stared, fingers in mouths.

The shape in the second bed did not stir. 'Nastasia?' I said experimentally, 'Nastasia Beyer?' But whoever it was remained silent and still. The woman, still talking excitedly, touched her lips with her finger and shook her head.

'Is she asleep?' I asked, and rested my cheek against my hand.

The woman replied at length. It sounded like a bitter complaint, against illness, against life, against her unknown neighbour. I held my hands out, palms down, in a placatory way and backed out of the little room. The staccato voice followed me.

If it was Nastasia, she was sharing her tiny ward with a strange family: man, woman, and children. I wondered how she felt about it or whether she was too ill to care. But I could not be sure who the huddled shape under the sheet was. I could not be sure of anything. This was Never-Never Land – maps lied, embassy officials lied, there were no buses, people turned up in all the wrong places. An American woman lay in a hospital bed and did not show her face. Maybe I had seen her; maybe I hadn't.

One thing you could rely on, though, was the children. They assembled apparently out of thin air and formed their jeering, hooting throng as I plodded wearily down the hill to lower Arba Mintch and then up it again to the bar. It was only about twenty minutes' walk, but the bag gathered weight at every step. The camera and binoculars I had thought essential at the beginning were nothing but a burden.

I stopped for a breather at the stall and bought another can of Chinese pineapple chunks. The proprietor still wanted to sell me fish hooks and I was too tired to make another attempt at asking for fly spray.

The children, sensing weakness, gathered closer and took more liberties. Sly fingers searched for the zip of my bag, they poked and prodded me up the hill.

I arrived at the bar soaked in sweat and goaded almost beyond endurance, asking myself if I was still the same woman who had been so shocked when the Moyale policeman had thrown stones. If I had been in possession of a stick or a stone I might have done the same thing. I was tired of them and their constant attention. They were a hazard, a menace. They were worse than the flies because I couldn't brush them away.

The only times I could be alone were in the fetid little bedrooms where I was harassed and goaded by the crawling, biting things that inhabited the walls and bedding.

22

Crawling things. Lice. Typhus. You catch typhus from lice. Or rather typhus is carried from person to person by body lice – worse, by louse shit. An infected louse takes a meal from a healthy person and defecates. The person scratches the infected faeces into the irritating bite. Typhus enters the bloodstream.

The louse is almost transparent, so you won't see it easily. It won't see you at all because most lice are sightless. But you'll feel it all right – it has large claws and a very well-developed piercing and sucking part at its front end. It is only about four millimetres long and should not be confused with the woodlouse which does nobody any harm and is anyway not a louse at all – more a sort of land crustacean.

I did not know what to do next, so I sat undecided on the edge of the dirty cot and thought about the cool, moist places where you might expect to find woodlice: under rotting logs, in the holes and crannies of stone walls. Woodlice do not like the sun. They seek out damp shadows.

The woodlouse brought me to an even more comforting subject – trilobites. A trilobite looks like a flattened woodlouse. The one I have comes from the family *Aulacopleura*. It might have come from North Africa, from around here in fact, and it is about four hundred million years old. It cost me ten pounds, nearly half a week's wages at the time, but it was worth it because it is so beautiful. Dark grey, like polished slate, it emerges from its sedimentary bed like a half-finished carving by a jeweller.

Thinking about fossils was a waste of time. I was frightened by what the doctor had said. I didn't know if he meant there was an epidemic of typhus or dysentery in

Arba Mintch. It looked like a likely spot for both. And I wondered if the flies crawling round my plate were the same ones which had been on the mule carcase or swarming on the *shintabite*. Flies are so mobile.

But at least you can see them. I couldn't see what was living in the bedding. I couldn't see what had infested my clothes.

I closed the door and shutter and undressed. My pale skin was covered with angry lumps and swellings.

The towel I was using as a wash-cloth was filthy, my clothes were stiff with dust and sweat and something was living in the seams. No wonder Sister Ingrid treated me with disdain.

I used the cleanest corner of the towel and a little drinking water to wash with, and then smeared insect repellent all over. The last of the spray went on clothes and bed. It was not enough.

The tick bite was so raw and pus-filled I could scarcely touch it, but it had to be cleaned too.

At that moment I would have sold my soul for a cool bath and a clean towel but there were no offers. I had become too poor a specimen even for the devil.

I still did not know what to do, so I took up a pad and pen. '*Dear Tony,*' I wrote. '*By now you will have read my letter from Kenya. I take it all back. I was restless. I wanted to do something different. I couldn't bear the thought of another February in England with no light and no lights and everyone moaning about the miners and the Arabs.*'

I tore that up, and started again. '*Dear Mum, What can I do about my clothes when there's no water to wash them in?*'

There are rambling roses growing up the post my mother suspends her washing line from. On a windy day the wet laundry tangles with the roses, and often my father's shirt-sleeves have little tears in them from the thorns.

'For God's sake prune those bloody roses,' Dad bellows

when yet another shirt has been sacrificed. But Mum doesn't agree with pruning.

'When does nature prune?' she asks placidly. 'It doesn't seem right to cut a good plant back to an ugly stump.'

She isn't very keen on weeding either. 'They may be weeds to you,' she tells my grumbling father. 'But they're wild flowers to me. What would England be like without its hedgerows?'

'I'm not arguing with hedgerows,' says poor Dad. 'I just want a decent lawn like everyone else. I don't want a bloody meadow. And why is the rockery covered with parsley? What's wrong with alpines?'

All the neighbours get their parsley from Mum. She lets it seed wild, and thick green clumps of it turn up all over the place. There is nothing wrong with the topsoil in *her* half-acre.

'Dear John and Bill,' I wrote to the twins, *'Correct me if I'm wrong, but you two only got as far as Marrakesh, didn't you? Salute your intrepid sister currently hoofing it through darkest Ethiopia.'*

They sent us postcards when they remembered, from Paris, Marseilles, Algiers, and Casablanca. They would have gone on to Israel but they ran out of money in Marrakesh, and came home brown and sinewy, with strings of cedar beads, hideously carved camels, and a couple of rather lovely kaftans. Dad wired them the fare.

'Never mind,' he said, wincing tolerantly. 'At least they kept out of jail.'

I was at school at the time and I was deeply shocked by one of their souvenirs. They brought back well over an ounce of Moroccan hash which they smoked in a locked bedroom with the window open. I expected them to turn into drug-crazed lunatics in front of my very eyes. But all they did was laugh a lot and play Jimmy Hendrix records. In the end I overcame my doubts and begged to try it too. But they wouldn't let me.

I tore up the twins' letter. I didn't have anything to say to them either.

Like my mother, the twins are big-boned and red-headed.

'Auburn,' Mum says huffily. 'Red may be all right for men, but it simply won't do for women. Remember, Fay, your mother has *auburn* hair.' And so she does. Now. A picture of her and Dad taken just before the end of the war shoes something a lot lighter and wilder. He is still in uniform, dark, neat, and apprehensive – not a fighting man, just a bright young engineer whose brains had rescued him from an internment camp in Wales, and whose know-how with bridges bought him a uniform. They never talk seriously about the war or about how they met, and there are a lot of things I don't know about them and the families they came from.

There is another picture, much older, of Mum's parents: red-headed Joakim Perieras and his tiny wife holding my infant mother who seems to be swathed in a tablecloth. No one says anything about Mum's mother and, looking at her faded portrait, you can see something a little different about her. All we know is that she came from Cuba and she died when Mum was still a baby. The woman we refer to as Grandma P was her stepmother, and she died in Miami only last year. Grandpa P still lives there.

I am supposed to take after my father. And it's true that we are both dark-haired and dark-eyed. But his hair is straight and he is quite tall. Sometimes I look at the picture of Mum's real mother and wonder.

23

It could have been thoughts of home and family which gave me such a strange dream that night.

I found my tiny grandmother embedded in shale on a Chencha hillside. 'Don't you worry, Granny,' I said. 'I'll get you out and take you home. Mum'll know what to do.'

'Fay's so stupid,' John said to Bill. 'Granny's been dead for four hundred million years. What would we do with a fossil gran?'

The fossilized grandmother laughed, and shattered into hundreds of tiny splinters which fell like obsidian rain into the Rift Valley. I ran after them and tried to collect them all up.

'I can't just leave bits of her in Africa,' I cried.'I've got to take them all home.' But it was like a jigsaw with lots of pieces missing, and I had a hole in my pocket so I dropped as many as I found.

In the morning, I tried hard not to think about Nastasia. I asked everyone I could find with the barest smattering of English about transport either to Dilla or Gidole.

Who were these informants? Well, none of them were women or girls, that's for sure. And they were not the men with bare legs who wore robes. No, a white shirt and trousers seemed to be the mark of an English speaker. One man told me that in four days someone was going to Gidole. Another said that there might be a boat to Dilla in two weeks. No one confirmed what anyone else said. Each had his own information and it was unique. Not one of them ever said, 'I don't know.' They would always begin by agreeing with me. So, 'Is there a bus to Dilla?' would be answered by 'A bus, yes.'

'When?'

'Oh, maybe ten days. There is a river – ' shrug – 'no bus can go there.'

There was a matter of style or manners that I hadn't grasped yet.

My conclusion was that on that specific day there were no buses to anywhere I wanted to go.

I had to admit, even though I had promised the doctor, I did *not* want to go to Chencha. It was close by, but short journeys on the map could turn into very long ones on the ground. Also I had sworn to myself that I would only travel south. Chencha was north, about forty miles up a white road, almost a quarter of the way back to Soddo. By now I had an almost superstitious reluctance to go in the wrong direction.

But in the end I went. To my shame, my motives had less to do with any wish to help Nastasia than with my desire to leave Arba Mintch. There was an uneasy feeling about the town, and three times I saw soldiers in their vehicles speeding down the road towards the bottom of the hill.

I was almost annoyed with poor, sick Nastasia. Pity is such a frail thing, so easily crushed by one's own fear or need. Well, in my case it was. People like Sister Ingrid acted on it in their own way. They stuck it out for years in places that finished me off in a single night.

There were thirteen of us packed into the Toyota to Chencha. All the men were armed with their long, stout staves or with rifles. When I asked my patient little friend why, he said at first, 'Crocodiles,' and then, cautiously, '*Shifta*.' The *shifta*, it appeared, were sort of all-purpose bandits who were both feared and admired by ordinary people.

The journey took over three hours. We crawled up hills fit only for goats, and ground through dry river beds. We swayed and lurched and breathed pure dust. But as we climbed, the country grew more beautiful. The earth was

112

rusty red. There was some grass and trees, and far below, even muddy Lake Abaya looked clean and blue.

It was cooler in the hills and the light had a sparkling mountain quality. At altitude, the coolness is deceptive, the air is thinner, and there is less protection from the sun. But I didn't care. In spite of the dust the air smelled clean. There would be no epidemic here.

Chencha itself was on the top of a gentle hill. Behind it, in the distance, blue and purple mountains rose like a fence to protect it. To the east the ground fell away sharply in a series of steep steps to the bottom of the valley. Late afternoon sun slanted down the broad red street, and on either side were low mud buildings.

The children herded me, like a single sheep, into the largest of three bars on the main street. No time to stretch or look around, there was only one place for *ferenj* to go and she went.

The dim room was unusually chilly and the madam wore a shawl over her black dress. She sat like a queen in a straight-backed chair and although she was broad in the haunch her face was long and fine-featured. I smiled. She gazed back out of the deep-set black eyes and the corners of her mouth twitched up. When I greeted her and asked for a room she did not scream with laughter or look blank like some of the other madams had. I had amused her but she was not at all disconcerted.

The girl she summoned was about my own age. She wore the traditional calf-length white dress, but covering her hair was a tricel scarf with a random and very loud pattern of pink and green geometric shapes – cheap and very western.

I was tired. I seemed to be getting tired earlier each day and it occurred to me that, small as I was, the unchanging diet of lentil sauce with the *injera* pancake was inadequate. All I wanted to do was lie down for a few minutes, so I didn't notice much about the girl or the compound she led me across.

Apart from diet, it was the feeling that I was giving a

public performance that was wearing me down. To be ceaselessly followed, stared at, whispered about, laughed at, is exhausting. There are actors and singers who must be used to it, who even court it, but I was finding it very hard to bear. And when the girl showed signs of wanting to stay in the cramped little room to watch while I sorted myself out, my patience snapped.

I put her out as politely as I could. When she had gone, I suddenly and without any particular reason burst into tears and cried without stopping for nearly half an hour. I couldn't think why I was doing it and I couldn't control myself either. All I could do was close the door and shutter and bury my head under the sleeping-bag. It was a peculiar enough thing to do; I didn't want to make a lot of noise about it as well.

24

It was evening and I knew I should leave the room and get something to eat. I had to find Victor Bartholomew. But that meant talking to people and I simply couldn't face it. With the tears, it seemed, my reserves of courage and sociability had seeped out too.

The room was airless but it was getting cold as well. I didn't want to stay in it: I didn't want to leave it. It was a dirty claustrophobic shell I had crept into to hide. Go or stay, stay or go. I simply couldn't decide which would be worse.

I must have gone to sleep because all of a sudden there was an Ethiopian judge in there with me. He wore the scarlet of an English judge, but instead of a wig he draped a white shawl over his head. And for a gavel he held a stick. The little room had become a cage with rows of ragged children pressed up against the bars, watching and muttering, '*Ferenj, ferenj.*'

The judge banged his stick on the floor and said, 'Why have you come?'

I tried to answer but my tongue was paralysed and I could only gargle.

'You are wasting hospital resources,' the judge intoned. 'And you refuse to entertain the people.'

My tongue loosened and I told him that I knew it was an important production, but really I was only responsible for ironing the ruffs and sewing sequins on the costumes. I wasn't an actor.

'It's not enough,' the judge said, pointing an accusing finger. 'What they should do is build a modern highway.'

'I know,' I said, trembling. I was guilty and I knew it. 'But there isn't enough topsoil.'

'Then why are you here?'

I woke up as suddenly as I had dropped off. Someone was tapping at the door. I lit the candle. The door opened and a round face and coloured headscarf appeared. She brought her hand up to her mouth and made eating motions. I nodded.

She had soft blunt features, very pretty, with no trace of solemnity. Her eyes invited laughter and, looking at her, I felt oddly forgiven. She watched while I wiped my face and brushed my hair. She wanted to touch but she restrained herself.

When I was ready she blew out the candle and, with a piece of my sleeve between thumb and forefinger, led me across the dark courtyard, to the lamplit bar. She brought my food and stayed to watch me eat. She only took a morsel when I offered her the plate, but to my embarrassment she began to feed me, expertly tearing off little bits of *injera* and popping them into my mouth.

There were other girls in the room, and a few men too and I started to wonder if perhaps she had made a mistake about me, that in spite of having watched me brush a great length of hair, she had taken her clue from the jeans. On the other hand the mistake could have been mine and feeding someone a normal friendly action between two women.

I was relieved when a man, who could only have been a teacher, sat down at my table and brusquely sent her away. She pouted and went as far as the doorway.

I was right, Tadesse Gebre-Mariam was a teacher, and like the others he came from the north. He was a small, anxious man who had just had all his poultry killed by mistake. 'It is the malaria eradication programme,' he said mournfully. 'I tell this man he must spray at water places for mosquitoes but he sprays instead my hen house. It is so stupid. Now it is Lent and I cannot eat the hens.'

'Also they would be poisonous,' I said, making sympathetic noises which to my horror sounded almost like clucking.

'Poison, yes,' he agreed, looking puzzled. 'How can

malaria eradication be scientific when uneducated men spray poison on hens?'

'Is malaria very bad in Chencha?' I asked. It wasn't as if I had neglected to inquire after Victor Bartholomew. It was just that the question had been ignored.

'Chencha is once capital city of Gemu-Gofa,' he said. 'There is much disease, so the capital is moved to another place.'

This was the first time anyone had volunteered any local information. I must have looked surprised because he said, 'I am historian. Do you know we have in Ethiopia the oldest civilization in the whole world? The Majesty Emperor Haile Selassie is related to the King Solomon.'

'Ah yes,' I said. 'You mean the Queen of Sheba . . . ?'

'You ask of my friend Mr Victor,' he put in suddenly. 'He is at this time at Arba Mintch.'

'Arba Mintch?' I said, feeling very tired and confused.

'Arba Mintch is now capital of Gemu-Gofa. You must visit. There are forty hot rivers in the ground.'

In the days I spent in Chencha, whenever I came across Tadesse Gebre-Mariam, he often rendered me speechless by dipping into his bran tub of conversational openings and presenting me with unanswerable statements like: 'Ethiopian Christianity is the one true Christianity in the world,' or 'In the thirteenth century Amda Tseyou vanquishes sixty Muslim warlords,' or: 'Ethiopia has the healthiest climate on earth,' or: 'When the King of Kings, The Majesty Haile Selassie opens our modern dam on the Blue Nile we will be the most modern agricultural and industrial nation in African continent.'

He presented Ethiopia to me as a dream of all that was ideal, a perfect land which a few stupid peasants were trying to hold back. His anxious eyes willed me to believe him, and I became anxious too. It was the same sort of anxiety I feel when faced with a Christian Scientist who says categorically, 'There is no such thing as sickness, disease, or death.' While finding the words, in the face of the evidence, unintelligible, I am forced to respect the

117

belief. I do not think it is my place to contradict. After all, what do I know about other people's faiths? – or about Ethiopia for that matter? Was a dam being built on the Blue Nile? I never found out.

But he was wrong about Victor Bartholomew. He was not still in Arba Mintch and he walked into the bar about nine-thirty.

25

Tadesse Gebre-Mariam made a long formal introduction which he obviously enjoyed. Victor enjoyed it less.

'Hi,' he said, rolling his eyes up to the ceiling and sitting heavily on a stool at our table. He called loudly to the girl who brought a fresh carafe of *t'etch*. She was delighted at the new diversion and sat herself down on his knee till he crossly pushed her away.

'That Abbavich,' he said, annoyed. 'She can be a goddamn nuisance. So, how're you doing? What's new?'

I stared at him in astonishment. He seemed to have only one nostril. His nose was so bent to the left that, full-face, just the right one was visible.

'Er . . . well, fine,' I said. After an hour's conversation with Tadesse, Victor seemed unbelievably casual. 'I just came up from Arba Mintch.'

'Yeah,' he said. 'You would have. What a hole. So what's going down? I heard there was some trouble.'

It was one of the things I wanted to ask *him*, but I said anyway. 'Well, there are a lot of soldiers about, but I don't really know what's happening. They say the teachers are on strike.' I looked expectantly at Tadesse, but he sat prim and upright, saying nothing. 'Students too,' I went on. 'And the phones are out. And there don't seem to be any buses.'

'Yeah, forget that,' Victor said nonchalantly, 'It's Lent. And if it wasn't Lent there's a whole bunch of religious festivals to gum up the works.'

'St George is our patron saint,' Tadesse said, nodding.

'Really?' I asked. 'He's ours too.'

'Soldiers, huh? I heard there was some sort of demo in Addis and a couple of kids got shot. Were you there?'

'No, I haven't been there.'

'Addis Ababa is meaning New Flower,' Tadesse said, looking discouraged. 'There is the home of my family.'

'So how did you get here?'

'From Kenya.' I looked from one to the other. Each seemed to be in a world of his own. 'Listen,' I addressed myself to Victor, 'the doctor in Arba Mintch sent me to find you. He wants to get in touch with Nastasia Beyer's family but apparently you have her papers.'

'Who says?'

'The doctor,' I said with that familiar sinking feeling. 'The doctor said you took her to hospital.'

'You mean Stasie? Isn't she better yet?'

'The doc says she's got typhus.'

'Typhus – no shit!' Victor looked concerned. 'Good thing I had my shots. Wow – typhus: that is *heavy*.'

'Yes. So the doctor wants to get hold of her people.'

'Yeah, right,' Victor said. 'So maybe you could take her stuff when you go back down the hill.'

'Well, yes,' I began, startled, 'except I haven't any transport of my own, and it's a question of waiting for buses. I was told you have a Jeep.'

'No kidding! This isn't a place for no wheels.'

'I know, but I had to leave my car at the border.' It was too complicated to explain, and he didn't want to know. He said, 'Well, hey, I got to hit the sack now, but I'll talk to you in the morning.' And he went.

26

In the night the tin roof crackled and sounded tantalizingly like rain. Twice I stumbled out to the *shintabite* and was violently sick. I wondered vaguely if it was anything to do with the altitude, and tried not to think about the first symptoms of typhus. I could not get typhus, I told myself firmly. I had been vaccinated.

But the morning was clear and clean and there was a frosty zing in the air, so although I was tired and weak, I felt encouraged. When Abbavich came to my door to summon me to breakfast she brought with her a little girl, no more than ten years old. The child wore a yellow dress with a bow at the waist. It was like a hand-me-down party dress. Abbavich straightened the bow and petted the child's face, and then pushed her forward to shake hands. They both giggled merrily.

It became a morning ritual to shake hands with Abbavich and Wobit. I don't know if Wobit was the child's real name or a nickname, but that is what everyone called her, and it suited. She was a quick-moving sprite who turned up in all the photographs I took of Abbavich and the other girls. There is Abbavich, trying for once to look serious, and in the background a bright-eyed blur that is Wobit. And Hijibatchaw, who was never anything but serious, and brought a chair out into the sun when she posed for her picture, is staring gloomily into the lens while behind her dances laughing Wobit. Lielit was the one who was not pregnant. Hijibatchaw looked as though her baby should have been born weeks ago and Abbavich sported a small roundness which was probably only four months old.

Abbavich was a true extrovert. The others were always shouting at her because she was lazy and never finished a job properly, Madame scolded her, Victor called her a pest, but she was the one who, through sheer good spirit, broke through the language barrier and made me feel I had found a friend.

She teased me, she laughed at me, she tried on all my clothes, she was insatiably curious, but she also washed my hair. And she went to the market with me and bartered for a shawl so that I could keep it clean. Without her, I would never have discovered how to ask for fly spray.

What a woman. She insisted on wearing my shoes even though her feet were too big. She trod down the heels and pinched her strong straight toes, but it gave her a pleasure I couldn't understand. My hair was a source of wonder to her, but she found my whiteness hilarious. When at last curiosity overcame her and she looked under my shirt at my flat, pale belly she laughed till she cried. She proudly displayed her own – bulging and shining with health – as a demonstration of how things ought to be. Hijibatchaw frowned, at her immodesty I supposed, but she didn't care. And nor did I. Hijibatchaw and Lielit tried to take me in hand. They showed me the dreadful secrets of the cooking shed, the fermenting batter from which *injera* is made, but Abbavich always claimed me back. I was *her* friend, *her* pet.

Of course we never really exchanged a word. According to Victor, she didn't even speak Amharic properly. 'In Ethiopia,' Tadesse told me proudly, 'are fifty-two different languages.' But in her own way she was a far better communicator than he was – or Victor for that matter.

Victor. He did not turn up to talk things over that first morning. I waited for him in the bar and drank coffee quietly with Madame but he did not come. After a while I went out to look for him.

The warning call, '*ferenj*', went out, and in an instant my excited escort gathered. There would be no quiet stroll through Chencha. They wore ragged shorts and sweaters with holes everywhere. The leader had a pair of basketball boots, unlaced, and a knitted cap. I spoke to him and asked for Mr Victor's house, but he was too overcome by laughter to answer. Eventually he led from behind, for when I started off up the street, he and the rest of the mob ran around me and turned me in the opposite direction. They wanted to follow, but they were the ones who knew the way. If there was a turn to be made they acted like an army of shepherds, encircling their single sheep and funnelling it in the right direction. I felt absolutely ridiculous. If only the children had got used to me life in Chencha might almost have been pleasant. But they never did. I was a circus animal and that was all.

We went downhill into a maze of beautifully woven cane fences. Except on the main street, the people of Chencha lived behind these fences in small houses. They were like flimsy fortresses guarded by emaciated dogs, and hedged by banana leaves. Shading the houses were tall eucalyptus and casuarina trees. The effect was pretty and defensive. It reminded me of England.

Victor lived in one of these houses. His gate was secured with wire. There were tyre tracks outside but no vehicle. He was not at home. The children chivvied me back to the bar.

He did not come that night or the next day either. I thought he must have gone to Arba Mintch. But he hadn't. He breezed in on the third night when I was eating supper, with Abbavich and Wobit in close attendance. Wobit disappeared immediately. Abbavich stayed. When he tried to get rid of her she put her arm round me and laughed at him.

'Still here?' he said as he sat down. Lielit brought over a bottle of *t'etch* and a glass.

'Well, yes. I'm waiting for transport to Gidole, and Chencha's a better place to wait than Arba Mintch. How is Nastasia?'

'Who?'

'Nastasia Beyer. Didn't you go to Arba Mintch to see her?'

'I had business in the west,' he said vaguely. 'Why do you want to go to Gidole?'

'It's on the road to the border,' I told him.

'Never heard of it,' he said. 'Me, I only go to Addis.' He drank deeply. I waited. In the end I asked, 'Who is she?'

'Who?'

'Nastasia. I've been following her all the way from Nairobi and I haven't a clue who she is.'

'Why?' he asked, looking puzzled. I explained about the letter I was supposed to deliver in Addis, and about the trouble that had turned me aside in Shashamane.

'She from Nairobi, then?' he said. 'She didn't say. I picked her up in Shashamane. Her boyfriend ran out on her – took the Jeep and left her. Don't know why, she was kind of a sweet chick.'

'Took her Jeep?'

'I dunno whose Jeep it was. She was travelling with him, they fell out, and he dumped her.'

Poor Nastasia. To be dumped anywhere is a misfortune: to be dumped in Shashamane was a disaster.

'But why' I asked, 'didn't she go to Addis?'

'Search me,' he said. 'I didn't know that's where she was going. I'd just come from there. She bummed a ride and that's all I know.' He drank in silence for a few minutes. 'Look,' he went on, 'some chicks just hate to travel alone. They'll go anywhere so long as it's in company. I'm not responsible for her.'

'But you've got her gear,' I said. I couldn't get over how nonchalant he was.

'Oh, I'll bring it round in the morning.' He got up to go. 'Say, tomorrow is market day in Dorse. You could stop by there on your way down. It's kind of interesting.'

27

He did not come in the morning and again, when I went there, his house was empty. Tadesse said he had gone to Arba Mintch, but Tadesse had said that before and been wrong. I asked him about the market at Dorse and he told me that the market in Addis was the biggest in the world. I decided to go to Dorse anyway.

There was no transport. Anyone who was going went on foot. I looked for Dorse on the map but it wasn't there so I simply followed the little trail of burdened people out of town and down the hill. We took the main track to Arba Mintch but the further we went the more I noticed the tiny paths that joined it. People trickled out of the hills like water – bands of sturdy hill-people who carried sacks lashed with string to their backs, men on mules or donkeys, children driving goats, townswomen who sheltered from the sun under ragged umbrellas. If you were to believe the map you would think that Chencha was the only town between Arba Mintch and Soddo and that the hills were uninhabited. But there were hundreds of people on the road and they all came from somewhere.

After an hour I was exhausted. Little old ladies were overtaking me with humiliating ease. I would have turned back except that Chencha was uphill all the way. I struggled on and became caught up in a group of mountain-women. They could see I was flagging so they gathered round for encouragement. They laughed like birds and their eyes sparkled. But it wasn't their eyes I looked at. It was their legs. I had never seen such strong legs in my life. To say that I envied them would be an understatement. Down we went – me stumbling, they bouncing from rut to ridge. They wanted their photographs taken. I barely had the strength to lift the camera.

For them it was a day out, a holiday, probably a rest from the daily grind. For me it was becoming a nightmare.

'Endurance,' I said under my breath. And then with each painful step, 'En-dur-ance . . . en-dur-ance.' I couldn't understand what had happened to my stamina.

The market spread out on a field shaped like a horseshoe in the middle of town. The harsh brown grass was worn dusty by thousands of feet. I made my way over to a tall dead tree under which a woman was selling *talla* from huge earthen jars. While she stared in amazement I drank three glasses straight off. Then I sat in the shade to rest. But a crowd gathered to watch me resting so I got up and moved on. Staring faces swam by. I wondered vaguely if I should buy a mule to carry me back to Chencha. But if I couldn't sell it there, I thought, I would be completely broke. Would a mule owned even for a single day by a *ferenj* be worth anything to an Ethiopian? Mule for sale, I gabbled to myself: one careful lady driver.

The mules was scabby and had sores on their backs and hind legs. Their heads drooped heavily in the sun. They had nothing to eat or drink. I dragged myself slowly back to the dead tree.

But now there were a lot of people sitting and standing under it. A musician had set his chair there and was playing a wavering tune on a one-string fiddle. A man wearing grey flannel shorts and black wellington boots got up to dance. He jumped, with his feet together and arms stiffly by his sides, up in the air like an arrow. He jumped with his feet apart. He jumped with one leg bent, and he jumped with both legs bent.

The wailing fiddle, the jumping man, and the *talla* combined to settle a fog of unreality over everything, and when I saw Mel's face in the crowd I thought it was the effect of heatstroke. But he saw me too.

I pushed my way out and we met by a woman who was selling black pottery. He had a full beard now and he looked like a muscular scarecrow.

'Back from the jaws of death, back from the mouth of

hell, Mel,' I mumbled, grinning idiotically. 'What on earth're you doing here?'

'Strewth, Fay, you pissed or something?' he asked with characteristic tact.

'Amazing! I thought I was seeing things.'

'You probably are,' he said, grabbing my arm to stop me sitting abruptly on the dusty turf. 'Well, blow me! – little Miss Fay grogged to the eyeballs.'

'I'm not grogged,' I said indignantly.

'Don't spoil it,' he muttered and, still with a firm grip on my arm, began to fight his way out of the audience we had collected. 'Old Pommy-face got to see this.'

'Graham?' I was overjoyed. 'He's here too? What about Peter?'

'Had to leave him in Shashamane. Broke a leg when the bloody askaris charged. Get a move on, Fay. Can't you even walk straight?'

As a matter of fact I was having difficulty walking at all. My feet felt like raw meat and my legs had a will of their own.

'Keep moving,' Mel urged. 'That seems to be the secret of success in these parts. You never get where you want to go – not bloody likely – but it's less trouble than stopping still. I dunno about you, Fay, but the minute we've stopped to draw breath the bloody soldiers move in and it's shove on or get clobbered. I thought maybe we could cross into Sudan and shift north that way – no chance. I dunno what's wrong with this country . . . keep the legs going, Fay . . . but I've never been stuck like this before.'

'It's Never-Never Land,' I burbled.

'Too right,' Mel exclaimed. 'Never bloody come here or you'll never bloody get out. Going round in a fucking circle, that's what we've been doing. If I'm not careful, I'll end up back in bloody Kenya.'

'Oh I do hope so,' I said. 'Where're we going now?'

'Another excremental fleapit,' he told me. 'Old Pom-pom's feeling a bit crook – got the squitters.'

We had crossed the field. Now he pushed and pulled me between the shacks and into a narrow doorway.

'Hey, Pom,' Mel shouted into the gloom. 'Look what the old possom dragged in!'

Graham lifted his head from his hands. His face was yellow and unshaved.

'My God!' he said. He got up, but instead of coming over he made a dash for the back door.

'Off to the shit-house,' Mel said cheerfully. 'Park your arse, Fay, before you tip over. Where's that bloody bottle of yours?'

I waved my hand in the general direction of Chencha.

'Typical. The only time it's fucking wanted . . .' He went to the door and yelled, '*Buna!*' at the top of his voice. 'Chop-chop, where is everybody?'

A wrinkled old woman in a filthy white turban brought coffee for me and *talla* for Mel. Her expression was of cold dislike. Mel's charm was having its effect here too.

It was the drabbest, dirtiest bar I had yet been in, but it was such a relief to be out of the sun and off my feet that I soon began to revive. The black, sweet coffee helped too. I said, 'Will Peter be all right? Was he badly hurt?'

'That's the trouble with you, Fay,' Mel grumbled. 'Always worrying about someone else. How do I know? He only broke a leg, didn't he? We got him to a clinic, but we couldn't very well stick around and watch it mend, could we?'

'I thought you all might be dead,' I burst out. 'I shouldn't have walked off and left you.'

'Why the hell not? I would've. Anyway, you didn't do so badly. That Irish gag took the sting out for us. Quick thinking. The rest of us was shitting ourselves. It wasn't the mob that got Peter – it was when we were all running like fuck from the soldiers.'

'What happened?'

'The bastards fired into the crowd,' Mel said soberly. He drank some more *talla*.

Graham came back, slightly bent and holding his belly.

I couldn't help remembering when I had first seen him singing 'Cockles and Mussels' and washing his face in Moyale. By contrast, the light-brown floppy hair was stiff with dirt and sweat and his rather benign neutral expression had given way to one of petulant suspicion.

'Where are you staying, Fay?' he asked without greeting me. 'Is it any better than this?'

'Chencha,' I said. 'Yes, it's all right up there.'

'I'm going through there.' Mel pulled a map from his back pocket. It was the same one as mine. 'I'd've gone through today but the bastard Toyota stopped here for the market.'

'I don't think you can go through,' I said.

'Why not? Look, there's a road.' A thick finger came down on the paper like a hammer. 'This here's the back road to Soddo. And then there are plenty of other roads to Addis. We don't have to go through Shashamane again.'

'Well, as far as I can see the road stops at Chencha.' I had walked it the previous day in an attempt to shake off my escort, and the road had ended in ploughed farmland. I went on, taking a tiny footpath that wound up into the hills. But the path stopped too at a strange oval building. This was made of closely woven cane and intricately thatched. There was nothing inside except for a curious decoration of red ribbons tied to the walls and beams. I didn't go in because I thought the place might have some religious function. Except for the ribbons, I don't know why I thought that. But at the time a funny buzzing sound started in my ears. It was funny because the building reminded me of an old-fashioned beehive. There was no one to ask – the boys had left me at the end of the town. But I didn't want to offend anyone by going in, even if there was no one present to be offended, so I turned round and went back. The buzzing in my ears faded as I left.

'Another false trail,' Mel said furiously. 'So what the hell are you doing there if there's no way out?'

'Well, I'm not going north any more,' I explained. 'I'm trying to get back to Kenya, only . . .' But I was too tired to go on. All I wanted was to get back to Chencha and sleep.

'What about your friends in Addis?' Mel asked. 'Did you manage to contact them?'

'I don't have any,' I said tiredly. 'Where did that story start?'

Graham said, 'You were carrying a letter to someone in Addis. Peter saw it.'

'Well, I've still got it,' I told them. 'If I can't get to Addis I can't very well deliver it, can I? And besides, the woman it's for didn't go to Addis either.'

'She didn't?' Graham asked. 'Then where the hell is she?'

'Here,' I said. 'Well, Arba Mintch. She's got typhus and I still haven't seen her.'

'Some letter,' Mel said. 'You follow some chick all this way to deliver a letter . . .'

'No, I didn't.' I couldn't imagine why they were so interested. From the first none of them had believed all I wanted to do was see the Rift Valley. Now these two didn't seem to believe all I wanted to do was go home. 'Forget the bloody letter,' I said. 'I just want to go home.'

'So what are you doing in Chencha?' Graham asked. 'Your movements haven't been very logical, you know.'

'Well, have yours?' I was exasperated. 'I only wish I *could* be logical.' Just then I heard a car horn. I jumped up and ran outside. Hearing a motor vehicle was such a rare event I couldn't waste the opportunity of finding out if there might be a lift in prospect. I was lucky. It was Victor in his Jeep stuck behind two over-laden donkeys.

'Victor!' I shouted. 'Are you going home?'

'Want a ride?' he called.

'Yes, please.' It was a godsend. My legs still felt like jelly.

'Oh, I see,' Mel said from behind me. 'A man. I might've bloody guessed.'

'Hang on a minute,' I said to Victor and, ignoring Mel, I ducked back into the bar.

Graham was sitting hunched where we'd left him. I said, 'I've got to go now.' His face creased in a spasm of pain.

Mel said, 'Give it up, Pommy. She's got a fancy American with a Jeep.'

'Shut up, Mel,' I said wearily. 'Have you got anything to take for your guts?'

Graham shook his head. Mel said, 'The Yank's got a clean shirt too. Poor old Pom, it's no contest.'

'Shut up, Mel,' Graham groaned. I said, 'I've got some Kaolin tabs up in Chencha. Can you travel?' He travelled in a rush to the back door, clutching his stomach.

'Kaolin tabs!' Mel sneered. 'What he needs is a load of quick-drying concrete up his . . .'

'Mel,' I interrupted, 'just for once be a mensch. Come with me and pick up some tablets for him.'

'You're kidding. If there was a road through Chencha I'd come but I wouldn't go back. As there ain't I'm hotfooting it back to Arba Mintch.'

'Please, Mel,' I said. 'It won't cost you more than an hour.' That was a lie, of course.

'I'm not a bloody boy scout,' he grumbled. 'Just because we happen to be on the road together doesn't make me his nurse.' Outside, Victor leaned on his horn.

Energy is like money – if you haven't got it you can't spend it. I didn't have enough to be angry. I didn't have enough to walk up the hill, so I didn't have enough to argue with Mel and risk losing my ride. I walked out. I may have muttered something like, 'Up yours, mate,' as I went.

To my great surprise, Mel followed and hopped up beside me in Victor's Jeep. He said, 'You can't trust a chick about roads. Some things you got to see for yourself.'

28

Victor pulled away fast, making chickens squawk and dogs bark.

'This is Mel Poole,' I said to Victor. 'Don't worry about him, he's rude to everyone.'

'I'm not worried,' Victor said casually. 'Because if he's rude to me I'm big enough to toss his butt out.'

We drove all the way to Chencha in silence. I was glad. My head felt like a heavy piece of fruit on a thin stalk.

When he dropped us off at the bar Victor told me he'd bring Nastasia's things over later. I no longer believed him but I didn't say anything. That too would have been a waste of energy.

Abbavich and Wobit, eager to see the newcomer, followed us across the compound. Abbavich took the mickey out of my limp by imitating it. She sat on my bed while I sorted through my toilet bag, and even crunched up one of the handful of tablets I was pouring into an envelope for Graham.

Mel leant against the door jamb, watching, 'Why do you let her take advantage?' he asked.

'Tell him to take two every four hours,' I said, and handed him the envelope. Abbavich was pulling horrible faces. I gave her the water bottle and she drank some to take the taste away. But she didn't like my water either and showed it.

'She's bloody laughing at you,' Mel said. 'Can't you see that? She thinks you're ridiculous.'

'She laughs at everything,' I said. 'It's why I like her.'

'You're so naïve, Fay,' he sneered.

'Would you like a drink before you leave?' I wanted him out of my room. His dark shadow in the doorway was like a blackout curtain.

'You got any salt?' he asked, eyeing my toilet bag with interest. 'I've been getting cramps in my calf muscles last couple of days.'

I made faces at Abbavich to warn her about the salt tablets, but she took one anyway. She even pretended to like it. Just after that, fortunately, she found the Lifesavers which I had forgotten all about. Abbavich and Wobit loved them.

'The things you lug around,' Mel said. 'You're crazy – you know that?'

Then Abbavich uncovered the cigarettes. She gasped dramatically and made a big show of throwing them on the floor in disgust. But when she wagged an admonishing finger in my face her eyes were quite serious. She had her foot lifted to stamp on the carton when she had another idea. She picked it up and, very sweetly, handed it to Mel.

'Don't mind if I do,' he said, looking puzzled.

'Be my guest,' I was almost speechless with laughter. He gave me an angry look and, stuffing the carton under his shirt, retreated across the yard. Abbavich, Wobit, and I followed, sucking Lifesavers and giggling.

When he was gone Abbavich tutted and murmured over my blisters. She called a conference with Hijibatchaw and Lielit in the ghastly kitchen shed, from which they eventually emerged bearing a blob of evil-smelling, fatty paste on a green leaf. Lielit smeared the concoction on my heels.

I wish I could say that this local medicine worked like a charm. I seem to have inherited from my mother an almost superstitious faith in folk remedies. To my fathers' disgust, we both show far more enthusiasm for comfrey than for penicillin. In this case, however, it was weeks before I could wear proper shoes again. The blisters did not heal miraculously, but they did not fester either. They remained open sores on which flies collected like pigs around a trough. But the sore on my shoulder which I had treated with antiseptic cream gave me much more trouble.

At the time, though, I was most affected by their kindness. Up till then Ethiopia had not struck me as a country where kindness had much place. It was a hard land and people led hard lives. Everyone, including foreigners, seemed on the edge of survival. When anyone stopped to help me it was not the lazy kindness of the rich. Help was something that cost the helper in time and trouble not easily afforded.

Did I, for instance, show much kindness to Graham by doling out a few tablets for Mel to take down the hill? I did not. It was something I would do only if Mel did the walking. The thought was mine but the effort was his. I was willing, he was unwilling, but he delivered the goods. It didn't cost me a thing.

29

Victor did not come that night either and by the next morning I was worried. I could not stay in Chencha much longer. Money was running out and I was afraid of missing transport from Arba Mintch. More than a week had passed and, as far as I knew, nothing had been done about Nastasia.

I kept telling myself that it wasn't really my problem. I had come to Chencha and explained it to Victor. What else was I supposed to do? I couldn't very well break into his house and abscond with Nastasia's possessions even if I knew which they were. I couldn't force him to act – I do not have a very forceful personality.

Victor's coming and goings were quite mysterious. No one could tell me where he went or what he did. The school in Chencha did not seem exactly to be on strike but there wasn't much activity there either, and the children spent most of their time on the street. Tadesse Gebre-Mariam, most often, could be found in the bar or wandering around like a lost soul mourning his homeland and his chickens.

Maybe it was the time of year. Certainly nothing was growing in the fields, and only rarely did I see someone hacking painfully at the dry earth. There was nothing soft or giving about the soil around Chencha. The men attacked it as if it were an enemy, and like an enemy, it resisted.

The men, in fact, did not seem to be doing much of anything. It was probably because I was living in a bar that I saw so many idle men, but it did seem that life in Chencha was oddly dead. Men did not talk much to each other. They drank a little, and if they were huddled in a group you could be sure they were listening to the radio.

The women were busier. Except in the bar you never saw a woman who was not carrying something. They did their washing in a stream on the downhill side of town, and eventually I plucked up courage and joined them. Armed with a gritty bar of yellow soap Abbavich lent me and my stuffed bag of filthy garments, I knelt by the stream scrubbing and rinsing with the rest. It was a great relief to see the dirt disappear downstream. The women watched covertly. I could see they were annoyed because I had brought with me my usual escort of rowdy children. They were shooed away eventually, but while they stayed they were an added source of embarrassment.

I don't know why what other people wear is of such interest, but my tangle of bras and briefs, shirts and jeans served as great entertainment. In the main the other women were washing simple lengths of fabric which were employed as shawls or dresses or whatever was required. Nothing else was needed, and as I wrung out the litter of underwear under so many curious eyes I couldn't help feeling how unnecessary it was. Bras are tight bands which trap sweat, and lice love them.

Briefs . . . well, never mind what they trap – but it seemed probable that what I was wearing only made life more difficult for me. I would have been a lot more comfortable and healthy in something loose and airy.

But bras and briefs are what I'm used to. Without them I feel unprotected and indecent. It isn't reasonable, I know, but in a strange land I seem to cling more than ever to what I'm used to, even if, as in this case, what I'm used to is uncomfortable and unhealthy.

The other major insecurity was money. Most people, when they travel, take more than they need. It is extra insurance so that, if they have to, they can buy their way out of trouble. Here there was nothing to buy. I couldn't hire a private Toyota because there wasn't one, or better my diet because there was no alternative to *injera* and *wat*. And anyway, because of the miscalculation over the car, far from having brought too much money, I had brought

136

too little. I had not reckoned on paying for room and board every night. Nor had I reckoned on not finding anywhere to change traveller's cheques.

Room and board were wretchedly cheap but they were eating away at my small stock of currency. At the beginning, fortunately, everyone took or exchanged Kenyan shillings, but those had run out long ago. Every morning I paid Madam in worn-out notes and thin burnished coins, and every morning she gave me a cup of coffee by way of receipt. It was a ceremony she enjoyed more than I did. I liked Madam – she was quiet and dignified, and she had beautiful hands – but I didn't like to be reminded how uncomfortably close to flat broke I was.

Whatever Victor chose to do I had to leave. Arba Mintch was the capital of Gemu-Gofa and, although I hadn't seen one, it stood to reason that there must be a bank or exchange bureau there.

30

The day I left, Abbavich and I exchanged gifts and cried on each other's shoulder. She gave me her scarf with the pink and green pattern on it, carefully washed and folded. For various reasons I am rather ashamed of what I gave her. She wanted a simple cotton shirt on which I had embroidered roses and I gave it to her. But at the last minute I unclasped the thin gold chain I always wore and hung it round her neck.

On this gold chain was a little engraved Victorian locket. Tony gave it to me for my twenty-first birthday. He had taken a lot of trouble to find it because, he said, I was his old-fashioned girl. In fact, it is his attitude to me which is old-fashioned, but it was a beautiful locket and a sentimental gift from a very nice man. To give it away was an act of disloyalty, and he would be very hurt when he found out about it.

But there must be something of my father in me after all – a belief in the saving power of gold. And although I knew Abbavich could take care of herself and it was none of my business anyway, I had become anxious about her baby. It would be months before it was born, but one night I had a dream in which the soldiers came to the compound and ripped it out of her arms. The next night I dreamed I was at home watching television with the rest of the family. The programme was about the Ethiopian famine of last year, and among the helpless starving faces I suddenly saw Abbavich carrying a dead baby. 'That's Abbavich; I know her!' I cried in the silly way one does when one sees a familiar face on the screen.

'But, darling,' my mother said, 'the poor child looks so hungry. You really should have asked her home for tea.'

Any way you look at it the little gold locket was an

inappropriate gift. On the one hand it was too much and yet, in the light of the dreams, it was too little. Perhaps it was the locket's fate to be passed from hand to hand for the wrong reasons.

So we smiled and cried and said goodbye, and I never saw her again.

The armed Toyota driver packed his passengers like kippers into the dilapidated four-wheel-drive and bounced out of town. Victor intercepted us on the first hairpin bend.

'You off?' he yelled to me as the Jeep and Toyota stood nose to nose. 'If you're passing the hospital you might as well drop this off.' He got down and came to the back of the Toyota with an electric-blue backpack – one of the deluxe models on an aluminium frame. He dumped it on my knee.

'Okay,' I said feebly. I was dumbfounded.

'Well, have a good trip,' he called, climbing into the Jeep and revving away. We all choked on his dust. 'Give my love to Stasie if you see her.'

He was waiting for me to leave *before* he gave me Nastasia's stuff, I thought. Why? I gripped the tailgate as we lunged dangerously downhill. If I had left days ago he would have given it to me then. And all the time I had been waiting for him. So much time lost. Nastasia's time.

I did not understand Victor. From the first he had been elusive and evasive about a very simple matter, and like a fool I had hung around waiting for him. For the first time I began to wonder about his behaviour towards me. I had come to find him, and I had expected, before we met, that he would be someone to talk to, someone who might have given me a clue as to what was going on in the country. He had been in Chencha for at least a year and he could speak Amharic. Clearly he knew how to cope. It must have been obvious to him that I didn't and that I was having a hard time.

I never expect anyone to be particularly interested in me, but I was, as far as I knew, the only other completely fluent English-speaker for miles around. Although this isn't in itself a recommendation, I was still surprised at his total lack of interest. Maybe he thought that if he showed an interest I would become a burden to him. That seemed to be his attitude to Nastasia. 'Hey, kid,' he had said once when I tried to pin him down, 'so I spend a couple of days on the road with a chick. That doesn't make me responsible.'

But he had taken charge of her luggage. Maybe the doctor asked him to. That didn't make him responsible either, but at least he could have given it back when asked. Especially as I had told him how ill Nastasia was.

As the Toyota lumbered slowly down the hill I thought suddenly about what the doctor had called Nastasia's 'superficial injuries', and it struck me that Victor might have caused them. Suppose he had beaten her up. Suppose in their few days on the road together there had been a violent sexual encounter. Or suppose he had robbed her. If he had been involved in anything like that it would be reason enough to avoid the very thought of Nastasia.

But Victor was a Peace Corps worker and they are likely to be idealists. In a suffering world, they are on the side of the angels. I changed my mind. Maybe I had misunderstood what seemed to be Victor's casual attitude. Probably he was so busy with his work in Ethiopia that he saw the problems of people like Nastasia and me as frivolous.

The heat of the valley rose up like steam from a cooking pot and as the Toyota descended into it my ears popped and bubbled as if water had seeped in. I yawned and blew my nose, but by the time we reached the floor of the valley I was nearly deaf. Once again my physical discomfort turned my thoughts inwards.

Warm almond oil, I thought helplessly through the pain of earache. Warm almond oil dripped slowly from an eyedropper or a teaspoon held by my mother.

It was the change in altitude, I thought. I would soon get used to it, and the pain would go away.

A group of seven soldiers met the Toyota when it

stopped near the bar I had stayed at previously. They were looking for someone. We climbed out nervously, clutching bags and bundles to our chests and the Ethiopians melted away. For once there was no welcoming committee of small children.

With Nastasia's backpack, my own bag, and the water bottle clasped precariously in my arms, I made straight for the bar. It was no time to appear hesitant. The soldiers followed me with their eyes but made no move to intercept. Someone was in trouble but it was not me.

The women in the bar gave no sign that they recognized me. They were uneasy, and the madam did not want to let me have a room. But I could go no further. There was too much to carry and my ears were screaming and pulsing, so I stood where I was, pretending not to understand until she reluctantly gave way. But she doubled the price and wanted her money in advance. Even if I couldn't hear her properly, there was no misunderstanding that. She cleaned me out.

I had to find somewhere to change a traveller's cheque. It was now vital. I lay on the filthy cot waiting for the pain to subside and the heat to lift a little, and tried to make a plan. It was really very simple, there must be an official part of town, and it stood to reason it would be somewhere near the hospital. I could take Nastasia's things to the hospital and inquire there – kill two birds with one stone. But far from being able to kill a single bird, I was not even up to ruffling a sparrow's feathers. So I waited and mercifully dozed off.

When I awoke it was cooler and the screaming in my head was reduced to a dull roar. I did what I could to refresh myself with a damp towel and a hairbrush.

Judging by the way the straps on her backpack were adjusted, Nastasia was several sizes bigger than I was. But the bag was heavy and I guessed that she too had packed for motor transport. I toyed with the idea of just sorting out her papers instead of lugging the whole thing to the hospital. But when I had changed the length of the straps it balanced quite nicely, and I trudged down the U-shaped road like a hiker.

The soldiers had gone but still there was tension in the air, the children who followed were subdued. Heads poked from doorways, and people stopped work or conversation as I passed. There was something wrong with my ears, but the quiet seemed so troubled I was sure there was something wrong with Arba Mintch too.

Walking slowly but purposefully. I tried to resist stopping to glance over my shoulder. I did not want to look uneasy or shifty in a place where already I stood out like a flowered hat at a funeral.

I arrived at the hospital exhausted but unmolested. The doctor, when I found him in his office, did not at first recognize me. He, although recognizable, looked twice as tired as I had remembered. His skin was like yellow rice paper stretched over a skull.

'Is Nastasia any better?' I asked.

'No,' he said shortly. 'You should not have brought that.' He pointed to the electric-blue backpack. 'There is no place for it. Too many sick people are here.'

'Well, I can't keep it either,' I told him. 'I'm leaving tomorrow.'

'I want only a telephone number to call.' He rubbed his face gloomily. 'One day last week – one day only – is the telephone working. Also to pay her bill.'

'Her bill?'

'Here is not your National Health,' he said, pinching his nose and opening his eyes very wide. 'Here is only Charitable Subscription. Anyone who can pay must pay. Please.'

The zipped compartment in the lid of the pack seemed the likeliest place to start and sure enough I soon found a green United States passport with a thick wad of Ethiopian money folded into it. I gave both to him. He took the money but pushed the passport back across the desk, saying something I didn't catch.

'I'm sorry,' I said. 'My ears have gone funny.'

He looked surprised but said loudly, 'Please to write particulars. Capital letters would be helpful.'

Inside the front cover was Nastasia's passport number, her address in the United States, and a message that read, 'In case of death or accident notify the nearest American diplomatic or consular office and . . .' There followed another name and address. I copied everything on the pad he provided. Meanwhile he was looking up records and counting Nastasia's money. He wrote out a receipt and scrupulously counted the money again, taking only the amount he had stated. 'Sign, please,' he said at last. I wondered if I was doing the right thing, but I signed. There was still a healthy wad to put back in the passport. I folded the receipt into it too so that Nastasia would know how her money had been spent.

'Thank you so very much,' the doctor said. 'You think I am hard perhaps? But if a person has no money of course we will treat them. These are people with nothing at all. You understand?'

I did. In any case Nastasia had plenty of money left so I wasn't too worried. I would have asked him to look at my ears if I'd had any of my own. I asked him instead for directions to a bank and left quickly before he noticed I wasn't taking the backpack.

31

The green, gold, and red of the Ethiopian flag hung limply from the flagpole. The building that was supposed to be a bank had its door firmly locked and a soldier stood, feet apart, on the steps. There were several official-looking buildings with flags on flagpoles but they were all closed and guarded. No one to talk to, no open door to walk through, and no money.

I walked from one end of the municipal row to the other and then back. I was very close to tears, and a cold cloud of fear seemed to be following me. I wanted to beat on the bank door till someone let me in, or run and not stop until I reached England.

It doesn't matter, I kept saying to myself. Come back in the morning – it'll be open then. You've already paid for room and board, there's nothing to worry about till tomorrow. But the sight of all the shut doors and the soldiers acted like a bad dream. The deafness too made me feel cut off, separate, isolated, and the hair on my arms stirred. I began to shiver as I walked away.

I went briskly down past the hospital and on into the lower part of town. The shopkeeper with the pineapple chunks called to me as I passed. I waved and went on. There was no money to buy with and I couldn't talk to him anyway. By the time I reached the bar my teeth were chattering.

To my astonishment, when I got there, I found Graham seated at a table. He leaped to his feet and I saw his mouth say, 'Fay! Hello,' but I didn't hear him. I forced myself to smile through the lockjaw. I said, 'Hi. Be back in a minute,' and went through to the compound. In my room, with the door shutter bolted, I wrapped the sleeping-bag tightly round my shoulders and curled up on the cot.

Within minutes I was drenched with sweat but the hair on my arms still stood upright like the fur of a scared cat. I could not let go of the sleeping-bag nor open the shutter for fresh air. It was suffocating in the little room but I wanted it smaller and more airless. I wanted to be buried in a safe place no one could get into but me, and if that meant I couldn't get out, so be it. No wonder tomb rhymes with womb, I thought unreasonably. A room is a womb is a tomb: all safe places.

Graham tapped on the shutter and called something I couldn't hear.

'Just a touch of fever,' I said through clenched teeth. 'Be okay in a bit.'

My head sang. 'She died of a fever . . .' a little, thin voice only I could hear . . . 'and none could retrieve her . . .'

After about an hour he was back again and this time I forced myself to let him in. He brought in a bottle of water and a glass.

'Ambo,' he said. 'It's mineral water. If you've got any aspirin, better take some. You don't always remember to do the right thing when you're feverish.' He searched through my bag till he found some. I took them with the water. Why not? What I had looked like fever. It even felt like fever. But it wasn't. It was blind, senseless panic. So I took two aspirin for it.

Graham said, 'This isn't malaria, is it? You haven't forgotten to take your Paludrin?' I shook my head.

'No,' he went on, 'you're pretty shrewd, aren't you? By the way, thanks very much for the stuff you sent via Mel – it worked a treat. I thought I was about to end my days in a Dorse *shintabite*. Not a lovesome thing, God wot.'

'Where's Mel?' I chattered.

'Started out for Soddo two days ago,' he replied with a lift of the shoulders that looked very much like relief. 'He's taking another stab at Addis. If all else fails he'll charge through like a bull rhino, that boy. Women and children beware!'

'And you?'

'No point,' he said. 'This wasn't meant to be an assault course. I'm going back to Nairobi to catch a plane like normal people do.'

Nairobi. He made it sound so near, so possible. My teeth stopped chattering.

I asked, 'When does the bank open?'

'I don't know,' Graham said. 'The problem is that half Arba Mintch seems to be on strike and the rest is on holiday. I can't work out which is which.'

'Still no buses?'

'None. As far as I can tell the only way to get around is in these private enterprise Toyotas. The buses all belong to the Emperor, you see.' He paused, looking at me, I supposed, to see if I was up to serious conversation.

'Never mind that,' he went on. 'You get some shut-eye now, and I'll call you when food's ready. I'll leave the Ambo. Drink as much as you can.' He stopped in the doorway and added, 'I must say I'm very pleased to see you, Fay. I thought you might've slipped past while I was stuck in Dorse.'

'A *ferenj* can't slip anywhere,' I mumbled. 'The children see to that.'

'Too right, as friend Mel would say.' He went, leaving the door ajar. I closed my eyes. I was feeling better but I still didn't want to give up the comfort of the sleeping bag.

The worldless time in Chencha with Abbavich was over. It was like the end of a holiday. This town was real life, with its menace, its soldiers, its suspicion and barred doors. I was glad Graham was there. He didn't make Arba Mintch any safer, but he was company. I drank the mineral water gratefully.

I thought about Tony at home, and wondered if he was waiting for me. What had he thought of my letter from Nairobi? Perhaps he hadn't taken it seriously. Of course, the fact that he took very little of what I said seriously was one of the reasons I wrote it. He had assumed responsibility for me and he thought he'd taught me all I knew. So when any of my wishes or opinions differed from his he discounted them as minor aberrations.

It was my own fault. I was so thrilled to be loved I accepted the tyranny as part of the deal: it was the price I had to pay for his attention. I should have stuck up for myself more, but I hate discord, and besides, it seemed disloyal to protect myself from Tony who was always doing his level best to protect me.

He didn't want me to take the job in Kenya.

'It isn't final, is it?' he asked when I told him about the phone call. We were at his flat. His living-room was candlelit because of a power cut and we were waiting for the electricity to come on again so that I could cook dinner.

'I mean, you can ring back and cancel, can't you?'

'Why?' I asked. He had his arm round me and my head was on his chest. His heart pumped strongly under my cheek.

'Well, I'm going to my family for Christmas and the New Year,' he said. 'I thought you could come too – make it sort of official.'

'Oh,' I said.

'You don't want to go to Kenya by yourself,' he went on. 'We could take a trip together next year if you're still keen.'

'It isn't a trip,' I put in. 'It's a job.'

'Well, if everything goes right for me next year, you soon won't need a job. That's why I want you to meet my parents.'

The lights came on then and I didn't have to answer. He didn't, anyway, expect one. I cooked dinner – lamb chops, rice, and salad – and then I went home to my own room. Tony didn't like me to go home alone at night so he argued about that. But I wanted to be alone to think.

If he had won the argument and I hadn't gone home,

147

and if I hadn't thought what I thought then, I would never have gone to Kenya. And I wouldn't have written him a letter about independence and my right to make my own mistakes. It was so much easier to write to him than talk to him: he couldn't interrupt or influence me. I didn't know if he would take my written point of view any more seriously than my spoken one, but now in Arba Mintch, I hoped not. I hoped he would be there when I got back. If I got back.

32

Mr Latybalu greeted me like an old friend. 'You have a pleasant vacation in Chencha?' he inquired, shaking my hand. 'You meet my very good friend, Mr Victor? Very fine fellow, Mr Victor.'

A tray of *injera* and *wat* was on the table. We sat down under the weak glow of an oil lamp.

'Who is Mr Victor?' Graham asked.

'He will send me books when he returns to America,' Mr Latybalu said confidently. Judging by Victor's performance to date, I very much doubted it, but I said nothing and we began to eat. It was hard work. Not only were my ears letting me down but my throat seemed to be filled with phlegm and I couldn't swallow properly.

I had eaten nothing but *injera* and *wat* since crossing the border. It wasn't that I disliked it – at first I had even enjoyed it. But suddenly I couldn't take another mouthful. My throat closed and that was that. I went to bed as soon as I decently could.

Graham knocked on my door a couple of hours later. 'Are you all right?' he asked. 'Has the fever come back? If you want I could stay and look after you.'

'No . . . thanks,' I said, alarmed. 'I'm all right.'

'Well, see you in the morning then,' he said. 'Fay?'

'Yes.'

'We'll be travelling together now, so we ought to make plans.'

'In the morning,' I said.

'If you're sure you're all right.'

'Yes,' I said. 'Good night.'

In the morning the bank would be open. If it wasn't . . . if it wasn't, well, maybe Graham . . . But I couldn't think about that. It was far too complicated.

I dreamed I was standing at the bottom of a rift valley with Tony. It was very small, and the walls rose up like buildings on either side of a street. The heat from the ground was intense and I danced from foot to foot to avoid blisters.

'It's quite all right,' Tony said calmly. 'Rifting always generates volcanic activity.' I jumped up and down.

'Stand quite still,' he went on. 'Hopping around causes no end of trouble. It weakens the earth's crust. You could open up a vent into the magma chamber.'

But instead of a volcano erupting, the valley floor dropped. It dropped nearly a mile, so suddenly that we were left suspended in air. When I looked down, the Red Sea had already rushed in and was boiling like a cauldron. I plummeted towards the water, screaming for Tony. But he was no longer there.

I had forgotten, after the cool of Chencha, just how hot Arba Mintch remained all night, how sweat and bugs combined to give the sensation of a microscopic army manœuvring over your skin, and how, in these conditions, anxiety mounts until, in the morning, you are wearing it like a saddle on your back.

If the bank isn't open, I thought; if this bloody earache doesn't go away; if I don't get a decent night's sleep . . . and so on, pausing only for short peculiar dreams, until morning.

The little lad who had been my companion in Arba Mintch last time turned up long before Graham surfaced. We shared a hard roll, but even though I softened the bread in coffee it was still difficult to swallow. He told me his name was Taffera. I told him mine.

'Fa-ee,' he said, white teeth gleaming in fun.

'I'm going to the bank,' I told him, waving traveller's cheques. 'Money. I need money.'

'Money! Yes.' He grinned even more broadly. I stood up and he stood too. We both checked for soldiers with some caution.

'Soldiers?' I asked, standing to attention with an

invisible gun. He seemed almost to sniff the air before pronouncing the street safe for *ferenji*. I set out. I had only gone a few paces before Taffera decided to come too. I thought perhaps he knew a short cut but he didn't. We went quickly down into the depths of town, and toiled slowly up again past the hospital.

The bank was shut. I stood helplessly in front of it and wondered what on earth I was going to do. The soldier on guard glared at me. In an agony of indecision I took the traveller's cheques out of my shirt pocket and approached the soldier. Taffera retreated several steps.

'*Tenastilin*. Please could you tell me when the bank opens?' I asked. I held out the cheques and pointed to the door. The soldier glared even more fiercely. Abruptly, he thrust his rifle out at arm's length so that it almost touched my chest.

'*Yellem!*' he snarled. '*Heat!*'

I went quickly. Taffera had already gone.

He had nearly reached the hospital by the time I caught up with him. 'No money,' he said soberly.

'No,' I agreed. 'Not a penny. I'm stuck. Without resources. Done for.' We stood looking at each other. 'I'm desperate,' I told him quietly. 'If I don't go home I'm afraid I'll die.' I meant it. But it sounded such a silly thing to say, especially to a small boy who didn't understand a word, that I giggled miserably. He touched my sleeve sympathetically and I was ashamed.

'Cash,' I babbled. 'Beg, borrow or steal; I don't care any more.'

'Cash,' he mimicked uncertainly.

I turned out of the sun and into the shade of the hospital compound. There were more people than ever camped in the centre, and every room was filled to overflowing. I met Sister Ingrid on my way to the doctor's office. 'Ah!' she said brusquely. 'Already you are here. I am afraid to tell you this American friend is dead in the night.'

151

33

Sister Ingrid, the doctor, and I stood around the doctor's desk. Nastasia's backpack was on it. The doctor said, 'I will try again to telephone to Addis, but . . .' He indicated the dead phone with a weary hand.

'Always when a foreigner dies there is trouble,' Sister Ingrid put in. The words sounded harsh but her puffy face was tired and sad. 'And now things are everywhere bad. We do not even know what is her religion. Beyer – it may be she is a Jew.'

'You can't tell by names,' I said. 'It's no use guessing.'

'We will wish to do what is correct,' she said stiffly.

'You have already done all you can.' Somehow I had been put in the position of next of kin and I was not at all comfortable.

'Poor child,' said Sister Ingrid. 'So far from her home.'

'Yes.' I could feel tears pricking at the back of my eyes. They were not all for Nastasia – not even half of them. For the second time that morning I was ashamed.

'We must act quickly,' the doctor said. 'If only it is possible to speak with her family. You must take charge of her property.'

'Must I?' He was playing into my hands. I wanted Nastasia's money. I knew where it was because I had folded a wad of it into her passport yesterday. It was the only way I could see out of my predicament. 'Suppose something happens to me, and I can't return them to her family?' I didn't want to seem too eager. They might decide my need would make me untrustworthy.

'In a week perhaps you will be in Kenya,' the doctor said. 'There you can telephone. There is the Embassy. Here, it may be months before someone can go to Addis. I cannot guarantee what will happen to her property.'

'I can't either,' I told him. 'Also, I simply can't carry all her stuff as well as mine.'

'You do not wish to help?' asked Sister Ingrid.

'I do wish to help,' I said guiltily. 'But if I do, I can't give any guarantees, and also I will have to leave some of the bigger things behind.' I indicated the bed-roll as an example.

'I understand,' the doctor said doubtfully.

'You said this hospital existed by charitable contribution,' I went on. 'Well, surely you will be able to find a use for whatever I can't carry. And surely her family will understand.'

'I don't know,' the doctor said. 'I do not like to take the responsibility.'

We looked at each other.

'You must take what you can,' he said at last.

'We have need of clothes,' added Sister Ingrid.

'I shall make a list,' I said, 'of what I take and what I leave. You are a priest, Doctor, no one would accuse you of dishonesty. But me . . .' I left the sentence hanging.

'Very well,' he agreed. 'We must leave you here to do it. When you have finished, call us, and we will sign.'

When they had left I started with the cash. I did not want to be interrupted so I counted it quickly and then substituted it with a rough equivalent of my own traveller's cheques. It was nearly fifty pounds' worth – a fortune, or at least enough to see me to the border. I buttoned the money into my top pocket. It should have felt like robbing the dead but it didn't. Sighing with relief but feeling a little sick, I started to sort through her clothes.

Nastasia had three good pairs of shoes. Her clothes were well-made and all nearly new. Make-up and toiletries were top quality to. She was certainly not a penurious traveller. In one of the zipped compartments I found her traveller's cheques. All told, she had over fifteen thousand dollars. I looked at her passport again. She was only twenty-five, height – five feet six inches, hair – light brown, eyes – blue.

It seemed a lot of money for a woman only a few years older than I was to carry around, and I began to worry, genuinely this time, about taking care of it. There were two piles: one of Nastasia's personal effects – her papers, some notebooks, letters, driving licence, make-up, jewellery. The other – bed-roll, clothes, towel, shoes.

Sister Ingrid added two heavy gold rings and an ivory bangle to the personal pile. 'This is good,' she said, stooping over the clothes and shoes.

'Too good,' I said anxiously. 'Look, Sister.' I showed her the traveller's cheques. 'She had so much money.'

'She did?' the sister asked, surprised. 'She did not when she came, look like a rich girl.'

'I don't understand how this could have happened to her.'

'The wealthy die too, you know,' the doctor said from the doorway.

'But look.' I held up a piece of paper which showed that Nastasia had bought a Jeep in Nairobi. 'She owned a Jeep. It had cost her five and a half thousand pounds. From what Victor Bartholomew told me, it was stolen in Shashamane. Why didn't she do anything about it? With all this money she could've replaced it. She didn't have to hitch.' I couldn't adequately express the feeling that wealth and wheels should have given Nastasia an immunity from the disaster which had overtaken her, and which was threatening now to overtake me.

'Or why didn't she turn round and go straight back to Kenya?' I asked uselessly.

The doctor looked at the paper. He looked at the jewellery and the cheques. He looked at me.

'I can't take responsibility for all this,' I said. 'Nastasia was no ordinary traveller. It's too much.'

He fingered a filigrée gold necklace without looking up. Sister Ingrid fingered the shoes. I waited.

'You made the list?' he asked at length. I had. I had even made a copy: one for each of us.

'We will all three sign.' He sighed. 'You see, if this

chaos continues,' he said, 'who knows? How long shall we be here?' He looked pointedly at Sister Ingrid. 'What may happen to the Mission?'

I shivered suddenly. He picked up a pen and firmly signed his name on both copies. Sister Ingrid signed, and then I did too.

'Last night,' the doctor said, gazing expressionlessly at the necklace. 'Last night came a boy. We did what we could, but he too died. He was wounded from a gun. You understand?'

I began to replace Nastasia's valuables in the backpack. I didn't know what to say.

'These people will not steal from you,' he went on. 'But life is not of such value. It is more disgrace to steal than to kill. This is a time of trouble. You must leave soon.'

The small voice sang, *'She died of a fever and none could retrieve her, and that was the end of sweet Molly Malone . . .'* I shook my head, but the tune persisted.

34

The sun was directly overhead when I left the hospital. Taffera sat on the ground under the dwindling patch of shade in the doorway. Why had he waited? I was struck again by the way a few people showed friendship to someone who was at best a figure of fun and at worst a suspicious character – an outcast or freak.

There was one more thing to do before going back to the bar. Nastasia's backpack thumped against my shoulders as I hurried down the hill, propelled by a terrible sense of urgency. Taffera trotted by my side, and a hoard of strange children took up pursuit. A couple of them half-heartedly threw stones as I rushed headlong into the shop-keeper's open stall. Again he threatened the kids with his stick before turning his wolfish smile on me. I pointed to the dusty shelf of tinned goods. There were nine cans of Chinese pineapple chunks left. He reached one down.

'All of them,' I said recklessly, making a sweeping motion with my arm. '*Siteyn*, nine, all!'

Looking bemused, he took another can off the shelf.

'More!' I cried desperately. Taffera took up the appeal. The shopkeeper stared at me in astonishment. I struggled out of the backpack and opened the lid. Slowly, unbearably slowly, he took the cans, one by one, off the shelf. I snatched each one as it came and hid it in the bag.

I couldn't quite believe what I was doing but it was vital that I did it. When the last can was concealed I zipped the lid shut. I was soaked with sweat and utterly spent. Taffera showed me an amazed grin.

'What about you, love?' I asked in a weary croak. 'What would do it for you?' I gestured round the stall that now contained, to my eyes, only worthless trivia.

Hesitantly he pointed to a linen hat, the sort Australian

cricketers wear: a floppy thing that once had been white but now was yellowed by sun light and dust. He touched it covetously, and the shopkeeper raised his stick.

'Let him have it,' I said. I had satisfied my needs and I could afford to be generous with Nastasia's money. Taffera did not wear the hat. He folded it carefully and tucked it away under his shirt. During both transactions we had each studiously kept our backs to the audience on the street outside.

'Are we two of a kind?' I asked him as we left the stall and began the exhausting climb up to the bar. 'Are we both turning into squirrels? Or are you copying me? Do you think I have just demonstrated proper behaviour?'

Gleefully, he chattered something in return. I didn't understand him and he didn't understand me, but nevertheless he knew my secret and I knew his.

The bar was dark and stuffy. Graham sat facing the door next to Mr Latybalu and another teacherish man. There was a carafe of *talla* between them. Graham looked downright bad-tempered.

'There you are, Fay!' he said. 'Where on earth have you been? I've been waiting for you all morning.'

'Sorry.' I tried to edge past him but he stood in my way. 'I had to change some traveller's cheques.' I wanted to get to my room.

'Where?' he asked. 'I even went up to the bank to look for you. It was shut.'

'Oh, someone at the hospital helped out,' I said vaguely. I didn't want him to look too closely at the backpack. The shape of the cans might show.

'Who?'

'Look, I'll tell you later.' I sidled by, horribly afraid that the cans might clank and give the game away. 'I've got to lie down for a minute. That fever . . .' It was true that my legs were shaking and my hands trembled and perspiration was soaking my shirt, but when I got to my room I did not lie down. I bolted the door and shutter and, by the light of a candle, sorted through my treasures.

First I tipped all the contents of my own bag on to the bed.

The most important thing was to secure the pineapple chunks. I made a soft sack by tying up the neck and armholes of a T-shirt. I put the cans in and disguised the shape with dirty clothes. I was tempted to open one and drink the juice but Graham might come along at any minute. It could wait till nightfall. The sack looked, as I had intended, like a bundle of dirty laundry. It would be all right as long as no one touched it. I relaxed a little and turned my attention to Nastasia's possessions.

I made a similar sack for her things out of another T-shirt and searched through the many zipped pockets in the backpack to make sure nothing was overlooked. At the very bottom, wedged under the plastic tray that stiffened the pack and gave it its square shape, I made a remarkable find. It was a solitary krugerrand, a solid gold coin which gleamed softly in my hand. What, I wondered, did Nastasia want with a single krugerrand? I put it with the rest of her valuables. These went to the bottom of the bag. The pineapple chunks came next, and on top I packed my own things. The canvas bag was rolled up and strapped to the outside where the bedroll had been. The result was neat and terribly heavy. Something had to go.

If I ate one tin of pineapple that night, I reasoned, I would only have to carry eight, but it wouldn't make enough difference. What didn't I need? The answer was a pair of binoculars, *Seven Pillars of Wisdom*, and the book about East African flora and fauna.

I was about to remove these items when Graham knocked on the door. I started wildly and heaved the pack into the darkest corner.

'Let me in,' Graham called. 'I've brought you some more Ambo.'

'It's all right,' I quavered, looking quickly about to make sure everything was hidden.

'Come on, Fay,' he said. 'You're looking really ill. You've got to drink water.'

He would suspect something if I didn't let him in. I blew out the candle and fumbled with the bolt.

'Why do you lock yourself away all the time,' he complained as he came in. 'We're supposed to be together now, but you go off by yourself without telling me. Suppose there was a taxi out of here and I missed it waiting for you?'

'I was broke,' I told him. 'I couldn't go anywhere without changing a traveller's cheque.'

'Well, you might've told me.' He poured some Ambo into a glass. 'Aspirin?' he asked.

'All gone,' I said quickly. I couldn't remember where they were.

'What do you mean, "all gone"? You had masses yesterday.' He looked around the room.

'Sorry, did I?' I said stupidly. 'I'll look for them later.'

'Now,' he insisted. 'Where did you get the new rucksack?' He had found it.

'Graham!' I said in desperation. 'I was about to change clothes and wash. Please let me get on with it.'

'Oh, sorry.' He straightened up and turned away from the corner. 'But don't forget the aspirin, will you?'

I was feeling so bad about everything that I decided to make an honest woman of myself – at least about washing, changing and taking the aspirin. Out came the damp towel, sponge bag, and clean shirt. It was a good thing there were no mirrors – my ribcage felt like a curved washboard and all the skin I could see was blotched with insect bites, especially under the waistband and round the groin. Even by candlelight it looked like an illustration from a medical textbook. I rushed through ablutions and avoided looking too closely, but even so I disgusted myself. I didn't want anyone to see me. It was another of the things which made living in a country where I provoked such curiosity a painful matter.

Had this happened to Nastasia? The black and white picture in her passport showed a perfect skin, glossy shoulder-length hair, and confident eyes. Passport photos are not a very good indication – at least I hope not, mine has a scared childish look to it – but the impression was of a well-cared-for person who looked very much in control. Five feet six is a good height. I don't think a woman that tall is overlooked or talked down to. She would have presence, I thought. She would be visible. She would not have trouble ordering a drink at a theatre bar in the interval.

But she was dead. Lice had given her typhus, dirty food had given her dysentery. The confident eyes were sunk and closed. She had enough money to hire a private plane and get out to wherever was safe. But lice had got there first. Nothing can save you if you're ill at the wrong time in the wrong place.

The tinny voice crooned, *'Now her ghost wheels her barrow, through streets broad and narrow . . .'*

Would she be buried or cremated? Did Ethiopians wear black at funerals?

'Alive, alive-O.'

35

'Guess what?' Graham called through a crack in the shutter. 'Mel's back from Soddo. Better break out the Kaolin or he'll be a permanent fixture in the *shintabite*.'

Mel was lying on his cot groaning. Graham brought Ambo. I brought Kaolin.

'Fuck off and leave me alone,' he whispered after he'd taken everything on offer. 'And don't shut the fucking door. I may have to make a run for it.'

He lay with his boots on, his trousers undone, and a fistful of *Time* magazine at the ready.

'How are the mighty fallen,' Graham said, looking at him clinically. 'Bit of a laugh, wasn't it Mel, when I was suffering, eh?'

'Piss off,' Mel groaned weakly. He was noticeably humiliated as well as sick. I backed out into the yard and went to sit in front of my own door.

'Let's have a look at your map,' Graham said when he came to join me.

We pored over it. There was the route: Arba Mintch, Gardulla, Gidole, Conso, Yabello, Mega, Moyale. Nothing had changed on paper. Gardulla, Gidole: the names swam in and out of focus.

'I don't trust maps any more,' I said.

'They don't tell the whole story, do they?' he agreed. 'Where's Dorse, for instance? And another thing – these hot springs old Latybalu was boasting about. Where are they? I'd give my right arm for a soak. It's all eyewash.'

'No,' I said cautiously. 'It's the right sort of place – lakes, water-saturated rocks, igneous activity. This is a rift we're sitting on – it's unstable.' I stared at the silent ground. 'There's a lot of hot matter close to the surface and there may well be hot springs.'

161

'But where?'

I shook my head. 'Anyway,' I said, 'it probably wouldn't be like Bath Spa.' What was happening under our sweating feet? 'Most hot springs are noxious,' I told him.

'Like everything else in Arba Mintch.' He stared at me for a moment. 'You really do know something about geology, don't you?' He sounded surprised.

'Not much. I just collect fossils really.' I was thinking about T. E. Lawrence again, and the way he could, from a camel's back, distinguish the elements that made up the desert: porphyry, green schist, basalt. It all looked like sand and dust to me. And the rift wasn't anything like the pictures in the books I'd read. There was no fallen keystone here.

'It all looks so different in books,' I said sadly. 'In real life I don't know what I'm looking at.' Perhaps I shouldn't be so quick to jettison *Seven Pillars of Wisdom*. At very least it was a lesson in endurance. T. E. Lawrence hadn't abandoned either his curiosity or his ethics just because he was ill or in a tight spot. It was disgraceful to abandon his book for the sake of eight tins of pineapple.

'Well, look on the bright side,' Graham said with an effort, 'we may be in Gardulla this time tomorrow.'

'If Mel can travel,' I reminded him.

'Sod it!' he said, lowering his voice. 'The bastard didn't wait for me in Dorse. Anyway, for all we know he still wants to push north.'

I kept my mouth shut. Hidden in my cell was a secret stash of tinned fruit which I had no intention of sharing, so I was the last person to press the virtues of communal feeling on Graham.

Not that it mattered. Our frantic inquiries produced nothing. Traffic in and out of Arba Mintch was at a standstill.

36

On the evening of the fourth day something happened. The three of us were sitting silently on the bare earth outside Mel's door. Nobody had anything to say. Everything, except getting out, was irritating and irrelevant and we were all tired and depressed. The way you are when optimism has faded.

For two days a heavy cloud had hung over the valley making the heat even denser and more oppressive, so when a sound like distant firecrackers started we all looked first at the sky.

Two women emerged from the cook shed, hurriedly wiping their hands on their skirts. They ran across the compound into the bar and didn't come back.

The light was fading fast. Nothing happened for several minutes and then we heard what we all identified as a single shot much closer by. It was followed by the sound of running feet outside. Then shooting broke out further away in the lower town – a cluster of reports followed by tense silence.

We were on our feet now and we went, without speaking, into the bar. There was no one there. All the women had disappeared, the door was closed, and none of the lamps were lit.

We waited, listening intently. After several more minutes of silence Mel went to the door.

'Don't open it,' Graham said, his voice loud and rough. Mel ignored him and stepped carefully outside. I followed slowly, straining my eyes to see into the gloom. Something was on fire in the lower town, that was all there was to be seen, but the night was filled with the soft sounds of whispers and scurrying feet.

Then, without warning, it began to rain. It came down

with the force of hailstones as if someone up there had turned on a water cannon. There was a deafening roar as the water hit the tin roof. Within seconds the road was awash and water rushed like rivers off the roof and down the hill. Mel jumped back inside but after the initial shock I stood in the downpour until my hair and clothes were soaked. In two minutes I couldn't have been more thoroughly washed if I had stepped fully clothed into a lake.

After five minutes it stopped as suddenly as it had begun. Dead silence followed. The fire was out and I stood up to my ankles in warm mud.

'For Christ's sake, come in,' Graham called softly. I went in and he shut the door firmly.

'What the hell was all that about?' Mel asked. Nobody knew. We were all shaken. I went to the compound to find dry clothes. It was a good thing Nastasia's backpack was waterproof because the roof leaked and not only was the bed wet but the floor had turned to mud.

When I returned the men were arguing in fierce whispers. Mel had lit a candle and was ransacking the bar to find something to drink. Graham had no objection to a drink on the house but he was furious with Mel for showing a light.

'This bar is like a sieve,' he said. 'Any light'd show for miles. The last thing we want is to attract attention.'

'Stuff you,' Mel said mildly. 'I'm not getting my arse shot off without gargle in my hand.' His health had improved considerably but he was not yet strong enough to be as obnoxious as usual. If he had, there might have been a fight. We were all as nervous as zebras when they smell lion. Mel found a bottle of *t'etch* and blew the candle out.

Nothing more happened, and as we passed the bottle between us we began to relax. But the women did not come back, the madam was nowhere to be seen, and Taffera, who was usually hanging around somewhere, had vanished too. When at last I plucked up enough courage to examine the cook shed I found the fire out and the pots cold. There would be no food that night. So we sat and drank in the dark.

'I've been expecting something like this,' Graham said quietly.

'Like what exactly?' I asked, I was most unnerved, as usual, by my own ignorance. 'I mean, does this sort of thing happen regularly or is it abnormal?'

'It's been so bloody tense,' he said without answering my question.

'Shut up!' Mel whispered. 'Listen!'

A slow shuffling sound came from outside. We turned wordlessly towards the door. I held my breath. Something bumped against the door, slid, flopped.

We waited immobile on the bench. A moan, and fingernails scratching on wood.

I couldn't stand it and began to fumble for the matches. Graham's hand clamped like a trap on my wrist.

Silence. And then a low, continuous whimpering began.

'This is stupid,' Mel said. He grabbed the matches out of my paralysed hand and lit the candle.

'Don't be a fool!' Graham shouted, making me jump as if an electric current had passed from his hand to my arm.

Mel pulled the door open. And a body rolled inside. Mel dragged it out of the way and slammed the door shut.

'It's . . . it's . . . who the fuck is it?' Mel asked.

We peered at the swollen, mangled face – split lips, broken teeth rimmed with blood, eyesockets so puffed and cut that no eyeball showed. He wept blood from his nose and ears.

'Is it Mr Latybalu?' I asked.

'Who knows?' Graham said savagely. The shape of the head was so distorted that it looked like rotten fruit. But the mouth cried softly at each painful breath.

'What can we do?' Graham said. 'What the hell can we do?'

'First aid?' Mel rasped. 'Anyone know enough first aid

to deal with *this*?' He laughed, a dry retching spasm which shocked us all.

'The hospital?' I said.

'Are you kidding?' Mel asked. 'Do you want to go out? Well, do you? You'll get ripped to pieces. We've got to get him out of here. What if they're looking for him?'

'Who?'

'Whoever did this, stupid. What if it was the bleeding *askaris*? What will they do to whoever helps him? Tell me that?'

'You think it was the soldiers?' Graham asked.

'If it was the soldiers they'll cut us up for helping. If it wasn't, and they catch us here with him, they'll think we did it and they'll cut us up for that.'

'Let's get him into the yard,' I said. 'We can open another room and use more light.' The rhythmic whimpering was like sandpaper on my face.

'That wasn't Chinese New Year we heard down the hill,' Mel said to Graham.

'I know.' They both looked down at the crying man.

'Ambo,' I said. 'At least let's give him water.' It might have been the flickering shadows, I know I couldn't see properly, but Graham and Mel suddenly looked quite detached.

I stumbled to the back where the madam kept her stores and lit another candle.

Graham yelled, 'Put it out!'

I found and opened a bottle of Ambo and then blew the candle out.

'She's going to get us all killed,' Graham said.

I was afraid of touching the man. He was so badly hurt I thought he would come apart in my hands. I put my thumb over the neck of the bottle so that only a dribble of water dripped into his mouth. It washed the blood from his broken teeth. I wasn't sure if he swallowed. He stopped moaning.

His head rolled to one side and a wash of blood erupted from his open mouth.

'Help me!' I cried. 'He's dying.'

Mel had the door open in a trice. The candle went out.

When it was lit again the door was shut and barred. I was kneeling in a mess of mud and blood. The Ambo bottle rolled away into the corner.

'Internal injuries,' Graham said.

'Don't blame yourself, Fay,' Mel said. 'He was dying anyway.' Both their voices shook. They pulled me to my feet and steered me towards the yard. I thought – I still think – I heard fingernails scratching on the door.

37

Early next morning we got out. Taffera came to my door at daybreak and told me there was 'a bus'. He had to shout: sometime in the night my ears had gone bad again.

The madam and one of the women were in the bar. They said nothing. They didn't look at us. There was no breakfast.

Fresh earth had been sprinkled on the dark patch by the door. Outside the churned mud had dried and hardened. It was, in any case, red. We carried our bags across it. The walls of the building were stained to knee height with red where the force of the rain had kicked up mud, and to my feverish eye it looked as if a river of blood had flowed during the night.

Seven Pillars of Wisdom stayed in my room, and at the last minute I gave the binoculars to Taffera. He, quiet and subdued like everyone else, accepted them without enthusiasm.

The Toyota was waiting on the outskirts of town. We walked the half-mile to it without exchanging a word or a glance. Taffera did not come, and the band of children who roamed and catcalled behind us gave me the impression we were being chased out.

Do they know? I kept asking myself, as I looked from side to side hoping to see Mr Latybalu. Do they know?

But Mr Latybalu had never been around so early in the morning. It was only in the afternoon and evening he came for his carafe of *t'etch* and conversation – a man who thought the soldiers were paid too much, that teachers were paid too little, and who liked Americans unreservedly – a man who had listened politely when Graham tried to explain the National Health system and was too courteous to express his obvious disbelief.

Was it Mr Latybalu last night? I asked silently; and, of the children: Do they know?

If there had been three Toyotas going in separate directions Graham, Mel, and I would have split up that morning. But there was only one and we are jammed together with ten other travellers and driven south to Gardulla.

We didn't talk and I remember nothing about the drive except earache and the several stops the driver made by the lake to take shots at crocodiles. He would stand, braced against the windscreen, to shoot off half a dozen rounds into Lake Chamo. The lake looked dead and empty to me, and I never saw a single crocodile.

I don't remember much about Gardulla either. We were stuck there without transport for three days. It was a pretty place, I think, but I didn't go out. I stayed in the compound with the other women and wore a skirt to dissociate myself from Mel and Graham. There was a baby there, and I remember that once or twice the women gave her to me to play with. I was grateful they trusted me. But it reminded me of dreams about Abbavich and made me want to cry.

'This little piggy went to market,' I intoned over soft fingers that curled like chrysanthemum petals. 'This little piggy stayed at home . . .' The baby cooed throatily but her mother watched with anxiety. Was I cursing her child? I handed it back. 'This little piggy went wee wee wee all the way home,' I prayed silently. My head felt like a balloon full of poison gas.

The daily business of inquiring about transport was something Mel and Graham did. They knew now that I was hampered by intermittent periods of complete deafness and that I would be useless at the question and answer routine they had to keep up with boys and teachers in order not to miss news of transport out. But they resented me. I was not pulling my weight.

And it was true. I withdrew. Sometimes it seemed too much effort to drag myself out of my cell in the morning. Fits of uncontrolled shivering and weeping plagued me.

169

I still could not swallow *injera* and *wat*, and after dark I would lock myself into the tiny room and secretly consume a whole tin of pineapple chunks. I counted and recounted the diminishing hoard. Each day Nastasia's bag weighed a little less. And each day my skirt hung lower on my hips.

Everything was running out. Mel finished the Kaolin. There was no more insect repellent or chlorine tablets. One day, sorting through my papers, I discovered my return ticket from Nairobi to London. The plane I should be on would leave in two days' time. For a couple of minutes I was almost jolted out of my lethargy. But what was the point of worrying about Nairobi and London when the short distance from Gardulla to Gidole was impossible to arrange?

There was a good reason for this, as it turned out. The map was wrong, and one of the towns did not exist. The similarity between the names should have warned us. Of course, nobody explained. It was something we eventually figured out for ourselves. Mel tore his map to pieces and used them in the *shintabite*. The desecration was caused as much by necessity as by anger.

So the next stage in the journey was Conso. We were given a lift out of Gardulla/Gidole by a cotton planter and later picked up at a crossroads by a grain convoy. The three trucks crawled laboriously along the rutted track, and we were so glad to be on the move again that we did not question what sort of area a grain convoy would be going to.

On the road we passed little groups of people, usually a man, a woman, and two or three children. Sometimes they were walking but more often they sat huddled by the roadside. They did not ask for a lift. They just watched the trucks go by.

At one slow bend of the track, I remember a particular family. The truck was in second gear with the engine howling, and I saw a woman crouched on the ground with a shawl held over her head like a tent, hiding her features, protecting herself from the noon sun. A small child with legs like a grasshopper squatted in the shade she provided. Neither of them looked up when the trucks passed, but an older child stood by the roadside and stared at us. Our eyes met. I wish they hadn't. Her mouth was set in an oblong rictus of misery, lips drawn down over her upper teeth, lower teeth exposed. She could have been crying huge black tears, but I knew they were flies that clung to her eyelids not water. I turned my head away and the truck crawled on.

A sudden, inexplicable rage shook me. Why were they just waiting there? Why didn't they do something? Why were they looking at me? They wanted my place in the truck and if we stopped they would take it from me. I clamped my fist grimly to the burning metal and hung on.

We arrived at the Norwegian mission just as the sun was going down. Three white women and a man met the convoy. They were obviously delighted to see it. But they were far from delighted with Graham, Mel, and me. We were met with a restrained anger which I did not at first understand.

'You cannot stay here,' the man said decisively as we crawled stiffly out of the trucks. He wore grey flannel trousers and a light tweed jacket.

'Wait till you're bleeding asked,' Mel said under his breath.

'Where then?' Graham asked more politely.

'The town is over there,' the man said, pointing across a steep and narrow cleft in the hillside to an untidy collection of buildings on the other side.

The track went in a half circle round the cleft, but Mel and Graham took the short cut straight across. I was still struggling with the backpack and they didn't wait for me.

A woman with a clipboard who had just finished checking the driver's bill of loading came over and said, 'You must not stay here.'

'I know,' I said, and started up the track. The gully looked unmanageable.

She said, 'I mean, this is a place where there is no food.'

I stopped. 'Famine?' I asked.

'It is not yet famine,' she said. 'So far only two hundred are dead. Not so bad, I think.' I stared at her. 'You must go,' she added as if I had not understood.

'Is there a bus?' I asked, 'or a Toyota, or is anyone going to Yabello?'

She shook her head. 'I have not heard,' she said. 'I am sorry.'

'We cannot walk to Yabello,' I said. I was wondering how to walk around the gully. The backpack hung like a sack of lead shot from my shoulders.

'I am sorry,' the woman repeated.

38

That night I made a list of Sea Areas around the coast of Britain, as far as I could remember them. It was to take my mind off the big problems. *Viking*, I wrote. *North Utsira, South Utsira, Forties*.

I had started by wondering about the seven seals in the *Book of Revelation*. This was because of what Graham had said when I told them about the famine.

It was dark when I stumbled into the bar in Conso. I could tell where they were by the raised voices.

'Ambo!' Mel shouted at the top of his voice. 'If you're too bloody tight to feed us, at least give us something to drink.'

A big-boned woman stood, arms akimbo, in front of her stores. She shouted too.

Mel had completely lost his head. 'You mean bitch!' he yelled. 'You charge way over the odds for this shit-hole and you have the nerve to say you won't feed us.'

'Shut up,' Graham said. 'She doesn't understand English.'

It was true. She did not speak English, but she understood Mel and she was furious.

I said. 'Famine. We've walked into a famine area.'

'Behold, a pale horse,' Graham said sarcastically. 'Or was it the black one?'

'What the hell are you chuntering about horses for?' Mel asked.

'The Four Horsemen of the Apocalypse, you ignoramus. One of them was famine.'

I couldn't remember who the fourth horseman was: one was death, one was famine, one was war. The four horses had emerged from the opening of the first four of the

173

seven seals. What were the other three? A great earthquake? Yes. What else?

I didn't want to remember.

Cromarty, *Forth*, I wrote, and then stopped. What came after Forth?'

If you spend a lot of time sewing you are often alone. And when the machining is finished, sometimes there is a lot of meticulous handwork to follow. Costumes for Elizabeth I, for instance, require thousands of pearls to be sewn on one at a time in intricate patterns. Although the result may be stunning, the work itself is not at all interesting, so you listen to the radio. I have heard the shipping forecast every day for months on end and you'd think I would know the Sea Areas and Weather Stations off by heart. But I don't.

They are repetitive, they always come in the same order and they are soothing. You know where you are with the shipping forecast.

I left a gap. *Dogger*, *Fisher*, *German Bight*.

Mel brought his fist down on the table with a bang. 'You filthy, whoring cow,' he yelled. It was something I could not prevent and did not want to witness. I dragged my bag through the back door and out into the dark compound. After a few minutes looking at the stars and listening to the roar of Mel's voice, my ears started to pop and hum and blotted him out.

A small shadow materialized at my side and a hand plucked my sleeve. She led me to a replica of all the other horrible little rooms I had slept in, and then she disappeared. There was no candle and I tussled with zips and buckles until I found my torch. Even though I had spared it as much as possible, the batteries were weak.

There were too many things I could not prevent and didn't want to witness: Mel's anger, those huddled family groups on the road, the man who vomited blood . . . *Lundy*, *Fastnet*, *Irish Sea*. No, that was wrong – I had missed out the South Coast.

This was not what I had been saving my batteries for.

174

I switched off and started again out loud in the dark –
Viking, Cromarty, Forth. My voice sounded hollow and
muffled; was I talking too loud, and what had happened
to North and South Utsira?'

Silently now I chanted: *Wight, Portland, Plymouth,
Channel Light Vessel.* Channel Light Vessel? Surely that
was a Weather Station, not a Sea Area. I squeezed my
eyes tight shut. Nobody – not even the most pathetic
ninny – cries because she has confused the Sea Areas with
the Weather Stations.

I did not know where I was – even with the shipping
forecast.

39

'Look presentable,' my mother advised when I was about to depart for my first job interview. 'Clean and tidy hair, clean and tidy shoes. If you get those right, people won't worry too much what comes in between.'

Presentable was the word my mother always used when she wanted me to make a 'good impression'.

'Don't overdo it,' she said, rejecting my best dress. 'You don't want to look desperate for a job, do you?'

I did not want to look desperate. I was going to the mission to ask for help, but I did not want to look as if I needed it. I wanted to look rational and respectable – not like someone who would become a burden.

Clean hair and clean shoes were impossible. I arranged a scarf over my head and put on a patterned skirt which might distract anyone from looking at the filthy sandals and blistered feet.

'It's got to be Fay,' Mel said reluctantly. 'She'll probably fuck it up, but look at her.'

Graham looked critically. 'Abandoned waif,' he announced. 'Well, she's got a better chance than the two of us.'

'Get going, Fay,' Mel said, 'and don't come back till they've promised us a ride or given you some food.'

They watched like two bearded terrorists as I left the compound. Watching even more closely was the weird child with the wart on his face. He picked the wart till it bled and then he sucked his fingers, staring all the time with dull and cretinous eyes.

I had no faith at all in my power to please or persuade. Sensing a lack of confidence, the children who followed me along the track threw a shower of stones. One hit the shoulder which was now red and swollen from where the strap of Nastasia's backpack had rubbed the infected tick bite. I did not turn round.

'*Shannon, Rockall, Malin, Hebrides*,' I intoned. It no longer mattered that the order might be wrong. The rhythm kept my feet going. '*Finisterre, Sole, Lundy, Fastnet.*' Anything would have done just so long as it kept me plodding onwards. '*Humber, Thames, Dover, Wight – Keep me marching through the night.*'

'Head up!' Mum said. 'Shoulders back. Deep breath. You can get any job you want. *I* know you can, so just relax and enjoy yourself.'

'Good luck,' said Dad, giving me a friendly wink.

'Knock 'em dead,' and 'Break a leg,' called John and Bill from the bathroom landing.

It wasn't much of a job, just a general dogsbody at a theatrical costumier's in the West End, but I wanted it badly.

I wanted to sit down and rest but with the children so close behind I didn't dare.

There was no one at the mission. The low white buildings looked abandoned. I wandered from door to door, knocking timidly on each one. Finally I chose a shaded porch and sat down with my back against a wall and watched long lines of siafu ants march through the dust.

'*The grand old Duke of York*,' I muttered deliriously, '*He had ten thousand men . . .*' and closed my aching eyes against the glare.

The sun was lower over the hills when the sound of a motor woke me. A Volvo drove into the mission yard and stopped in front of one of the bungalows. A fair-haired woman and two fair, pink children got out.

The woman saw me coming. She let the two children into the house before walking over to meet me. The children had plump legs and startlingly white socks.

'Excuse me,' I said. 'I'm sorry to bother you, but . . .' Suddenly panic overwhelmed me as it had once before in Arba Mintch. The woman's cool blue eyes gazed at me politely and my teeth started to chatter. What could I say

177

when her children's socks were so white and she put them in the house rather than let them meet me?

'I'm sorry,' I said again. 'But there are three of us . . .'

'Oh yes,' she said. 'Three hippies in Conso. It is a bad time to come.'

'Yes . . . but we didn't know . . . I mean, we are trying to get to Yabello.' In complete misery I stared at the ground. I couldn't meet her eyes. My hands shook and sweat dribbled down my ribs.

'You must understand,' the woman began, not unkindly, 'we cannot interrupt important work here.'

'*Sumburgh*, *Bell Rock*, *Dowsing*,' I whispered and clasped my hands tightly together to stop the trembling.

'Excuse please?' she said, looking very wary.

'I'm sorry . . . I mean, we would work for you . . . or anything . . . but we cannot get out unless you help.'

'To work will not be necessary.' She was embarrassed. 'Already we have too many. For the food, you understand. Otherwise they will starve.'

I am a beggar, I thought. Even as a beggar I am a failure. I haven't eaten for days, please, missus, spare us a couple of bob, hard times, missus, just a crust.

'Wait here,' she said, pointing to the ground. She went away into her bungalow. I stood on the spot and trembled. Please missus . . . but if you had to choose between the starving and the merely hungry which would you choose? I had no right to beg.

She brought a packet of custard cream biscuits when she came back. 'My husband says to tell you, on Monday he must drive to Yabello. You must come back on Monday.'

'Yes,' I said. 'Thank you very much . . . but, please can you tell me what day it is today?'

'Today?' She looked at me tiredly. 'Of course today is Saturday.'

'Of course,' I muttered unhappily. 'Thank you. Thank you very much.' She gave me the custard creams and watched until I was back on the track and limping towards Conso.

40

If you look like a hippy, act like a mental patient, and don't know what day of the week it is, you shouldn't be too surprised if people don't treat you with respect. In fact I thought the woman at the mission had been charitable to say the least. I did not expect her to recognize the inner me under the dirt and weakness. Further than that, the inner me was riddled with more weakness than I showed on the surface and now I did not want anyone to see it.

The stunned and grateful surprise I felt when Tony had found something special in mousy little Fay seemed laughable. The 'old-fashioned girl' who, he once said, would 'do anything for anyone' was a mask which crumbled under stress. Mel and Graham knew more about me than Tony did. They knew a lot more about me than I wanted anyone to know.

They had found the pineapple chunks.

'Thought we wouldn't find out?' Mel asked grimly when I staggered into the compound with the custard creams hidden under my shirt. They were sitting on the ground outside my door. The last two cans were displayed like evidence in front of them. One can had been opened. It was empty.

'You've been through my things!' I said, outraged.

'You've got gold, Fay,' Graham said. 'We could've bought our way out of here.'

'How?' I cried. 'What's to buy? And anyway it isn't my gold. It's Nastasia's and its going back to her family.' There was something like a clenched fist in the pit of my stomach. It held rage and fear.

'That sow has stores.' Mel jerked his thumb at the big-boned woman who was watching us greedily. 'She's waiting for us to get hungry enough to pay her fucking price.'

'You want to pay a speculator with a dead woman's gold!' I shouted. The fist was opening. 'Is there nothing we won't do? You aren't starving! She gives you one meal a day. It's not three, like you're used to. But it's one more than most people are getting round here.'

I shook like a machine and my ears exploded into a scream so I didn't hear what Graham said in reply.

'And in case you haven't noticed,' I went on, 'you're getting my share. I can't eat her food. The only thing I can get down is pineapple. Which means I can't eat biscuits either. So here . . .' I pulled the packet out of my shirt and flung it in Mel's face. It hit his mouth.

I snatched up the last precious can and kicked Graham's legs till he cleared the way to my room. He was trying to say something but I slammed the door and shot the bolt.

That was the last I saw of them that day. When I spied through a crack in the shutter I saw them arguing bad-temperedly on their way into the bar.

Of course the fight had been witnessed and enjoyed by everyone in the compound. The strange boy with the bleeding face was stamping on an old tractor tyre and watching my door with slitty eyes. The big-boned woman, who now had nothing better to amuse her, knocked him off it with a blow from her hard hand and laughed as he sat confused in the dust.

And from the kitchen shack, a half-grown girl with hair plaited like raked gravel giggled behind her hand.

In this compound the kitchen was a thatched round hut so small that you had to crawl through the doorway. I took refuge in it during the storm which broke about half an hour later. Rain hit the tin roof like bullets and found its way on to the bed. The mud in the compound sucked the sandals off my feet. Mel and Graham were in the bar, making that enemy territory, but the kitchen girl peeped out of her hut and beckoned, and I ran through the wall of falling rain to join her.

181

She was cooking *injera* – slap-happy, and full of good cheer – and letting her misshapen black pot of *wat* boil over. The straw fire kept going out and she was in perpetual motion trying to keep it alight, slapping *injera* and stirring *wat*. It was so smoky that even the goat had watery eyes. The girl blew her nose on a dress that must once have been white, but now was nearly not even a dress – just a rag held together by a stitch here and there.

The thatch did a better job of waterproofing than tin and after a while I stopped shivering and earned my keep by stirring the *wat* with a stick while the girl breathed life into the fire.

She must have breathed a little life into me too because I was much calmer when the rain stopped and I went back to my room. It was a comfort to know there was someone in the compound who would share her dry kitchen with a distraught *ferenj* and a goat.

41

Acts of kindness were few and far between in that compound. The men who drank themselves stupid in the bar bullied the big woman, and she bullied unmercifully the girl and the odd child. He, in turn, beat the goat whenever he could get near it. The goat was fairly evil-tempered too, but then there was nothing for the poor creature to eat. It nibbled on the kitchen thatch, the old tyres, and even gnawed at wooden door frames. There was nothing for it to drink either.

On the morning after the rain the earth was as cracked and dry as it had been before. Not a puddle remained. There should have been gutters and rain barrels; there had been enough water the night before to fill a hundred tanks. But the bar woman bought water from an old lady who dragged it in gourds tied to her back from far away at the bottom of the hill. The old lady was bent like an angle-iron at the waist. If you saw her on a London Street you would have offered to carry her handbag, but no one in the compound so much as helped her take the heavy gourds from her back. She was paid a few coppers and sent to the bottom of the hill again for more.

I watched the compound from the crack in the shutter. And the weird child watched me. At least he watched my door. Even a closed door with a *ferenj* behind it was more interesting than nothing. Except for thirty-seven bottle tops and an old tractor tyre his life was completely empty. I knew about the thirty-seven bottle tops because my life was empty too, and I counted them one day when, tired of staring at me, he started to play a game with them. It was the only time I saw him play with anything.

Behind my bolted door, I was avoiding him as much as I was avoiding Mel and Graham. I know it sounds stupid, after all he was only about seven, but he frightened me. His crazy, blank gaze was unnerving and I began to think he was ill-wishing me. He knew all about me and he was punishing me for it: I know you, his eyes said; you're dirty and infected just like I am. You're too frightened to help a dying man. You hoard food. You steal a dead girl's money. *You don't care a damn about me*. So I curse you.

It was only when he was temporarily out of the way and the men were elsewhere that I ventured out of my cell. I carried the tin of pineapple under my shirt like a shameful secret and stole like a thief through Conso till I had shaken off the escort of stone-throwing kids.

Up the hill, in the opposite direction from the mission, the track led between bare fields. They were proper fields, walled with dry-stone, not simply patches of earth ploughed into the hillside. Serpentine layers of low walls snaked around the hills surrounding the town. Some of them were crumbled, spoiling the graceful line, but this was a bold and beautiful example of contour farming.

It seemed so unjust. Conso was the only place I had seen where an attempt had been made to preserve the topsoil, to hold back water, and yet it was in the middle of a famine.

The sun, which is such a blessing in the chilly north, burns like a flame-thrower here. It cracks the earth, and shrivels the seed in the ground, and dries the soil to dust. It shatters the hopes of men who work the land. It burns the grass and starves the beasts. It dries up mother's milk. Even the furthest fields are never green. Range after range of brown and purple mountains reach helplessly for rain. And even the lakes somehow fail to look like water. The sun transforms them into hot, grey stone, a home for mosquitoes and parasites and crocodiles.

The sun cooks the brain and makes the mind wander. I slid off my stony perch and limped back to the bar.

Concealed by the back door of the bar, I saw Mel and Graham emerge from my room. Mel was gesticulating frantically. Graham looked pale and ill. They had not found Nastasia's backpack which I had left for safekeeping with the girl in the kitchen. Maybe they thought I had run out and left them. Serve them right, I thought nastily. I bought a bottle of Fanta and sat on a bench. My hand played with the hidden can of pineapple, incubating like an egg next to my skin. It was a risk. If I ate it tonight and there was no ride out tomorrow there would be nothing left. If I saved it and carried it to Yabello . . . it might be a waste of energy.

The big woman charged a fortune for Fanta, but there was no tea or coffee except what she drank herself. *T'etch* and *talla* were relatively cheap but even a small amount of alcohol played tricks with me now.

Mel and Graham ducked in through the back door like two tattered pirates. They saw me in my shadowy corner and ran straight at me, saying things I couldn't hear.

'I can't hear,' I said, standing up. 'You've been into my room again. Do not go in my room.' I picked up the Fanta bottle and left them.

When Graham came half an hour later, the can was under the mattress and I had decided what to do.

He banged loudly at the door. I heard him but I didn't say anything. After dark, I was thinking. I'll eat it after dark.

His face appeared round the partly opened shutter. He had combed his hair for the first time in days and it stuck neatly to his head as if he had used Brylcreem. Making a good impression, I thought. How funny. Except for the beard, he looked like a salesman. He smiled a salesman's smile and pointed to the door. I got up and went out.

'How are the ears?' he shouted.

'Not too bad,' I said. 'Speak slowly.'

'I'm sorry we went in your room,' he began, enunciating very precisely. 'We thought you'd gone to the mission without telling us.' He composed his features but I could tell he was anxious.

'You didn't say what happened there yesterday,' he went on. He was trying to be casual.

'You didn't ask,' I said. 'You were too busy stealing my food and prying into my room.'

'Look, I'm very sorry about that. It was Mel's idea – you know what he's like. Aussies get a bit touched if they don't get steak and eggs three times a day.' He smiled nervously. 'Look, we've got to stick together, Fay. After all, I got you that lift out of Gidole.'

'And in return I didn't steal from you,' I said vengefully.

'I apologize! What more can I say? Look, we can leave Mel behind if you want to, but for God's sake tell me if you got us a lift.'

I was very angry. I said, 'Who do you think I am? I'm not leaving anyone behind. There is a lift.'

'Thank Christ for that!' He sat down suddenly in the dust and leaned back against the wall. 'When? Where?'

'I'll tell you in good time,' I said, hating him. Hating myself. 'Unless you start snooping again – if you do, or if you go on about Nastasia's jewellery again – I'll happily leave you to rot.'

He smiled up at me, hating me too. 'Honestly,' he said, spreading his hands – Look, friend, nothing up my sleeves. 'Honestly, I'll keep Mel away from you. Pax, Fay. All right?'

'Pax,' I said and went to the kitchen for Nastasia's backpack.

42

The dark hours crawled with bugs and sweat. I was up long before dawn, afraid of missing the fair woman's husband, afraid I had got the wrong day. It was still dark when we trailed across the gully and I led the way to the fair woman's bungalow. Lights were on in the house and through the windows came the cheerful sounds of a family at breakfast.

She was wearing a pink towelling bathrobe when she answered my knock. 'Oh yes,' she said, remembering. 'To Yabello, yes? Well, in an hour, perhaps he will go.'

We waited. 'What's this "perhaps", Fay?' Mel whispered. I pretended not to hear. I was hoping it was just her English. Perhaps an hour, not perhaps he will go. Cold with sweat, shaking with anxiety, I gazed at the lighted window.

But after a while the husband came to the door. He wore a grey sweater with leather patches at the elbows and he smoked a pipe. He did not look at all like a missionary, more like my father on a Saturday afternoon.

'Good morning,' he said, looking us over carefully. 'You wish to go to Yabello?'

'Good morning,' I said. 'Yes. It's very kind of you to take us.'

'You have been in Conso since the grain came?' he asked. I nodded, and he looked at us even more carefully.

'Then perhaps we may offer you some coffee,' he suggested.

We trooped wordlessly into his kitchen, stunned by the smell of cooking. It was a clean, shiny European kitchen, with a cooker and a sink with taps. I hardly noticed though, because the remains of the family breakfast were still on the table: eggshells, toast crusts, ham, cheese, jam.

I tore my gaze from the table and found him looking at me.

'Perhaps a boiled egg with your coffee?' he asked gently.

I cleared my throat. 'Please don't go to any trouble,' I whispered. Mel kicked my ankle and said, 'That'd be just fine. Sir.'

We had boiled eggs, soft white bread, and jam with our coffee. And as the sun came up we climbed into a Jeep and we even smiled at each other.

'You nearly blew that, Fay,' Mel muttered as we arranged ourselves in the back. 'Crawling only takes you so far.'

'You called him "Sir",' Graham said softly. 'I heard you.'

'Any man with that much tucker's a sir to me,' Mel retorted.

I had Nastasia's pack on my knee and I leaned forward resting my head on the rolled sleeping-bag and closed my eyes.

An egg. A soft-boiled egg with the white just set and the yolk still liquid. A spoonful of egg which slipped painlessly over the tongue and down the throat. A quiet, bland, gentle egg against which the throat did not rasp and tighten or the stomach rebel. Nursery food. Sickroom food. Food of nourishment and comfort and airy darkened rooms. A cool hand on a hot brow. Chilled glasses of lemonade. Clean sheets.

Snatches of conversation between Graham and the missionary: 'Land . . . reform?' '. . . internal politics . . .' '. . . actually pay tithes to their Church . . .'

I would never leave home again. Return and never leave. How many days to Kenya now? Two? Three? Don't count on it . . . *Fair Isle, Faeroes, South-east Iceland*.

When I opened my eyes again we had left the hills far behind and were in a flat waste-land of dead and withered thorn. The sun was overhead and reflecting off the dust and shingle with an aching glare. Both Graham and Mel were asleep but the missionary hummed tunelessly as he drove straight ahead at a steady twenty miles an hour.

The brim of his linen hat touched the bridge of his sunglasses, and I loved him. I almost wished something would go wrong with the Jeep so that I could put it right for him.

The scrub seemed quite empty, and after a while I asked the missionary about it. 'Drought,' he answered. 'All dead or migrated. I cannot remember when we last saw game. The nomads also. And the little villages. One we found – no one knew it existed – we found accidentally, yes? Sixty-three inhabitants, all dead of starvation. People in Europe do not know the meaning of remote.'

'But *no* one knows,' I said. 'I mean, I asked at the Embassy because of the famine last year and she said there was no more famine. It was all over.'

'They wish perhaps to encourage tourism,' he said with the first and last laugh I saw him give. Then more soberly he went on, 'The Ethiopians know and they do not know. They take it for a fact of life. If it is Europeans you mean, well, we have no journalists or TV people here. We are far from Addis. It is worse that we are far from the people also. They come if they know about us and if they can still walk. We go to them if we know they are there. But often we do not know. No one knows how many people live here and so no one knows how many will die.'

Scilly, Valentia, Ronaldsway. You sit in a Jeep with an egg in your belly . . . *Tiree, Butt of Lewis.*

'In England,' I said, 'every house is on a map somewhere. Every name is on a census.'

'Ah, yes. But two hundred years ago, perhaps, when harvest failed, people starved there too. Only a little time ago. You must not judge.'

'I wasn't,' I said. 'I was only dreaming.'

'When I came at first – ' he smiled – 'I used to dream also.'

It wasn't even a proper desert. In better times, when the thorns were green, it would support animals and people –

people whom nobody knew about. People who lived so far from society that they had no back-up when things went wrong – no network distributing surplus food or medical help or fuel. When your waterhole dries up, when your crops don't grow, when the game goes elsewhere, when you've slaughtered your domestic animals and burnt your own house for fuel, you die. You die because you don't know where to look for help and help does not know you exist.

There must have been a time when everyone lived like that: from one crop to another, at the mercy of the sun and rain. We've built guilds and unions and social services and groups to protect ourselves. It has taken centuries and now most of us can't live without them. I can't. A month in Ethiopia has taught me that.

'I couldn't live here,' I said.

'You do not have to,' the missionary replied. 'Tomorrow, perhaps you will be in Kenya.'

43

The first time we came to Yabello, we came too late and left too early to see it. We stopped only for a few hours' sleep on the way north. That time Gabriel was in a rush to get home. And Peter had been with us. I wondered if Peter was still in Shashamane or if he had managed to get a message to his rich father. And if so, what would his father have been able to do?

'Back at the berloody beginning,' Mel grumbled. 'It's taken us bloody weeks to get back where we bloody started.'

'What're you going to do?' Graham asked.

'Dunno. My guts are still a bit crook. You wouldn't think a guy who'd had no food could shit so much.'

'Spare us the details,' Graham said. 'You could probably waltz straight through to Addis if you wanted to. I shouldn't think trouble lasts long here.'

'Trying to get rid of me, are you? You two Poms want to hightail it back to civilization, eh?'

'Yes,' I said.

'Think your car'll still be in Moyale?'

'Yes.'

'Fat chance.'

'No,' I said. 'Ethiopians don't steal.'

'Aw, give it a rest about that sodding pineapple,' Mel complained. 'Tell you what, Fay – you get us a ride as good as the last one and I'll buy you a crate of the fucking stuff. Whaddya say?'

I said nothing. As usual we were sitting round a table in a bar. The men were drinking beer and I had a small bottle of Ambo. I was dog-tired. But breakfast at the mission had done something for all of us. It wasn't just the food, I thought. Eating off china plates with cutlery and egg cups, and being forced by the presence of the missionary and his wife to behave like well-mannered people had reminded us of what we had in common – not what divided us.

'She still looks kind of respectable, doesn't she, Pom?' Mel went on.

'Better than us, at any rate,' Graham said.

'I haven't grown a beard, if that's what you mean.' It was the only difference as far as I could see.

'C'mon, Fay. We aren't asking you to tart for us.'

'No?' I said. 'Well, okay, I'll try. But you'd better try too.' Apart from the missionary's Jeep I hadn't seen a single vehicle in Yabello. There were plenty of donkeys and mules, even camels, but there was a distinct absence of motor traffic. Certainly there were no buses, and I had been counting on a bus to get us back to Moyale.

There were nomads in Yabello – women who walked softly behind the camels, straight slim women who wore black and red shawls, and whose arms and legs clinked with brass, copper, and silver. Maybe they would walk to Kenya.

I followed one for a few paces, but her long leisurely stride was deceptive. She was walking much too fast for me. It reminded me of how weak I was and I turned away in another direction.

At the north end of town I discovered the dance. First I saw a huge crowd of women, then I heard the screaming. I was about to run for cover when I realized it wasn't screaming – it was ululation. The men were dancing and the women had formed a circle round them.

To begin with, I could see only the men's bobbing heads. Some of them had plastered mud in their hair and decked the mud with ostrich feathers which bounced as they jumped up and down, stamping, clapping, and thumping with sticks. One in particular had a tall head-dress of curled feathers and the tip of his stick was decorated with silver coils and scarlet dyed horsehair. But when I edged between the women for a closer look I saw he was

wearing a black jacket, khaki shorts, and plastic shoes –
north and south of him at total odds – and I couldn't
make up my mind which half was in fancy dress.

Sometimes the men's circle collapsed inwards like a
bouncing ball, and then it stretched out again, thumping,
stamping, clapping. And all the time the women screamed
their high, thin trill.

For once no one noticed me, and I was suddenly very
happy. This was where I liked to be – on the edge,
watching – not performing in the middle. I could have
stayed for hours, but the light was fading so I slipped out
of the crowd, and ran straight into two khaki uniforms.

'American?' said one. They were not carrying rifles but
they both wore holsters. I was a lone *ferenj* again – no
longer part of a crowd.

'English,' I said. 'How do you do? I mean, *tenastilin* . . .
er . . . *denada*.'

'Tourist?' he asked.

'Er, yes . . . but now I'm going home.'

'You enjoyed your vacation in our beautiful country,'
he said. It did not sound like a question.

'Oh yes,' I said enthusiastically. 'It's wonderful.'

'But now you leave?'

'All good things must come to an end,' I mumbled
stupidly.

'To where?'

'First to Kenya, then home to England.'

'You will come with us.' His broad face split into a
grin.

'What for?' I asked, my heart thumping like part of the
dance. I was too frightened by the uniform to realize he
was offering me a lift. I thought he was arresting me.

'You will go to Moyale,' he said, looking puzzled. 'In
the morning, we will go to Moyale. You may come.'

'Oh,' I said. 'Oh, I see – ' I was silly with relief. 'I
thought you were police.'

He said something in Amharic to his companion and
they both started to laugh. 'Customs and Excise,' he

explained, tapping himself on his shinily buttoned chest. 'We go to the border for contraband.'

It was not to be a free ride, I gathered, but since what they asked for was comparable to what we had paid for buses and Toyotas I agreed immediately. And when I told them there were three of us, they were delighted. 'Three, four, five . . .' The one who spoke English spread his arms expansively. We shook hands and I took them back to the bar for a drink.

Having myself recovered from the shock of the two uniforms, it didn't occur to me that Mel and Graham might be similarly affected. They reacted characteristically.

'Berloodyell,' Mel said, leaping to his feet. '*Askaris!*'

Graham sat very still and his face went quite expressionless.

I said quickly, 'These two officers are from Customs and Excise. They have offered us a lift to the border tomorrow.'

Graham was very good. He got up slowly and said, 'Good evening, gentlemen. Will you have a drink with us?'

They drank the most expensive German bottled beer and I explained tactfully about the fare. Soon afterwards I extricated myself and went to bed. Mel followed me as far as the back door. He said, 'You want to scare me hairless, Fay? I thought you'd turned us in or something.'

'Beggars can't be choosers.' I was exhausted and in no mood to defend myself. 'It's the only game in town – take it or leave it.' I pushed by and went through the compound to my room. The meeting with the two officers had reminded me of another problem.

When I got to Moyale I wanted to step across the border without any hassle or argument or delay. I didn't think I could stand to be held up for a single minute. The border officials who liked to play games and entertain themselves with the travellers passing through their hands would have a field day with the extra set of papers, traveller's cheques, and valuables that were Nastasia's. They could hold me up for a week while they elaborated on the difficulty those would cause. It was a horrible thought and I spent most of the night scheming how I could pass Nastasia's property through without anyone noticing.

There was another, even more pressing anxiety. When I got undressed that night I discovered that the tenderness from my tick-bitten shoulder had spread into my upper arm. And more puzzling but no less worrying were the hard painful lumps which had come up in my armpit. I remembered how the missionary, when he said goodbye to me, had lingered for a minute and then said, 'When you arrive in Nairobi you should see a doctor. It would be unwise to delay.' He didn't say anything more specific than that but it was enough to be frightening.

44

With my head pillowed on the bag I slept most of the way to Moyale. I couldn't keep my eyes open or talk to the men. It was as if poisoned cotton wool had been stuffed into my ears and the drug was seeping into my brain. I was overcome with alternate waves of nausea and fatigue. Sometimes I did not believe we were going south, that the border was coming closer. We were simply travelling, in perpetual motion. Ethiopia would never let us go.

It was getting dark when we arrived in Moyale and the police chief who was looking after the car did not recognize me. I had to produce the papers for him. Mel did not wait. He said, 'They'll close the border any minute now, and I'm fucked if I'll spend another night here.'

Graham stayed for a while and then followed. 'See you on the other side,' he said cheerfully, and left me. He said nothing about his own wrecked Land-Rover. Like Mel, it seemed he would pay any price rather than stay longer in Ethiopia. I didn't have the choice: the DKW was my only asset.

Fortunately, the Customs and Excise men also wanted a word with the police chief so he let me go after a few more minutes.

I unlocked the DKW. Weeks of accumulated heat hit me as I opened the door. The smell of petrol and hot plastic was too much for me and I hung retching over the door.

But the engine turned over at the third attempt. I couldn't believe my luck. I drove away from the police house towards the immigration shed. Just before I got there I stopped, and by the light of a rising moon I unpacked and redistributed my possessions, taking all the precautions that had kept me from sleep in Yabello.

Leaving Ethiopia, after all, turned out to be no problem. Entering Kenya, however, was fraught with difficulties. I could not exchange the remainder of my Ethiopian currency for Kenyan shillings. The temporary export licence on the car had expired and the Kenyan immigration officer made a fuss about the exit stamp the Ethiopian official had put in my passport. He said it was out of date, and of course he was right: it was still 1966 in Ethiopia. We had what seemed like an endless discussion about Gregorian and Julian calendars which he thoroughly enjoyed and I barely survived. This must have been a game he played with everyone who came south.

Sharp at six-thirty, though, he stamped my passport and slammed down the grille on his desk. It was time for him to go home. That left me with the customs officer who also wanted to leave. He took the keys of the DKW and said he would inspect it first thing in the morning.

I was in despair. I had no Kenyan money. I couldn't leave the DKW unlocked and unattended so in the end I crawled into the back seat, curled up, and spent the night there, outside the customs shed. Mel and Graham had not waited. I imagined them flagging down a ride to Nairobi or tucked up in a Kenyan hotel or eating and drinking in a proper restaurant. The lights of Kenyan Moyale were bright and I caught snatches of music and laughter from the bars down the hill. The Ethiopian side was black and silent.

I was alone. There was no place to go. I had crossed the border but I could still be sent back. Perhaps there was a secret place nearby where people who had not quite left Ethiopia were put, where they kept people who were not quite English, not quite Jews, not quite Kenyan, where they made us carve little stone pots out of soft stone that looked like human flesh. The dark shape of the prison loomed between me and Ethiopia. I was not quite in prison, not quite free. You travel but you never arrive, I thought; there is always one more place to go, one more step to take. No place is home.

My fingers crawled up under my shirt. The lumps had invaded both armpits now and were spreading down my sides: little knots, nuts under the skin, growing, cancerous. The DKW became a hospital ship swaying sickeningly on a flat, dusty sea, and the inner voice sang, 'My body lies over the ocean, my body lies over the sea.' Pipes wailed. 'Dust to dust, sand to sand,' the captain said in a dry husky voice. They tipped the coffin and a body with a face like rotten fruit slid out into the desert. The sand opened with a languorous ripple and down he went, his bloody teeth gaping, his mouth full of dust and blood. 'Next,' said the captain, and Nastasia stood straight and tall on the plank wearing a dress of swarming black flies. 'Jump,' said the captain, 'we can't wait all day.' And then she was gone too and the cloud of flies hovered over a dent in the sand.

In the morning the customs officer read aloud from a list of things I might not import into Kenya. I couldn't hear most of it, but I shook my head every time he looked up. He opened Nastasia's bag and spread my dirty clothes out in the boot of the car. He examined my papers, the car's papers, he grumbled about the temporary export licence. But his heart wasn't in it. He was spinning his job out in order to delay the driver of a soft drinks lorry who was heading north. He watched the impatient man out of the corner of his eye and a secret smile twitched like a nerve in his cheek. He did not take the car apart and find my cache, as I had feared he would.

Then Graham and Mel turned up. Mel said, 'There was no traffic south last night so I found a boarding-house.'

It was astonishing the difference a single night in Kenya had made to them. Graham had shaved and they had both washed their hair. No longer was it hanging in greasy strips over their collars. They both had on clean shirts, but most of all, they looked rested. The hollow-eyed, hungry look was almost gone.

Graham said, 'We saw your car here last night so we knew you hadn't gone far.'

'Let's hit the highway,' Mel said. He dumped his pack in the boot and climbed in.

'I've got to get some petrol,' I told them. 'I had half a tank but either it's evaporated or someone's siphoned it off. And first I have to change some money.'

'We'll go shares with petrol,' Graham said, hopping into the back. The sun was high and the heat intense, but I put the night's horrors behind me and tried to act competently.

That was where the trouble started. Neither of the two filling stations was open, and as we toured around Moyale the reason gradually emerged. We had spent weeks without any news so we didn't know that sometime in the past month the OPEC countries had quadrupled the price of oil.

The Kenyan Government would not accept the new price, with the result that there were petrol shortages everywhere, and Moyale was completely dry.

'I don't believe this!' Graham said, speaking for all of us, as we came to rest once again near the prison. 'Talk about out of the frying-pan . . .' We had failed to buy, beg or steal so much as a teaspoonful.

I switched off the engine. The needle of the fuel gauge stood in the red.

Between Moyale and the next town, Marsabit, stretched one hundred and fifty miles of desert. Only a raving lunatic would attempt to cross it without a full tank. I leaned my head against the steering-wheel and shut my eyes.

'Well, sorry, folks,' Mel exclaimed suddenly. 'I'm off. It's the old thumb for me.' He opened the door and got out. My eyes were tight shut so I didn't see him walk away.

'Rats and sinking ships!' Graham said philosophically. 'Tell you what, Fay, I'll have a wander round and see if there's anything to be done.'

The back door slammed and I was alone.

199

After a while I wiped away the tears and set out to change some money. There were not many traveller's cheques left. If the price of petrol had increased, and supposing I could buy some, it would take nearly all the money I had left to get back to Nairobi. There would be very little for food and lodging. This meant I would have to sell the car very quickly when I got there. Life seemed unbearably difficult.

With money in my pocket again I stopped at a *duka* and bought some more tinned fruit. The shopkeeper had a tea stall at the front and I sat under his faded canopy with a huge mug of tea and tried to put my thoughts in order. Could I phone someone? Who? The British Embassy? Would they send someone with petrol? The idea almost made me laugh, and my head swam.

I drank some hot sweet tea. If petrol was scarce there was bound to be a black market operating. Someone somewhere must have some. It was a question of who, where, and at what price.

When the shopkeeper came to refill my mug I asked, '*Petroli uko wapi?*' He laughed and replied in English, 'No gas, miss.'

'No gas? None at all?'

'No gas,' he told me firmly.

I went back to the car and opened a can of pears for lunch. A dog as thin as a toast rack sat with dreadful patience at my feet while I ate.

Graham came and went without any more news.

The prison warder did not recognize me and offered some more Kisii-stone pots, but no tea or petrol.

A truckful of soldiers arrived to patrol the border for *shifta*. The officer said they had no spare fuel.

I spoke to a priest, a policeman, and two more shopkeepers, and after every interview retreated to the car for rest. I thought they were all laughing at me.

45

Graham returned at sundown. He said, 'What're you going to do?'

'Stay here.' I swept my arm round the square with all its official buildings. I was too tired to move and I couldn't waste any money on lodging.

'No, but really,' he said, 'if you can't get petrol . . .'

'I don't know.' If there was no petrol the car was useless. All my savings were in the car. I would have to sell it in Moyale. But Moyale was little more than a village. Who would want a DKW, even if it had been modified for a Safari Rally? Maybe there was a plot afoot to break me.

'Well, come and eat. There's a curry place a bit further . . . Jesus! Look who's here . . .'

Mel, powdered from head to toe with dust, strode across the yard. He flung his pack on the ground and squatted down.

Graham said, 'I thought you'd be half way to Nairobi by now.'

'Got as far as the next construction camp,' Mel growled. 'But there wasn't anything going south today. Got you some gas, though.'

'What?' The beard suddenly made him look like a messiah.

'Got talking to the Wop engineer who brought me back. They've got a fuel dump at the construction camp.'

'How far's that?' I asked.

'Dunno – 'bout forty miles. But the deal is, you pay the Wop for a full tank. He gives you one gallon and a chit for the rest, see? You get to the camp on the one gallon, hand over the chit, fill the tank, and off you go.'

'Oh yeah?' said Graham. 'What if the chit's a phoney?

Fay loses money and gets stuck forty miles into the desert.'

'Take it or leave it,' Mel said, giving me a bad-tempered scowl. I said, 'Thanks, Mel. That's the best offer I've had all day.'

'The only offer,' he said, unmollified. 'Talk about helpless chicks sitting around waiting to be rescued.'

'You can put as much energy into failing as succeeding,' Graham retorted. 'No one's been sitting around waiting. When's this Italian coming?'

'Morning,' Mel said. 'Thought I'd stick around till then.'

'I see,' Graham said sarcastically. 'The gallant colonial boy's looking after number one, as usual.'

'That's fine,' I put in hastily. 'That's great, Mel!'

'Well, you Poms're short on gumption.' He yawned gustily. 'You got a camp bed, eh? Thought I'd stretch out for a bit.' He hauled the camp bed out of the boot and assembled it next to the car. Graham watched him suspiciously. It was as if each of them suspected the other of scheming to leave him behind. And I didn't want to leave the car. It had become not only my transport but also my bank roll.

In the end the area round the car became a campsite. Mel lay snoring on the camp bed. Graham spread his sleeping-bag on the groundsheet on the other side. And I curled up again on the back seat.

46

The moon rose. Crickets rasped out their song, mosquitoes whined. Behind was the dark, unexplained mass of Ethiopia where travellers became lost or sick or died. Its power reached across the border still gripping and holding me close, like a vast quagmire you can never quite escape. The more you struggle, the deeper you sink, down, down into the dark.

The hospital ship was sinking. 'Get up,' whispered the captain, 'you're next, get up.'

'No!' I cried.

'Shut up,' he whispered, 'or I'll cut your stupid throat.' The sharp point dug in just below my ear.

'Get up,' Graham said softly. I opened my eyes. The ship swayed.

'Do what you're told and you won't be hurt.' It was very dark. I cringed away from the sharp point.

'Get out of the car.'

I slithered along the seat and staggered out. It wasn't a nightmare. Someone gripped my arm so hard the flesh was pinched.

'The keys, Fay,' Graham said hoarsely. He was behind me. I couldn't see anything. 'Give me the keys.'

The cold sharp thing stung my neck and my fingers scurried like frightened mice into my pockets. Graham was going to steal the car.

'What about petrol?' I tried to say.

'Shut up.'

The keys were wrenched from my hand. Footsteps. The sound of the boot being opened. It wasn't just Graham. There were others.

'Got it.'

'Let's go!'

My arm was freed. I was just bringing my hand up to massage the hurt place when a slap knocked me sideways. The blow landed on my cheek and ear and I reeled into the car bonnet and fell to my knees. Graham crouched beside me. I knew it was him, the smell of his sweat was familiar.

'That's for Conso, and the *askaris* in Yabello,' he said softly. 'And if you make any more trouble for us you'll be dealt with properly.' He went away. I began to vomit. An engine roared and twin beams of light swung across the compound and away down the hill.

I lay in the dust. Whirling nausea made the ground heave and ripple like lava. Lying with my ear to the ground I heard the earth moan. Dogs were howling too.

Then I thought I heard someone say, 'Oh shit . . . Oh Christ.' It wasn't me. I stayed very still.

'The fucking bastards,' said the voice in the dark. 'You still there, Fay? Got a torch or something?'

I crawled on hands and knees to the car door and fumbled under the dash for a torch. The thin wavering beam picked out the camp bed, broken and on its side like a dead insect. Mel lay on his back. His nose was puffed up and blood dribbled from his nostrils into his ear. I dropped the torch.

'Water,' he said.

I found the water bottle and crawled over to him. It gurgled while he drank. Shaking like a leaf, I groped for his hand.

'Lay off!' he said, and drank again. He was all right.

'Don't start snivelling,' he said. I felt around for a towel and helped him clean the blood off his face. We pulled the camp bed upright and he sat down heavily.

'Bastards broke my nose,' he said. 'Got any grog?' He reached for the torch and turned it on me.

'I'm sorry,' I said. 'There's only water.'

He sighed. 'Looks like they tried to cut your throat,' he said. 'What happened?'

'I don't know.'

'Well, fucking take the torch and look.'

I staggered dizzily to the back of the car. The boot yawned like a gaping mouth. It was empty. Mel absorbed the news in silence.

'I don't understand,' I said.

'Don't give me that.'

'What?'

He was suddenly furious. 'The bastards broke my nose,' he shouted, 'and you have the nerve to play ignorant! I always said you were up to something. He knew that as well.'

'Who?' I quavered.

'Don't take me for a sucker!' He shone the torch in my face again. 'Bashed you up too?' he sneered. 'Well, poor little you. That's what a dumb little sheila gets when she tries to be clever. What's the time?'

I didn't understand a word he was saying and I couldn't see my watch because he had the torch. He answered himself. 'Three forty-five. That's good going. If that Pommy bastard phoned his pals this morning when he was sure we were stuck, they made Nairobi to here in fifteen hours. Some driving.'

I sat down suddenly on the groundsheet and fumbled with the water bottle. Mel snatched it from me. 'Look, you dumb bitch,' he hissed savagely, 'if I'm getting my snout clonked on account of you I want to know sodding why.'

My face began to ache. I put my hand to my cheek and found my ear was swollen too. No one had ever hit me before. What had I done?

'He said, "That's for Conso, and the *askaris* in Yabello," ' I mumbled.

'What?'

'He said . . .'

'I heard what he said, stupid. Why . . .'

'I don't know. I don't know . . .'

'Ah, shut up,' Mel said. 'You're getting hysterical.'

After a while he gave me the water bottle and I drank.

'Let's get some shut-eye,' he advised. 'My nose feels like an elephant stood on it.'

I crawled into the car. He said, 'It's that fucking friend of yours. Nastasia.'

I stared up into the darkness, my mind instantly clear. Graham had taken Nastasia's backpack, but Nastasia's property was still where I'd hidden it. I still had what Graham wanted.

I could hear Mel snorting to clear the blood out of his nose. He said, 'You were following that Nastasia, and he was following you.'

If I still had what Graham wanted he would come back.

'The keys,' I said. 'Did he take the keys?'

Mel turned the torch on again and pointed it at the back of the car. 'Still in the lock,' he said. 'No, you don't. I'm keeping hold of them, just in case you're thinking of running out on me.' He switched the torch off and I heard him stumbling about in the dark. The boot slammed.

Mel wanted it too. He was waiting for me to show him where it was. Then he'd steal the car and leave me. He was only pretending. Graham had left him to spy on me.

I was glad I was thinking so lucidly. I could easily have made a mistake and told him about the extra petrol tank Mr Singh had put in for the Rally. It was no longer used and the fuel line had been cut. But it looked like a petrol tank. It had a proper opening with a cap on it and if you didn't know about the cut line you could easily mistake it for the real thing. The customs official had.

Mel settled back on the camp bed. 'He wouldn't go to all this trouble for a few gold trinkets, would he?' he asked. He sounded so weary I was almost fooled.

'I don't know,' I said. 'I don't understand anything.'

'Christ!' he exploded. 'You really take me for a wombat, don't you? Who the hell was Nastasia and why were you trekking all over the bloody bush after her?'

'I wasn't . . . I told you . . .'

'You bloody were. I saw the letter myself in Conso.

That Pom knew you were up to something and he was right.'

They stole from me in Conso. They both said they were travelling overland to Europe via Addis. At Yabello Mel had another chance to push north but he hadn't taken it. Liars never believe people. Graham and Mel had never believed me. Mel and Graham were liars. Thieves and liars. And yet I was being blamed. Graham hit me. 'That's for Conso . . .' What had I done? I hadn't shared the pineapple, and I had kept the lift secret as a guarantee of their good behaviour.

'Who is this Nastasia?' asked Mel, his voice rough with fatigue and impatience.

'I don't know,' I said slowly. 'She's an American and she's dead.' My mood of cool detachment disappeared. My blind fingers had discovered that the lumps under my arms were swelling even as I spoke. They had grown from nuts to fruit. Rotten fruit. I said, 'It's Ethiopia. I don't think anyone wanted to go to Arba Mintch, let alone die there. It's just that wanting and willpower aren't enough in Ethiopia.'

Ethiopia crouched like a giant behind me. I had to get away.

'I notice you haven't suggested calling out the police,' Mel said. I was startled. I hadn't even thought of it. Hours of questioning loomed. They might even search the car. They might send me back. Mel was being very clever. If I called the police and they sent me back he could just walk off with the car. But if I didn't he would take it as an admission of guilt. Guilt? What had I done?

'Do you think we should?' I asked. I could be clever too. He sighed. 'Not on your life,' he said. 'We do that and we'll never get to Nairobi.'

I should move now, I thought. It wasn't safe simply to stay and wait for Graham to come back. But I had no petrol, and Mel had the car keys.

'That Italian,' I said. 'Are you sure he'll come in the morning?'

'He'd better.' Mel's voice sounded like radio interference. 'Shut up, will you, or you'll be wrecked tomorrow.'

There was nowhere to hide. Mel had never liked me. When someone dislikes you and is angry, and there is nowhere to hide, you are not safe.

A procession of four, Nastasia, me, Graham, Mel, ran in tightening circles in the desert. Dip, dip, dip, my little ship, sailing on the water, like a cup and saucer, you are It. Nastasia was eliminated, tagged, sent off. Graham, Mel, and I made patterns in the dust. One potato, two potato, three potato . . . close your eyes, don't look, I'll give you a hundred . . . coming! ready or not . . . Tyne, Dogger, Fisher, German Bight.

47

In the grey dawn, while Mel squatted over a tangle of wheel tracks in the compound, I tried to rinse the blood off my collar with a little drinking water. The stain spread like rust. All my spare shirts were gone. Graham had them.

'What d'you say?' Mel called. 'A Land-Rover. I'm pretty bloody sure it was a Land-Rover.'

He came back to the car. A red and purple blob that had once been his beaky nose swelled between his eyes and mouth. The bruising leaked into his eye sockets making him look like a black-eyed and dangerous animal. I buttoned my shirt hastily.

'Did you see anything?' he asked, rotating his head and trying to massage the stiffness out of his neck and shoulders.

'Fuck me!' he said, wincing. 'They didn't have to break my bloody nose.'

'How many were there?' I asked.

'Must've been three at least.' He fingered the blob. 'Came at me in the dark. Never said a word, just biff-bam. Bastards. How many did you see?'

'No one. Just Graham. He shone the torch in my face so I didn't see anything.'

'Gave you a thick ear an' all.' He looked satisfied. 'I dunno, though, after they bopped me and I was lying doggo, I could've sworn it was one of those safari jobs. Y'know, Land-Rover painted like a giraffe.'

'Reticulated?'

'What?' He stared at me, eyeballs red. 'God, you dumb Pom. Does it matter what sort of giraffe?'

I looked at the ground. Why had Graham hit me? 'That's for the *askaris* in Yabello . . .' It wasn't my fault

the Customs and Excise officers looked like police. I
hadn't alarmed him on purpose. What would he do when
he came back? I looked down the hill hoping for a sight
of the Italian.

'Dynamite bloody driving,' Mel said. 'Nairobi to
Moyale in fifteen hours.'

'We couldn't do it in fifteen hours,' I said cunningly.

'Don't see why not.' He stared aggressively at the
DKW. 'If they can, we can.'

'It took *me* three days.' I didn't mention stopping to
see the game reserves at Samburu and Marsabit.

'Three days!' Mel sneered. 'What were you doing? –
stopping for a piss every five miles?'

It took us over an hour to reach the construction camp.
With only one gallon in the tank, I had to save fuel and
switch off the engine on downhill slopes. Mel wanted me
to drive flat out but I refused. It was my car and I knew
its consumption rate. Even so, we were in the red again
by the time we arrived.

'You drive like an old woman,' Mel said, furious with
impatience. I didn't care. I was terrified of running out
of petrol and being caught, helpless, miles from anywhere
when Graham came looking for me.

The camp was behind a high wire fence. It was in a
swirling fog of cement and desert dust churned up by the
giant wheels of the earth-movers. While we negotiated at
the fuel dump, I strained my eyes through the curtain of
dust to the road a quarter of a mile away.

A Frenchman and another Italian checked and double-
checked our chit before allowing us to fill up.

'You'd think it was liquid gold,' Mel complained. I said
nothing. I had just seen a telltale cloud of dust from the
road. Someone was driving north very fast. I pushed my
sunglasses up for a better look. Was it a Land-Rover –
marked like a giraffe? There was too much dust. Well,
that meant they couldn't see us either. If it was them.

And if it was them, now they would be behind us. I would have to watch in both directions.

'You've had your turn,' Mel announced, and dropped like a stone into the driver's seat. 'Reckon we can't do it in fifteen hours? – Well, watch the expert!'

He drove like a charging bull. Rocks battered the chassis unmercifully as we careered, one wheel up on the ridges, from one rut to another.

We took the stretches of corrugation at forty miles an hour, and the boiling wind screamed through the open windows, sand and dust grazing our skin and stiffening our sweaty hair till it whipped like leather. The only obstacles were sand drifts where the desert was white and brown, and pumice boulders were scattered randomly as far as the eye could see. In these places lines of camels strode casually past us and Mel raged and hit the steering-wheel in frustration until the tyres could grip once more and we crashed on to the hard core. We did not speak. The wind and pounding blocked my ears. The harsh white light blinded.

Our first puncture came just before Marsabit and the twenty minutes we spent in the blazing heat to change the wheel exhausted Mel. His face was raw from the wind. He lolled beside the car incapable of any effort. I had a nosebleed while straining to tighten the wheelnuts, and I drove us into the filling station at Marsabit with blood drying slowly on my mouth and chin.

I washed my face, but the taste of blood stayed in my mouth – metallic, like the taint of a tarnished fork. I drove for three hours while Mel slept, his head bouncing and jerking against the hot leather. He was ugly, his mouth gaped, his beard was caked with grime, his smell was rank, but he was my only ally. I couldn't trust him but I had to rely on him to get me south when it was my turn to collapse. Far from sleeping while he drove, I dared not close my eyes. If Graham was behind us, if Graham caught us, what then?

There were moments when I didn't care, when I

thought the danger was an illusion. The journey was so punishing it seemed that there was nothing Graham could do to make things worse. If he killed me, I thought it would only mean I would not have to drive any further. I wondered if this state of mind was what people meant when they spoke of death as a merciful release. When the moments passed I thought of them as nothing but laziness. How could anyone want to die to avoid discomfort? And then I remembered a story told to me by an electrician at the Colosseum about a friend of his in the army, and how they had been pinned down by snipers somewhere in Malaya. They knew that in order to survive they must remain absolutely motionless, but after several hours of lying like corpses the electrician's friend raised a hand and scratched his nose. The snipers shot him. 'I never could understand it,' the electrician said. He had told the story many times and always with the same disbelief in his voice. 'It was only half an hour to nightfall. You'd think he could've held out till then. Fancy being killed for an itchy hooter!'

I had never really understood that story. An imaginary itch is not irresistible. Heat, when you are not hot, seems bearable. The aches and bruises sustained in a jolting car are not major injuries. But they add up. And in the end you would rather stop no matter what the consequence. I would have stopped if it had not been for Mel. Without him I would never have reached Nairobi that night, and, whatever he might have said, I don't think he would have made it without me.

We came to the tarmac just after Isiolo and a strange unearthly silence descended on the car. The road was smooth and we could drive steadily in fourth gear. Mel took the wheel for the last time. I wanted to sleep then but earache kept me awake. And then came the second puncture. It was dark. Mount Kenya had passed like a great black shadow in the dusk and we were speeding downhill towards Nyeri.

'Slow down!' I yelled as the juddering began. 'You'll wreck the rims.'

He shouted something back but my ears were boiling too loudly to catch what he said. I was stiff from hanging on, and sore all over from the pounding.

'Civilization!' he cried at the top of his voice. I heard it as a muffled roar as the lights of a service station swam into view. The car limped and shuddered into the floodlit forecourt.

It took the mechanics an hour to mend the tyre. Mel reeled away, dazed with fatigue, to find something to eat. But I stayed, close to the road, to keep an eye on the DKW and watch out for Land-Rovers. I wasn't hungry. I hadn't been hungry for days. A steady queasiness had taken the place of hunger.

The mechanics sucked their teeth and tutted over the battered rim. It would do as a spare, they said, but only in 'the gravest emergency'. How much damage had Mel done, I wondered. Was he just impatient, or was he in a hurry for some other reason? He could be rushing me towards some new danger.

I'll leave him here, I decided, as I watched the road for Land-Rovers. He'll be all right this close to Nairobi.

When the mechanics levered the DKW down from the jack there was still no sign of him. He's phoning ahead, I decided, as I paid for the repairs and more petrol. I'll show him. I got in the car and drove gently out of the garage.

I saw Mel a hundred yards further down the road. He was sitting on the verge with his knees drawn up to his chest. The lights of a bar illuminated his bowed shoulders.

He hasn't seen me, I thought as I drove past. Thank God he hasn't seen me. What's the matter with him?

The car seemed to stop of its own accord. I was almost in tears as I put it into reverse and drew up alongside him. He crawled into the passenger side.

'Monkey meat,' he groaned, and folded both arms across his belly.

'What?'

'Monkey meat . . . in the bastard curry.'

'What were you doing eating monkey?' I checked the mirror for chasing headlights but we were alone on the road.

'It's cheaper than goat,' Mel said, and curled himself as best he could against the door.

'Bad luck,' I murmured, grinning nastily into the dark. He won't give me any trouble now – all his plans wasted – I'll drop him where I like and his reception committee can wait all night.

'*Two lovely black eyes*,' I sang, putting my foot down hard on the accelerator. There was no one behind me, Ethiopia was hundreds of miles away. '*Oh, what a surprise . . .*'

48

The lights of Nairobi revived him. He sat up, moaning weakly, and said, 'Where are we?'

'Nairobi.'

'Where are you taking us?'

I didn't answer. To tell the truth, I hadn't even thought about it. My hands seemed stuck to the wheel. I couldn't imagine what I would do if I let go. I drove twice round the Murango Road roundabout because I couldn't think what to do next. Nairobi! – and now I was there I didn't know where to go, or how to stop.

'There's a lodging-house on River Road,' he suggested. Never! I brought the car back on to the proper side of the road. My mind was wandering.

Nairobi was like a ghost town in the dead of night – only a few lighted windows, a couple of late taxis – otherwise the town was asleep.

'Where're you taking us?' He made an effort to straighten up.

'The YMCA,' I said at random, and sighed with relief. It was miles from River Road.

'That's miles from River Road,' he said.

'Take it or leave it.' I drove on, laughing out loud.

'You're crazy – you know that?' he said when I dropped him on State House Road. 'Where *are* *you* going to stay?'

'YWCA,' I said craftily. That would make sense – It was just up the road – And it was miles from the Quaker House – He'd never find me there.

'Okay,' he said. 'Well, see you in the morning – if I haven't already left for Mombasa.'

Mombasa! Who did he think he was kidding? I drove away, giggling. He couldn't follow me: he had no car. And with the boiling corruption of monkey meat in his

215

guts he wouldn't be good for anything for several hours. I was free, and alone in Nairobi: a wanderer come home to no particular home. The car wavered in the road and a couple of late revellers turned to watch. They thought I was drunk too.

'I'm not drunk,' I called out of the window, but they had gone. Or rather I had driven past. I brought the car back under control and wove a random course which, in spite of blurring vision, took me to the beginning of the Ngong Road.

49

If you are the sort of person who is rarely listened to you lose the habit of telling anyone very much. In my case this was turning out to be an advantage. I racked my brains but I was almost sure I had told neither Mel nor Graham about the Quaker House. It was a long way from the area of Nairobi where tourists or travellers usually stay, and its guests tended to be foreign students who were staying for several months. You did not have to be a Quaker to get in.

Rajib opened the door. He knuckled his eyes and yawned hugely. It was still dark. He did not recognize me.

I had to say, 'Rajib, it's me – Fay,' before he stood back to let me in.

'My God – Fay – I thought you went to Somalia.' He turned on the hall light.

'Ethiopia.'

'Well, yes, somewhere like that. How was the trip? What has happened to you?' Even though he had just got out of bed his dark head was sleek and his skin looked polished.

'I need a bath,' I said.

'Well, yes,' he agreed politely. He was one of the most fastidious men I had ever met, but he also had wonderful manners.

'Are there any clean towels?'

'Yes – laundry came yesterday. But, Fay, you must try to be quiet. Everyone is still sleeping, and the plumbing, you know . . .'

'I can't help it, Rajib. I'm sorry.'

He looked worried but said, 'Some Americans left yesterday. There is a room.'

'Thank you,' I said. 'And, Rajib, you haven't got a spare shirt or something, have you? Everything was stolen in Moyale.'

'My God, Fay, you *have* been in the wars.' He was being as concerned as he could without coming too close. 'Have a bath and I will sort something out.'

I had two baths, but no amount of washing removed the certainty that I was dirty through and through. I could see it in the yellow mass just beneath the surface of my shoulder and in the red streaks that ran down my arm. I had clean hair, clean skin, clean finger and toenails but corruption was in my blood. I filled two plastic bowls with soapy water and drowned what I had been wearing. I even soaked the towels I had just used, and scoured the bath. Whatever infected me should not be passed on.

Rajib knocked and handed me a pair of cotton pyjamas round the door. He was waiting for me with a cup of tea when I came out. We went along to my room to drink it. The pyjamas trailed on the floor and hung below my hands.

'Oh dear,' he said, standing in the doorway. 'Now that you are clean you look, if possible, worse. Are you ill?'

'I don't know,' I told him. 'I think so . . . do you know a doctor?'

'What about money?' he asked. 'Was that stolen too?' Doctors do not come free in Kenya, so it was a pertinent question.

'It wasn't stolen,' I said. 'And when I sell the car there'll be more.'

'There's a very good man in Machakos. I will look out his address for you.'

'And if you know anyone who wants a car . . .'

'Yes, well . . .'

'Thanks, Rajib.' I could see he wanted to go back to bed.

I had everything I'd wanted for so many weeks but still I couldn't sleep. The bed seemed to pitch and yaw and the road ran like a movie on my retina. Ruts and ridges, flying stones, dust, and streams of tarmac rushed through my head.

The sun came up and I began to hear the plumbing, the slam of the bathroom door, the kettle whistling. Early risers feel they have a moral obligation to let the sounds of virtue resound like church bells to wake the lazy.

I got up and locked my door before opening the curtains. Was I safe? The window overlooked a large patch of ground which had been divided up into allotments. Some people had goats and dogs tethered. There were hens too and any intruder was greeted noisily. I was safe enough.

Nastasia's property was still knotted into the T-shirt sack I had made in Arba Mintch. The sack smelled of petrol and peppery Ethiopian dust.

First things first – I opened the undelivered letter.

Dear Nasty [it read], I have already written by regular mail, but you know how reliable that is! There's a kid driving to Addis so I thought a touch of 'belt and braces' would do no harm.

This is to warn you – You already know what happened to Josh. Well, they've sent someone out after you too, so don't linger longer (ha ha) in Addis than you can help. (I know how you like the night spots.) Get back to London PDQ, and then bury yourself. I'll be in touch you know where. I don't know when – I'm busy keeping my head down and cursing you like the rest of the wolves.

Don't go near Barclays or the London office. Keep it under floorboards, it's safer. See ya. XXX. PS. Don't get greedy and bury yourself too deep!

The letter was typed and unsigned.

What have you done? I asked the passport photograph. Nastasia Beyer, age: twenty-five, height: five feet six . . . What have you got me into?

Letters from her mother. *'It's fifteen degrees outside and your father still complains every time I touch the thermostat . . . I hope you are enjoying your trip . . . The card with the flamingoes was lovely.'*

Letters from a boyfriend. *'Darling . . . It's been so long . . . Christmas was hell without you . . . Everyone wants to know when you are coming home.'*

A notebook filled with addresses and telephone numbers – large, loopy handwriting – green ink. The numbers danced in sinuous snake patterns, and I closed my eyes.

50

Knuckles rapped on the door and I started up in bed. An American voice said, 'Hi, Fay. Rajib told me you were back.' It was Caroline from Indiana. I rolled out of bed. All my joints were aching, sweat streamed into my eyes. I crept to the door.

Caroline called, 'You okay in there?' The doorknob rattled. Stealthily, I checked the key in the lock. I didn't want to see Caroline. More than that, I didn't want her to see me. She was shaped like a Christmas pudding and had a generous jolly personality. Of all the guests at the Quaker House, she and her husband Max were the only Quakers. I couldn't stand the thought of her Christian judgment.

The doorknob turned. 'The door's locked,' Caroline said. 'I guess she's asleep.' I tiptoed back to bed. Caroline's footsteps retreated from the door. I closed my eyes. I never wanted to see anyone again.

It was late afternoon when I woke next. The house was alive with the sounds of people coming back from wherever they had been all day. Caroline knocked and called through the door. Tom Okolo's bass voice boomed from the kitchen, 'It's good that she sleeps,' and Caroline went away.

Rajib came once. 'Do you need anything, Fay?' he asked. But I would not answer him either. I pulled the damp sheet around my ears and willed them all to leave me alone.

The sounds of the house faded in and out, like a poorly tuned radio. My ears ached and throbbed. Supper-time came and went but I wasn't hungry. I slept again.

A cicada rasped in the dead of night, and I stole from the room to rinse my face and hands and drink from the tap. Everyone else was asleep, so I was safe from prying eyes.

But next morning Rajib mobilized his family, and I awoke to hear Gita's soft voice saying, 'Fay. Fay-ee. Open the door. You have slept enough.'

'All across town we have come to see you,' Shanti wheedled. 'Come, let us in.'

'We came in taxi,' Gita supplied. 'Very expensive.'

'So we will stay till you open the door.'

I crawled out of bed and let them in. Silk and perfume wafted in accompanied by the soft chorus of voices.

'Oh dear, dear, dear,' Shanti cooed. 'It is the fever, yes? Rajib did well to call us, isn't it?'

'Put water in the bath, Shanti.'

'And these . . .' Shanti plucked at my sopping pyjamas.

'But I haven't any clothes,' I stammered at last. 'In Moyale . . .'

'Yes, shshsh, stolen, Rajib is telling us.'

'Never pay no mind,' Gita purred. 'He told us and we have brought.'

I burst into tears.

Later, when they tucked me into clean sheets, I said very clearly, 'Thank you both so much, but really it doesn't matter. You see, I've got cancer.'

'Listen to her,' Shanti said imperiously, 'she is talking nonsense.'

'They rave sometimes,' Gita replied. 'With the fever everything they think is rubbish. Rajib!'

Rajib poked his head cautiously round the door.

'Lazy boy!' Gita cried. 'Didn't I tell you to bring tea and cut up mango.'

'It is done,' Rajib protested. 'Fay, don't let them bully you. You see how they are.'

'Silly girl thinks she has got cancer,' Shanti told him. 'You should telephone to Dr Lal.'

'Dr Kekri is better.'

'No, no, no. All those Africans he works for! Dr Lal has aquarium in his waiting-room. He is very good.'

'Dr Kekri,' Rajib said firmly, and went away to pour the tea.

Afterwards, after the peachy sweetness of the mango, when Shanti and Gita had gone, leaving only the heavy scent of patchouli behind, I picked up Nastasia's pen. It weighed a ton and my fingers seemed bruised.

I wrote a list in no particular order: Ticket, Car, US Embassy, Doctor, MONEY. I was writing on Nastasia's paper with Nastasia's ballpoint pen. Camera? I wrote. I couldn't remember if the camera was in the backpack or whether it was in the car. I ought to search the car.

I was lucky in that my own passport and the car's papers had been in my pocket during Graham's raid.

Assets, I wrote: Car, camera? Liabilities: no bag, no ticket, sick, tired, Graham, Mel. AVOID BEING SEEN, I wrote and then stopped. I crawled back into bed. Would any of it matter if I had cancer?

'Blood tests are expensive,' Dr Kekri said sympathetically. 'But I can tell you now what I think is wrong.' He had a light voice, cool fingers, and thick, black eyelashes. During his examination he had included some old-fashioned techniques like looking at my tongue and the colour of my fingernails. Mother would have approved of him.

'It is almost certainly mononucleosis; that is glandular fever to you British. Also anæmia and severe undernourishment. And if we do not treat this shoulder very quickly we may also include blood poisoning.'

'Wonderful!' I said, almost light-headed with relief. 'I thought it was cancer – the lumps, you see . . .'

'Ah no.' He smiled. 'Just overactive glands trying to combat infection.'

'And the deafness?'

'It will clear up with the fever.' He began, with swab and knife, to clean up the shoulder. While he worked he talked. 'You have a most interesting name,' he began.

'Jassahn is also a town close to the border of Iraq and Iran. You are Moslem perhaps?'

'Well, no,' I said, embarrassed. I hate to talk about these things – they are so divisive. Possibly Dr Kekri was a Moslem and he wanted to talk about what we had in common, but if anything it would have the opposite effect. How could I explain my father was a sort of Jew with a Moslem name, and my mother was – well, what was she?

'I'm a bit of a mongrel,' I said in the end.

'You should not refer to yourself as a dog,' he admonished gently. 'Speak rather of United Nations. At the moment you are depressed because of the sickness and you are seeing things in the light of that. It will pass.'

'Nations are not very much united at the moment,' I pointed out.

'No,' he agreed. 'It is sad.' He worked on in silence. After a while he said, 'Ethiopia – that is a much troubled land. I believe there are some riots there.'

'To tell you the truth,' I said, 'I didn't understand what I saw. There were no newspapers to tell you what it was all about. There *was* some violence.' I shuddered involuntarily.

'This will hurt,' he said. 'It is inevitable.'

'Doctor?'

'Yes?'

'If a man has been beaten up, and you give him water, and immediately after that he coughs up masses of blood – have you killed him?'

He dropped the dirty swab into a metal bowl and looked at me intently.

'This happened?' he asked.

'It's just a question,' I stammered.

'I cannot answer without more information,' he said. 'You should not think of such things now. You must rest and take a good, high protein diet and not worry about those things you have no power to alter. It will be difficult because for this shoulder I am giving you drugs which may depress you further. For the mononucleosis there is nothing but time and rest . . . Oh yes, and perhaps brewer's yeast.'

Brewer's yeast – my mother would definitely approve of Dr Kekri.

'Mono? That's what they call the Kissing Disease,' Caroline said from the door of my room. 'What *did* you get up to in Ethiopia?' She looked interested.

'There wasn't a lot of kissing,' I said. 'But it's very infectious, so . . .'

'Yeah, I'll keep out of your hair.' She waved two envelopes at me. 'These came while you were away. I guess you didn't look at the letter-board.'

'*Dearest little Fay*,' Tony wrote. '*I was surprised and a bit disturbed by your letter from Nairobi. I can understand that you might want to try your wings before settling down, but do you really know what you are doing? . . .*'

'*Dear Fay*,' wrote Mum. '*What a splendid time you are having. I do envy you all that sunshine and the wild animals. There was a wonderful programme about the elephants of Tsavo on television last night but unfortunately the power was cut half way through . . .*'

In an otherwise empty notebook Nastasia had written: '*Shit, shit, shit, shit. It's all literally shit . . . the fucking kids are driving me wild . . . and where is this bastard Victor taking me? If I hadn't been so scared in Shashamane . . . I should go to Addis, but what is the point? I can't go back. I can't go back. I can't go back.*' The last of the repetitions was heavily underlined. Why couldn't she go back? Going back had been the saving of me. She couldn't go back and she died.

'*Four days ago I woke up with a headache*,' she wrote. '*I can't seem to shake it. I am held together by filth. Without it maybe I'll fall apart.*'

I could understand that. Since the bath I had felt as if my bones had melted and leaked away into the hot water. Perhaps the grime had sealed in my energy.

'*Trapped*,' she wrote, her loopy handwriting shaking

225

and sprawling across the page. *'I don't even like him any more. It's just he's American and I can't face being squashed in a bus with all those people.'* People had a wobbly but emphatic line under it. *'I hate men,'* she went on. *'They use you, they rob you blind . . .'* There she stopped.

I felt closer to Nastasia than I did to Mum or Tony, so I picked up her pen and wrote in her notebook:

Dear Mr and Mrs Beyer,

I am so very sorry about Nastasia. I do not know if you have heard from the hospital in Arba Mintch, but in case they have not been able to get in touch I will tell you what happened. I'm sorry if you've heard it all before.

Nastasia died in hospital in Ethiopia of a combination of dysentery and typhus. I cannot give you the precise date because I lost track of time. It was sometime at the beginning of March.

If the hospital has not informed you it is because there was some rioting and the phone never worked.

But anyway Ethiopia is a difficult place to travel in. You can become lost and sick very easily. It is not like Kenya and no one who goes there is quite prepared for how hard it is.

I never met Nastasia. I just happened to be in the same place at the same time. But truly I am sorry.

I left her clothes at the hospital for the poor people. I just couldn't carry them. I hope you understand. They did their best there. They are good people.

About the money. I had to take Nastasia's cash. Traveller's cheques to the same value are included but if this will not do please contact me at the above address and I will pay you back . . .

It wouldn't do. I knew it wouldn't do, but I couldn't think how else to say what had to be said. I added my parents' address and signed the letter. Perhaps the words would come tomorrow.

51

I delivered everything, including the inadequate letter, to the US Embassy on my way to Mr Singh's garage. There was some consolation in handing the responsibility over to someone else. If anyone wanted to steal Nastasia's things now, they would have to burgle the Embassy. I suppose I was suspicious of myself too – I was tempted to repossess some of my traveller's cheques. And the krugerrand seemed magnetic. It had come to represent safety – something small but valuable which could be hidden and converted when the need arose. It was too seductive and I was glad to pass it on.

The only thing I did not pass on was the unsigned anonymous letter. It hinted of things I did not think Mr and Mrs Beyer would want to know about their daughter.

In the end, it was the camera which was sold first. Tom Okolo bought it for twenty pounds, so I was able to pay the rent and buy the food Dr Kekri recommended.

There was a middle-class suburb about a mile up the road from the House, and on its edge a small shopping precinct and cinema. I stood in the air-conditioned butcher's and waited while the assistant cut half a pound of liver. Already my polythene bag contained milk, bread, tea, and green beans. The slice of liver flopped juicily on to a sheet of greaseproof paper, and the assistant wrapped it with two quick flips of his wrist. There was so much food and not a fly in sight. I stared at the bloody chopping-board while I waited for change. My hands shook.

Outside, in the glare of the sun, I paused for a moment under the awning of a flower shop. Inside were lilies, orchids, and long-stemmed red roses. My reflection in the glass showed the white of my blouse and the patterned cotton skirt Shanti had lent me. I could buy flowers if I wanted to waste the money. In the grocer's I had seen stack upon stack of tinned fruit, but I had hurried by with a shudder.

I turned away, suddenly exhausted, and walked back to the car.

The visit to Mr Singh's garage was badly timed. The East African Safari Rally was about to begin and some of the local drivers used the garage as base camp. The dusty red yard swarmed with men in turbans and overalls. Support vehicles and rally cars, bright with racing trim, cluttered all the available space. Some of the mechanics had rigged plastic shelters over their cars so that they could work under shade, and the yard looked like a shanty town.

'So sorry, Miss Jassahn,' Mr Singh said, pausing briefly on his way between an Audi and an Opel. 'As you can see, there is no time for discussion. Perhaps next week . . . yes?' He too was wearing overalls and had to shout to be heard over the clang and clash of metal on metal.

'I suggest you advertise in the *Standard*.' He moved on and was soon involved in excited conversation over the Opel's exposed engine.

It was an advertisement in the *Standard* which had brought the DKW to my notice in the first place. But advertising was out of the question: it would be like publishing my address for Mel and Graham to read.

John and Bill would love this, I thought, as I hovered indecisively behind the group around the Audi. There was a problem with a half-shaft – the discussion was in Urdu, but I know a half-shaft when I see one. I would love it too, I thought, if only the DKW were sold and I had a ticket home and didn't feel so ill. I turned away.

'Miss Jassahn!' Mr Singh stopped my by the gate. 'I am thinking,' he called, 'if you are not successful with the advertisement, come back. We may be of mutual benefit. Next week, yes?'

But next week was a long way off so I went back to the Quaker House and sold the Pentax to Tom.

'There is film in this,' Tom reminded me, so I spooled it back and took it out. I had taken only one roll of film in Ethiopia – some in the first couple of days in Moyale; some of Abbavich, Wobit, Hijibatchaw, and Lielit in Chencha; some, shakily, of the hill women on the way to Dorse.

'Mementoes of your trip,' Tom said cheerfully. 'You mustn't lose those. They say there is revolution in Ethiopia now. Perhaps at last they will overthrow the tyrant imperialist, Haile Selassie. If I had been there I would have joined the people in their struggle.'

'I'm a pacifist,' I said, 'not a revolutionary.'

'There's no place for pacifism in modern Africa,' Tom said severely.

'Is that why you are eating your cornflakes in a Quaker house?' Rajib asked. 'And don't drink out of Fay's mug.' Tom looked horrified.

By now they all knew I was infectious, and I had my own mug, plate, and cutlery which everyone else avoided. There were strict rules about cleanliness in the kitchen anyway because of the ants so I wasn't too worried about spreading disease.

'But really, I mean it,' Tom went on. 'We oppressed Ugandans are regrouping. We need strength and organization to fight. You Asians would not understand this. You are not interested in the political, only the mercantile. You will exist under any corrupt hegemony if you can make money. Power and idealism are required for revolution – guns and Marx.'

'And money,' Rajib said gently.

'But not liberals or pacifism. No, Fay, this is no time for pacifism. Lenin, Mao, Castro, these are the men we must emulate.'

'Not Gandhi?' Rajib asked under his breath, and winked at me.

52

The wide paved streets were lined with bougainvillæa, and tourists ambled sleepily in the heat, glancing one way towards the smart shops and then the other to the street traders who sold carved animals and batiks. This was the part of Nairobi where Europeans collected in the greatest numbers to shop or sit in shady cafés and bars. It was where Mel or Graham might expect to find me and I didn't want to be here except that this was where the travel agent was too.

The counter was stacked with leaflets and brochures offering safari tours and fishing trips. I glanced at them sadly while the bored young man behind the counter explained that if I could not produce my old air ticket he could not authorize a replacement. Besides, he pointed out, since the rise in oil prices fares had gone up and all the airlines had cut the number of flights. More travellers were competing for fewer seats and he could not possibly book me a place on any flight unless I could put down a cash deposit.

'But I had a ticket,' I protested. 'I booked and paid for it here in February. Surely that should count for something?'

Eventually he called the manager who leafed through a huge ring binder.

'Jassahn . . .' he muttered. 'Yes, Jassahn! We do have a record of the transaction – Nairobi to London changed from February to March, Correct? Well, I'll have to check with the airline whether or not they resold your seat before I can accept a refund as part of the deposit. If you will give me your address and telephone number I will let you know.'

'Er . . . well . . .' An awful thought had struck me.

Graham had my old ticket. It was in a folder with the name of the travel agent on it. I was being very stupid indeed. 'I'm on the move at the moment,' I said. 'Camping, you know. I'll call back in a week's time.'

'What about American Express or the YWCA or a friend's number?' He looked at me strangely. 'Somewhere we could contact you at short notice.'

'That's not possible, I'm sorry,' I said, backing away.

Another thought hit me while hurrying back to the car and I went on till I found another travel agent.

'Can you tell me,' I asked a well-groomed woman behind another counter, 'who has vehicles painted like giraffes?'

'Giraffes?' She looked surprised. 'You must mean Twiga Tours. They do camping tours in all the game reserves – small parties only. Would you like a brochure?'

The brochure told me that I was only a stone's throw from the Twiga Tours' office. It was without doubt an unhealthy part of Nairobi for me, and if the travel agent was on the phone now telling Graham I'd been in contact it would be safer if I never went back. And that meant I would lose the refund.

But if I could sell the car I wouldn't need the refund. All I wanted was a ticket home and enough money to survive on till I left.

'What you need is a loan,' Rajib said sensibly. 'With currency restrictions as they are you cannot, anyway, export all the money you would get for the car when you leave. If you use the loan for your ticket and running expenses, by the time you pay back you will have only a little left and that will be quite all right.'

'But what if I can't sell the car and therefore can't pay back the loan?' I asked.

'Then the lender gets the car,' he said patiently. 'The car is what you put up as collateral.'

I filled the kettle and thought about it. Rajib finished washing his shirt and wiped the draining-board.

'How do you go about getting a loan?' I asked.

'Oh dear, Fay,' Rajib sighed. 'Are you now telling me you have never borrowed money? Don't you live in the real world? Tell me, just what is it you do for a living when you are at home?'

'I sew,' I told him, embarrassed. 'I'm a dresser. I work in film and theatre wardrobe.'

'Fantasies,' he said. 'Such people can only make a living in places rich enough to give financial support to fantasies. Well, Fay – I do not want to influence you unduly, but if it were me who wanted money I would ask my mother's cousin in Machakos.'

'Not related to Dr Kekri by any chance?' I poured boiling water into the pot.

'No, no,' he said. 'Of course if you suspect I am only trying to drum up business for distant relatives, perhaps it would be better to look for a pawnbroker.'

'I didn't mean that,' I put in quickly. 'Besides, to be a relative of Dr Kekri is a recommendation.'

'A private loan can be cheaper,' he said, mollified.

'This would be a private loan?'

'Semi-private. Is there enough tea in the pot for two?'

No one in our family ever borrowed money. We never bought on credit, and I don't believe my parents even had a mortgage. I remember when John and Bill wanted to buy an Elan on hire purchase, Dad said, 'You don't own something you can't pay for. If it can be repossessed, it isn't really yours.' The twins bought a second-hand Mini Cooper instead.

And one of Mum's sayings is, 'Don't lend anything you can't afford to give away. It's better to lose money than friends.'

I poured the tea. The idea of borrowing money made me feel slightly faint so I sat down at the kitchen table.

Rajib said, 'I don't understand why you haven't advertised the car. You should have had dozens of applications by now.'

'There are people who know the car,' I explained awkwardly, 'and I don't want them to know where I am.'

'So paranoid!' He laughed. 'What crime did you commit in Ethiopia that you are so afraid will catch up with you?'

53

'Rest,' Dr Kekri had said. 'Complete rest.' But I was being forced into activity. It doesn't normally take much effort to get money. You can phone your bank or give a credit card number or write a cheque. But you have to make cash deals in person. People want to see your face and if you are putting up a car as collateral they will want to see that too. An air of confidence as well as integrity doesn't do any harm either. 'Don't look as if you need it,' Mum always says of job interviews. Well, not looking as if you need it, when in fact you're desperate for it, isn't restful.

I washed the car and drove it gently back to Machakos. The centre of town, where Dr Kekri had his surgery, bustled with life. It was a little like an Ethiopian town, with raised boardwalks and dusty streets, but the suburb where Mr Dar lived was sedate with its colonial bungalows and green lawns.

We drank tea in the garden at a white, wrought-iron table which was screened from the rest of the family by a hedge of rhododendron bushes.

'So you are the friend of Rajib,' Mr Dar said, his teacup poised between his vast waistcoat and a pair of smooth, plump lips. 'That boy should be living here where we can keep an eye on him. But now, he must stay near the university.' The shouts of children and the restraining murmur of women floated over the hedge like fairground music.

We had not yet discussed business. Mr Dar had a new Rover in his carport and I couldn't help wondering if I was in the wrong place. Shanti's clothes hung loosely, making me look like a child in fancy dress. I spooned some sugar into the tea. Sugar equals energy.

Mr Dar began in a roundabout way. 'In Nairobi I am known as a respectable businessman. Even after Africanization my business is quite good. Of course there have to be changes and this government makes it difficult for us, but we survive, we survive. From Rajib I hear you have experienced some difficulties too. That is so?'

'Yes,' I said. 'I spent much longer in Ethiopia than I planned.'

'That is a bad place.' Mr Dar frowned. 'If I were you I would never have left UK. But now you are here perhaps we can help one another. Are we not put there to help one another?'

'I always thought so,' I said.

'It is a small matter – one I would prefer to entrust to a member of my family. Yours is a small difficulty too. I do not normally interest myself in such matters, but you are a friend of Rajib, and if I cannot help my cousin's son, perhaps I can help his friend.'

I was not at all sure what he was getting at, but I said, 'Well, I am certainly in need of help and if there's anything I can do in return . . .'

'You see, my cousin's family, some are still living in Uganda. Some are fortunate enough to have been accepted into UK. But it is hard for them. Everything they own is still in Uganda. Families should help one another – is this not true? Well, this family is in a foreign country now. They are cold. They do not understand the ways of the British people. It is hard for them to get work.'

'I do understand,' I said.

Mr Dar searched through his coat pockets and produced a small spiral notebook and a gold propelling pencil. He laid both on the table.

'Write,' he said quietly. 'Write for me your father's name and his address in UK.'

I picked up the pencil and he watched carefully as I wrote. Then he studied the pad.

'Your father, perhaps, is not British?' he asked. 'Perhaps he also is immigrant.'

'A long time ago,' I said.

'A long time ago,' he repeated. 'Perhaps if he remembers, he would understand.'

'I think he remembers,' I said. The safe under the garage floor was the memorial.

Mr Dar closed the notebook. 'Well then,' he said. 'I think I may trust you. And if that is not so, then perhaps I may trust your father.' He put the notebook back in his pocket. 'To business,' he went on, his voice clipped. 'I will lend you what money you require. You will undertake to pay it back at five per cent per week. That is satisfactory?'

I nodded.

'However, if you wish, you may pay in sterling into an account in UK. Do you understand?'

I nodded again.

'This is trust,' he said. 'Do you understand?'

'Yes,' I said. 'In UK I am trustworthy. In UK there is no reason why I shouldn't be.' My mouth tasted foul and I felt sick. I didn't want to look him in the eye but I knew I must.

After the few seconds he lowered his gaze and poured some more tea. 'There is another small matter,' he said, slipping a thin slice of lemon into his cup. 'This five per cent. You are not well, I see. Perhaps it will be several months before you resume your work. A loan without interest might be preferable.' He stirred his tea calmly. The lemon slice spun like a roulette wheel.

I said, 'Five per cent seems most reasonable.'

'It is,' he assured me. 'However, if you would agree to deliver a small packet for me when you return to UK we might dispense with interest altogether.'

'The old fox,' Rajib said. He was leaning against the door and I was in bed. 'You know, they call him Diamond Dar in the market?'

'Diamonds!' I cried, horrified. 'I can't do that. It's illegal.'

'Sh! Don't worry. It probably isn't that. All the same, I hope you are keeping this package in a safe place.'

'I haven't got it yet,' I told him. 'It won't be ready till just before I leave.'

'Either you have an honest face or he must be desperate. I've never known him go outside the family before.'

'What for?' I asked.

'You must rest, Fay, if you are to get well,' Rajib said soberly. 'Don't waste your energy on what you do not understand.'

'What don't I understand?' I asked plaintively. But Rajib went away, closing the door softly behind him. It wasn't only in Ethiopia that people refused to answer questions. I went to sleep with Ethiopia on my mind and woke up two hours later screaming.

The man with the misshapen bloody head had become without question Mr Latybalu, and he followed, whimpering and weeping, wherever I went. 'We cannot serve your friend,' the waitress in a restaurant said.

'I'll marry you,' Tony said, turning away in disgust, 'but you'll have to do something about *him*. I can't marry both of you.'

And finally when, after a blood-spattered chase, I thought I had escaped, and locked myself in my bedroom at my mother's house, I turned back the coverlet and found Mr Latybalu crying and bleeding in my bed.

Gita shook me, saying, 'Wake up, Fay, wake up.'

I *was* awake but I couldn't stop screaming.

She said, 'Get some water, Shanti. She's burning.'

'No water!' I cried. 'Water killed him.'

'Don't forget to use her mug,' Rajib said.

'Hush, Fay.' Gita smoothed the hair away from my face. 'You have the fever. It is only a dream.'

'It wasn't . . . it *wasn't*! It happened. I gave him water and he threw up blood!'

'Who did?'

'Mr Latybalu – at least, I think it was him.' I opened my eyes at last. It was still daylight. Gita sat on the edge of the bed. Rajib leaned, arms folded, against the door-jamb. Shanti came back with some water and Tom followed her in.

'He was so badly beaten,' I went on, 'I didn't know who he was.'

'Then probably it wasn't Mr Laty . . . Mr Whoever,' Gita said comfortingly. 'Here, drink.' She held the mug to my lips. 'A drink of water never killed anyone.'

'And then they rolled him out into the rain and I know he was still alive.'

'If he was still alive you didn't kill him,' Rajib said reasonably.

'Hush!' Gita said. 'She has fever. This logic of yours is not helping.'

'Well it seems to me she's been acting like an idiot since she got back. I know she's sick but she hasn't helped matters by being so furtive. I think logic would help very much.'

'What did you dream, Fay?' Tom asked. 'There is truth in dreams.'

'Why don't you ask her why she didn't go to the police when her luggage was stolen?' Rajib said. 'It's a better question – or why she's too afraid to advertise her car. Or why is she so reluctant to claim a refund on her ticket that she goes to moneylenders instead?'

'Is this true?' Tom asked.

'You don't understand,' I said.

'What are we not understanding?' Gita held the mug steady while I drank.

'When I was trying to get out of Ethiopia I thought everything would be all right if only I could get to Moyale. But Moyale was too close to Ethiopia, and it wasn't all right. If I'd gone to the police they might have held me there forever. I'd smuggled Nastasia's things through the border, you see. I thought I'd be able to straighten it out once I got to Nairobi, but it's all following me around. I just want to go home.'

'You're lucky,' Tom burst out. 'If I go home Idi Amin will kill me.'

'One problem at a time,' Rajib said. 'There is nothing we can do about Idi Amin. And how lucky Fay is, is open to question.'

'Who is this Nastasia?' Gita asked. 'You never have spoken about someone called Nastasia.'

54

Rajib quite frankly did not believe me. Even with Nastasia's letter, by now creased and grubby, in his hands he gave me his coolest, most sceptical look. It was dark and we had just finished supper, a vegetable curry which Gita, Shanti, and Rajib had thrown together in a friendly quarrelsome fashion. The girls claimed that Rajib was a clumsy oaf who should finish his studies and go out to earn money the way men should, while he abused them soundly for being old-fashioned enough to think that a man could not take care of himself. Tom hung around looking superior. He would rather go hungry than cook anything himself. As usual, Gita and Shanti were uncomfortable when Tom was present but that night they were too intrigued to be reticent. The story I had told them was so different from what normally filled their days that it excited their imaginations.

'That Nastasia was a bad girl,' Shanti said. 'So many boyfriends she had.'

Tom, who seemed to like bad girls, said, 'It is different in United States,' and Rajib, who liked to be precise, put in, 'But which of the three men were actually boyfriends? The man who gave you this letter, Fay, said he was. But this . . .' He tapped the letter with his fingernail. 'This is not the letter of a lover. A conspirator perhaps, but not a lover.'

'How would you know?' Shanti asked, unwilling to give up her theory. 'All you know are these bluestocking girls at the university. You have never been in love.' She sighed and Gita sighed too.

'Well, anyway, we really do not understand this letter,' Rajib went on. 'Obviously Fay is the "kid driving to Addis", but who is Josh, and what happened to him?'

'I think,' I began, leaning my chin on my fist, 'I think Josh is the man, who was killed in Snake Park.'

'Yes,' Tom interrupted. 'You have said that the Englishman was most interested when this story was told in Moyale.'

'Adding two to two and making five,' Rajib said.

'Well, I think she's right,' Shanti said.

'Also, Rajib, this is something you can test,' Gita added. 'This famous library you are spending so much time in will keep all the newspapers.'

'All right,' Rajib agreed surprisingly. 'I will look it up. And then, Fay, when you know that this Josh was *not* killed in Snake Park, will you stop being frightened and advertise your car in the *Standard*?'

'I don't know,' I said. 'Graham thinks I've got something he wants and I don't want him coming here. I don't ever want to see him or Mel again.'

'Let them come,' Tom said. 'It's one thing to beat up a woman who is alone, but here you have friends.'

'He didn't exactly beat me up.'

'He hit you,' Gita said, outraged all over again on my behalf. I smiled at her. I was very tired, but for the first time since the beginning of the trip I felt comforted. I was part of a group again. We were sitting around a table like a family.

'I wish you could remember the name of the man who gave you the letter,' Tom said, and Rajib nodded. But I couldn't remember. The night we had met and talked at the YMCA seemed so long ago. Then I had thought he was a rejected lover, someone like Tony at home worrying about a woman who wanted to travel. I remembered the wine, and the kippers which I had hoped were holy wafers. It wasn't just that it was a long time ago, it was as if I was remembering someone else's memories.

'He must have been Nastasia's boyfriend,' Shanti said. 'These crosses here represent kisses, isn't it, Fay?'

'Yes, but it isn't always personal.' I tried to explain, but to Shanti kisses were always personal. For all I knew,

Shanti expected to kiss only one man in her life. Casual crosses in a letter were promiscuous. Perhaps Rajib thought so too, because shortly after that he called a taxi to take Shanti and Gita home. He said their father would give him trouble if his daughters stayed out late.

As I snuggled down into bed, feeling comfortably that a problem shared was truly a problem halved, I was struck by a sense of familiarity. The discussion reminded me of what had happened when at dinner with the family, I first floated my ambition to work in the theatre.

'Theatre?' my father asked, 'is that wise?'

'It isn't very secure,' Mum put in, looking anxious. After that the idea was out of my hands. John and Bill joined in, for once on my side and the discussion evolved without me.

'It might be a convenient use of her peculiar talents,' John said. 'She's got a good eye, she can sew . . .'

'She gets along with everyone,' Bill agreed. 'The theatre's a sociable sort of place, isn't it? It's not as if she wants to be an actress.' They both laughed.

By the time I went to bed my future had been wrapped up and given to me like a birthday present. Why had I struggled with a niggling sense of resentment? Why did I feel as if, far from giving it to me, they had taken my ambition away?

Of course tonight wasn't the same. In this case, I wanted the problems to be taken away. But in both cases I felt like a failure – a cosy sort of failure, protected but inadequate.

The next morning I kept my appointment with Dr Kekri in Machakos. He changed the dressing on my shoulder. 'You are not yet eating enough,' he said, shaking his head. 'Did I not say you should eat well and rest? How can the body fight infection if it is debilitated and tired? You are taking the tablets as instructed? Yes? And the brewer's yeast?'

'Yes,' I said.

'Then I would also add a little oral iron and also vitamin

supplement.' He began to arrange a fresh bandage. A wasp, as long as my thumb, crawled up the frosted glass window.

I said, 'Doctor, if a man has been very badly beaten up, what should one do?'

'You must monitor blood pressure in case of hidden injury. This is most important. There may be rupture to the spleen or liver.'

'But if there is no medical help?'

He stopped what he was doing and stared at me. 'You should ask yourself why you ask these questions,' he said slowly. 'Is it comfort you are seeking, or the truth?'

'It's just a question,' I muttered, looking away. The thorax of the wasp seemed tied to its abdomen by a long thread: there was hardly any communication between the two parts.

'If it is comfort you require,' Dr Kekri went on, 'it is better you do not ask a truthful man. You must rest and eat and become strong. Truth does not suit weak people.' He stood up and went to the window. 'The connection between the mind and the body should not be overlooked,' he said thoughtfully. 'You must believe you are worthy of good health.' He opened the window and the wasp flew away.

55

When I stopped at Mr Singh's garage on the way home the shantytown had been dismantled and most of the cars were gone. The rally had begun and a smudgy grey picture of the leading driver had appeared on the front page of the morning paper.

Mr Singh was in his rickety shed sorting through his accounts. His overalls hung neatly behind the door and his white cuffs were rolled back to save them from the ink. Ballpoint pens seem to melt in the heat of Kenya.

He said, 'Miss Jassahn, I was just thinking about you.' He pulled up a stool for me to sit on.

A copy of the paper lay on his desk, and to postpone the time when I would have to talk about the car, I asked him who he thought would win the rally.

'One of us,' he said proudly. 'A Kenyan. These Scandinavian drivers are very good, but they do not know the conditions as we do. If you should wish to bet, I advise you to put your money on Joginder Singh in the Mitsubishi Lancer. Certainly he will finish and probably he will win. It is the toughest race in the world. Out of ninety-eight starters, how many will cross the line? *That* is something I should not like to bet on.'

'Is Joginder a relation?' I asked.

'We Singhs are not all from the same family,' he said. 'But it was of family I was thinking before you came. For five years I have not seen my brother in Wolverhampton, but you, Miss Jassahn, may go there whenever you wish. You are fortunate enough to be British citizen. You may also come here for holiday. It is not so easy for someone whose status is not yet official. There are many restrictions for Asians who live in Kenya, and also if they live in UK but have come from Kenya or Uganda.'

'So I've heard,' I said. The sad word 'Diaspora' came into my mind. If you move from one country to another to escape hardship or to better your condition, it is the timing of your move which will determine how easy it is. If you go alone, when there is no mass exit from one place and entrance to the other the chances are your passage will be smooth. If everyone has the same idea, naturally, difficulties will arise.

'You will be in UK soon, Miss Jassahn,' he went on. 'I too would like to go to UK to be with my brother, but because of restrictions here, to go would be to leave everything my family has worked for for three generations. I do not wish to be a poor man. At my age, to start again with nothing would be hard.'

'I know,' I said, prompted by the memory of my father's safe, hidden under his garage floor. Was he afraid too that sometime, somewhere, he would be forced to start again with nothing? It gave me a peculiar feeling in the pit of my stomach to think of my father as an insecure man. It had never occurred to me before: a father should be a strong, sure person.

'When will you leave?' Mr Singh asked.

'I've borrowed money to buy my ticket,' I told him. 'But I can't leave until I've sold the car and paid back the money.'

'Ah yes,' he said. 'The car.' It was as if I had given him the opening he needed. He relaxed. 'Perhaps after all we may help one another. Perhaps I can offer you a very good price for the car.'

'No,' I said. 'Not "very good". Just fair.'

'Fair?' he asked. 'Well, we shall discuss it tomorrow. First I must speak to my uncle.'

Uncles and brothers – safety in numbers. The last time I had thought about safety in numbers was in Moyale, wondering whether or not to take a lift north with Gabriel. Then I thought that travelling with three white men would offset the danger of hitching in Africa. The dangers when they appeared were from war, famine, plague, and two of the three white men. Hitching had turned out to be the least of my worries.

The noonday sun beat down on the car and I parked it in the shade of an oleander bush behind the Quaker House. There was no one in. I took two of Dr Kekri's tablets and lay down to rest. The curtains were drawn to keep out the sun. Soon I would have to make some lunch but just then I was too tired. I'm ill, I thought, not lazy. But how long had I been ill? How much of what I hadn't done could I blame on illness?

The man with the pulpy face and bloody teeth rose up out of the darkest corner of the room and said, 'You didn't help me. You didn't even try. Now I am a poor man who must start again with nothing.' Blood flowed slowly out of his mouth and rippled lazily round my feet. A volcano erupted and I could not run fast enough to escape the lava.

Rajib said, 'Fay! We must talk.'

I sat up and wiped the wet hair out of my eyes. Rajib knocked again. 'Fay, wake up!' He came in and opened the curtains. The sun had moved round.

'This is bad,' he said, sitting down on the end of my bed. He had a sheaf of papers which he laid on the sheet between us. It was the first time he had come into my room. Normally he never came further than the door.

'The man who was murdered in Snake Park was indeed called Josh,' he told me, frowning. The papers he had brought were photocopies of the 'Body Found in Snake Park' stories from the *Standard* which told of the mutilated corpse of an unidentified man. A night watchman on his way home from work in the early hours of a Saturday morning discovered the body. At first it was thought to be a panga attack by a gang of nationalistic youths, but later it was discovered that the panga cuts disguised a bullet wound. Robbery was thought to be the motive, because the man's wallet and all his personal documents were missing. He was identified a few days later as Joshua Rollins, a representative of a local travel firm.

'Twiga Tours!' I exclaimed. 'Oh God!' Something cold crawled down my spine.

'It seems, Fay,' Rajib began slowly, 'that you were, after all, wise not to advertise your car in the paper. The Englishman and the Australian, if they work for Twiga Tours, are not to be trusted. Not only are they thieves, they may also be associated with murderers.' He was looking at me as if I was a complete stranger and I felt myself shrink.

'You must go home as quickly as you can,' he went on. 'By accident you have interfered with something dangerous.'

'I'm trying to go home,' I whispered. 'You know I am.'

'But meanwhile,' he said, his dark eyes remote, 'you have brought trouble to this house. I am sorry for you, but there are others I must think about. For instance, my cousins are coming for tea. Yes?'

I nodded. My cousins, he said, not Gita and Shanti. They were, once more, his cousins and not my friends.

'I think I must phone them to make some excuse. I will say you are not well enough.'

I nodded again and he got up from the bed. He said, quite gently. 'You do understand, don't you?'

'Oh yes,' I said. 'I do understand.' And I did, because I could see Mel's heavy hand strike Gita's flowerlike face the way Graham's had struck mine.

'You could go to the police,' he suggested.

'Yes,' I said in a dull voice. 'But then I would be here even longer. And what's worse, Graham said that if I made any more trouble for him he would deal with me properly.'

'You must go home,' Rajib said forcefully, and left me alone with the photocopies.

Mechanically I gathered up the papers and put them in order. I had enough money for the ticket, but not enough for the ticket and Dr Kekri. I might have to wait a long time for a flight and during that time I would need to pay for food and rent. Perhaps I could camp out at the airport

247

and wait for the first cancellation to London. But if Graham and Mel were still looking for me, wasn't it obvious they would keep an eye on the airport?

I sat in bed, with a neat stack of photocopies in my hand, quite paralysed. I did not know what to do or where to begin. Rajib came back and said, 'They have already left, Fay. They are on their way here.' Sickness made my head swim, and my ears, which had been much better lately, started to whine and ache. It occurred to me that I didn't want to hear any more, and I wondered foolishly why I hadn't gone blind as well. I started to get up. Rajib left the room quickly, closing the door behind him.

The only clothes that did not belong to Shanti were the pair of jeans and shirt I had been wearing in Moyale. I put them on and went to the telephone. The airport's number was engaged. I tried it three times. Rajib watched from the kitchen. I tried again.

Finally, and with reluctance, Rajib said, 'Who are you telephoning to, Fay?'

'The airport.'

'Why the airport?'

'Because all the travel agents I know are in the centre near the Twiga Tours office.' I sat down on the floor under the phone.

Rajib said, 'You think, if you phone the airport there will be a cancellation on a flight out tonight?' I nodded. He said, 'That is very optimistic, Fay. Since the shortage of oil the airport has been in a dreadful state. I shall make a pot of tea.'

The hallway was dim. It had no window of its own and the only light was from the kitchen. Sitting on the floor with my head in my hands, I thought again about woodlice hiding from the sun in cool dark places. They are primitive creatures which curl up when threatened and remain utterly inactive until danger passes. A lot of them get trodden on because they do not immediately scurry for shelter or fight back. You see them bumbling amiably along the carpets of country houses quite unaware that they inhabit the same world as giants with big feet. They come out from cracks in walls and skirting-boards, and people suck them up into vacuum cleaners. They are not welcome indoors even though they do no harm. But if they do no harm, they do not seem to do much good either. Woodlice are not like ladybirds, which are pretty creatures and useful too: they protect the roses from aphids.

'Come and drink your tea,' Rajib called from the kitchen. We sat in gloomy silence until Gita and Shanti swirled in with a swish of silk, bangles tinkling, bearing one box of honey cakes and another of cream pastries. Rajib tried to get rid of them. He told them I was not feeling well enough for company.

'Of course she is not well, silly boy,' Shanti said. 'It is for this we are bringing sweet things to feed her up. Look how thin she is. Take, Fay, take.'

'You're very kind,' I said miserably.

'Kind – pooh. When we want to see the film stars we arrange a visit for us.' Her arms jangled musically as she piled my plate with cakes.

Rajib got up and went out. He came back with the photocopies.

'Read,' he ordered grimly. They read with their shining black heads almost touching. At length, Gita said, 'This is the Josh in the letter? He is dead?'

'We think so,' Rajib said.

'What trouble a letter can bring!' Gita got quickly to her feet. 'Where is it Fay? You must destroy it immediately.'

'What are you talking about?'

'This letter, Rajib. I will burn it. It is bad luck.'

'My God!' Rajib exclaimed. 'For this my uncle paid good money to your school?'

'She is right,' Shanti put in. 'The day she took this letter was an unlucky day.'

'That is true,' Rajib conceded. 'But it will not help to burn it. Also you should know that it is perhaps the same people who killed this man who are looking for Fay.'

'They have not found her yet.' Gita sat down again and looked at him with wide, innocent eyes. 'Who would look here? No one lives here. You should not be living here yourself, Rajib. My father says it is disgrace you do not stay with your family.'

I had not seen Rajib grit his teeth before, but he did now. 'They may not have found her yet,' he said, 'but that is not to say that they won't. And what will happen when they come here and find my two stupid little cousins with her?'

'What nonsense you talk,' Shanti said uncertainly. 'Soon she is going to UK. What can happen?'

'Before I left Uganda,' Rajib said, 'some soldiers came in the night and took away my grandfather . . . *your* grandfather. He too said, "What can happen?" I know what can happen.'

'He's right,' I said. 'I know what can happen too.'

'Perhaps, after all, you should go to the police.' Rajib addressed me directly for the first time. 'If nothing else, it would show these silly girls how serious this is.'

'The police will do nothing,' Gita said. 'When that African stole Daddy's car they did nothing.'

'That is enough,' Rajib said, standing up. 'I'm taking you two home.'

56

Rajib did not come back after seeing Gita and Shanti home. I waited for him in the kitchen until Caroline and Max arrived and politely invited me to go to a film at the American Institute. It was seven-thirty by then and I was so much in need of company that I nearly accepted. But the American Institute was two minutes' walk from the Twiga Tours office so I pleaded tiredness and said I would go to bed. They were relieved because, although kind and well-intentioned, they had an almost superstitious fear of infection.

Tom came back briefly. He was on his way to a night-club but he had been drinking at the YMCA and had news of Mel.

'My informant was a girl who cleans the rooms,' he said, his deep bass voice vibrating off the kitchen window-pane. 'It is a typical result of colonial misrule when a woman must become one of a sub-class in her own country.' He looked at me severely, and then laughed. 'But you are not interested in politics, Fay. Just in saving your own skin.' He laughed again. 'Don't look so guilty. You are a small person, and small persons are afraid of everyone.'

Tom must have been afraid once or he would never have left Uganda. I said, 'Mel's big and tough, and he doesn't like me.'

'I am bigger and tougher,' Tom said. There were not many people anywhere who were bigger than Tom. I said so and he looked pleased.

'This girl at the Y, she too says the Australian is a bad man. She says the *mzungu* was filthy and that many people complained because he did not clean up after himself. She says he borrowed money and did not pay it back. He fought with another *mzungu* and left after two days.'

'That's Mel,' I said. 'He claimed he was going to Mombasa.'

'That she did not know.' Tom went to the door. 'He was dirty, he made work for her, she did not like him. That was all she cared about. She too is a small person.'

He left me alone to wait for Rajib. But Rajib did not come and next morning, before the heat became too intense, I drove over to see Mr Singh. He was in a jovial mood. The Rally was still going well for Joginder and this seemed to give him confidence. The interview with his uncle must have gone well too, because he bought the car for only a little less than I had paid for it. It was more than fair, considering how much chipping the paintwork had suffered on its way to and from Moyale.

There it stood in the bright orange courtyard, like a pale blue toad in a rusty pond, and it was not mine any more. I wondered what mistakes its next owner would make. 'Buy a car,' those nameless, half-remembered travellers at the Y had said. 'It's the cheapest way to see Africa.' And my imagination had done the rest. But I never camped by a lake. I never slept out under the stars. I never cooked on the campstove. The DKW had gone no further than the police compound in Moyale. It was a symbol of failure and I was glad to have the money instead. I could pay all my bills and move out of the Quaker House into a hotel if Rajib insisted.

Mr Singh interrupted my thoughts. 'This is not really a question of cars or money,' he said. 'I do not know why you wish me to buy your car. You could sell to anyone. It is not a hardship for me to buy it because easily I can find a buyer myself. Perhaps you wish to deal with me because you know me. Perhaps I wish to deal with you because you can do me a favour.' The sound of his voice hung in the confined space of his office like the smell of cooking.

'Yes,' I said slowly. 'There was a reason why I didn't want to advertise.'

'I will not ask your reason.' He fingered the car documents I had placed on his desk. 'And so perhaps, as a gesture of equal confidence, you will do something for me when you return to UK.'

Fleetingly I wondered at the interpretation he had put on my reluctance to advertise. Maybe he thought I was a criminal, or a snob, or afraid of meeting strangers. Something in my looks and air of desperation told him I was in his debt. Maybe a failed romantic or a team member who has let the side down gives off invisible signals that show she is vulnerable, vulnerable to offers that might allow her to make good again.

'Yes,' I muttered. 'How can I be of use?'

I left Mr Singh's on foot with a brown paper parcel clutched in my perspiring hand. The parcel contained, so Mr Singh told me, a glass jar filled with dry rose petals. The rose petals had been collected under the light of a full moon by a holy man and were a present from his aunt to Mr Singh's brother. She believed that an infusion of them would ward off the effect of chill and rheumatism – an ideal present for a relative in Wolverhampton. She did not wish to send them by post, Mr Singh said, for fear of breakage.

As I crossed the road to the bus stop I tried to imagine why he had told me this story. He surely didn't expect me to believe it. I was not offended though. Oddly enough it was like a gift: something I could believe if I wanted to. As once I had changed kippers into holy wafers, now I could turn whatever Mr Singh wanted me to smuggle out of Kenya into rose petals. He could smell my weakness as clearly as a perfume – the way animals can. I was grateful that instead of going for my throat he had given me something unbelievable.

There was a group of women at the bus stop, three of whom had babies on their backs. I joined them under the shade of a corrugated tin shelter.

I was exhausted already. I wanted to lean against the wall of the shelter, but it was too hot to touch. The murmured conversation of the women sounded like a church service – a musical verse followed by a soft response from the group. They touched each other when they spoke and no sentence went without an answer.

I had not been there five minutes when a white Datsun drew up alongside. The door opened and a man in a lightweight tropical suit got out. He approached me, laid a hand on my arm, and said, 'Enough's enough, Fay. Where is it?' The women moved politely away and left us alone in the shade.

'Don't touch me!' I cried, wrenching my arm out of his grasp. He took hold of my shirt instead. Although the women did not seem to be listening they moved even further away.

'Don't be stupid,' he said. 'I'm not going to hurt you, and it's too damn hot to run.' It was the same pleasant voice which had sung *Cockles and Mussels*. He was a little thinner perhaps, but the brown hair still flopped innocently over his forehead. It was only the suit which had put me off. A man in a suit is a completely different shape from one in jeans and a T-shirt.

'What are you doing here?' I asked breathlessly. The shock of his sudden appearance seemed to have sucked the oxygen out of the air.

'I've been keeping an eye on the garage,' Graham said. 'The chap you bought the car from told me. We traced him through the registration.'

'Oh,' I said, watching over his shoulder. A bus was coming. He turned and saw it.

'Please, don't,' he said wearily. 'I'll only have to follow the bus. Just be sensible and tell me where it is, and then we can all go home.'

The bus pulled up at the stop and waited while the women got on. I watched it go.

'Even if you run away now,' he said, his fingers on my

254

shirt, 'I'll only track you down again. So don't think you're safe even if you take it home to UK.'

'Don't ruin England too,' I cried. The street and buildings began to bleach – to turn white and starry. My head seemed to float off my shoulders. My knees crumpled.

57

I came to in the car. The air-conditioner was working full blast and we were driving slowly along a wide street with jacaranda planted in the dividing lane. I felt sick.

'I'm going to be sick,' I said. Graham swerved abruptly into the nearside lane and pulled up.

'Don't get out,' he warned. 'Take a few deep breaths and you'll be all right.'

I took them. It was a main road near the university. There were not many pedestrians. I wondered what had happened to Mr Singh's parcel.

'Where's my parcel?' I asked.

'For Christ's sake, Fay . . .'

'Graham!' I shouted. 'I don't know what you want! I never knew Nastasia. All her things are at the US Embassy. Just get off my back and leave me alone.'

'Don't come the innocent with me!' he said angrily. 'You were looking for her as much as I was. How come we all ended up in Arba Mintch?'

'That's where the bloody bus went!' I yelled. 'We didn't have any choice – you know that!'

'Coincidence!' he sneered. 'You knew where to find her. You were always talking to the kids and asking questions. They told you.'

'I talk to everyone,' I protested.

'Then why didn't you talk to me? And why were you so evasive in Arba Mintch? If you weren't hiding it, what were you so shifty about?'

'The bloody pineapple chunks, you fool! And I was right. You and Mel stole them in Conso.'

'Not *those* again,' he said tiredly. 'Jesus Christ, Fay, are you absolutely daffy, or what?'

'They were valuable to me at the time,' I insisted. 'Not

256

Nastasia's gold necklace, or her rings – I couldn't eat *them*, and they weren't mine anyway. Are you telling me they were yours?'

'Of course not!' He ran a hand through his hair and turned to look at me. 'I don't want you to come to any harm,' he said more quietly. 'But how the hell am I supposed to believe you? You say you never knew Nastasia, but you had a message for her. She goes to Arba Mintch: you go to Arba Mintch. You, just by chance, happen to come by her luggage. And when at last I get the opportunity to search it, blow me, the one thing I want has gone missing. How do you explain that?'

'I don't know what you're looking for,' I said. 'But I can tell you for nothing that there were at least two other ways it might have gone missing. There was the guy who stole her Jeep in Shashamane and there was a chap who looked after her things in Chencha.'

'The Yank?' he asked. 'Who is he?'

'I'm not telling you. This has to stop. You can't just run around threatening everyone who had anything to do with her.'

The engine purred and the air-conditioner blew. Outside in the bright sunshine people seemed to glide past without a sound.

'I can't work you out,' Graham said at last. 'Either you're very astute or you're unbelievably dim. You could get yourself off the hook by convincing me the Yank took it.'

'No. You've got to stop,' I repeated. 'It's lost – whatever it is – and you've got to accept that.'

'I wish I could.' He reached over and took a packet of cigarettes from the glove compartment. 'But I'm in trouble with my boss. He sent me to get it back. "Simple instructions", he calls them – and I can't explain what it was like back there.' He sighed and tapped a cigarette on his thumbnail. 'The trouble is I haven't felt at all well since I came back. I'm supposed to chase all round Nairobi looking for you but I haven't been sleeping well and sometimes I have barely enough energy to get out of bed in the morning.'

'Go and see a doctor,' I suggested. 'Have a blood test. I came back with glandular fever.'

'Really? Oh hell – we all ate off the same plate half the time.' He lit a cigarette and closed his eyes. 'That's all I need.'

He's ill, I thought, and I can smell weakness too. I said, 'What is it, Graham? What are you looking for that I'm supposed to have?' It was the wrong question. Knowledge is only power if you have the strength to use it. Otherwise it can be a danger.

'Curiosity killed the cat,' he said meanly.

'You're right,' I said. 'Don't tell me. I don't want to know. I just want you to leave me alone so that I can go home in peace.'

'Then you'd better leave us alone too,' he snapped. 'No funny business with the police or anything like that.'

I didn't bother to answer him.

'What would you have done to Nastasia if you'd caught up with her?' I asked instead.

'Done to her?' He opened his eyes and stared at me. 'What do you think I am? I'd've taken the consignment back to Nairobi, that's all.'

'Then what would Mel have done, if you're so civilized?'

'What's it got to do with Mel? You can't think I was associated with that berk, can you?'

'I don't know,' I said. 'After Moyale I thought you and he were a team.'

'I wouldn't belong to any team with him as a member,' he said decisively. 'You think I'm some sort of hard man, don't you? "What would I have done to Nastasia?" ' He mimicked me in a high girlish voice. 'If I was going to do anything to Nastasia I'd have done it to you too when I thought *you* were a team with *her*.'

What about Josh Rollins in Snake Park? I asked silently. Instead I said, 'You mean you believe me now?' I couldn't tell what he was thinking. The only expression on his face was of pained discontent.

'I don't know . . . I really don't know. I've spent so long thinking you were leading me by the nose . . . I still can't believe you're as inoffensive – as daft as you seem.' He rolled his head from side to side on the back of his seat. 'What am I going to tell my boss? He wants to know where the thing is and he wants to know who, in the firm, warned Nastasia. Can't you help me?' In spite of the cool air blowing from the dashboard his upper lip was covered with tiny drops of sweat and I suddenly believed he was feeling as ill as I was. It made us equal.

I said, 'How can I help? I swear I don't know what you're looking for, but it must have been lost in Ethiopia. You can't get it back now.'

'Well, at least tell me who gave you the letter to Nastasia. If I don't tell my boss something I'm in dead trouble.'

'If I tell you, what will happen then?' I asked.

'Nothing – I promise.' He gave me a long, level look. Nice hazel eyes, I thought. A quick salesman's smile. He was lying now. I was sure of it.

'But maybe whoever gave me the letter didn't write it.'

'Maybe not. It doesn't matter. It's just that I must tell my boss something. Help me, Fay.'

'And nothing will happen?'

'I swear.'

'Well then,' I said, taking a deep breath and looking him straight in the eye. 'It was just an ordinary chap called Josh Rollins.'

His eyelid flickered and the sweat dripped off his upper lip. Slowly and deliberately he reached into his pocket and brought out an old envelope and a pencil.

'Say that again,' he said. 'How did it happen?'

'Well, when I first decided to go to Ethiopia I advertised for a co-driver – someone to share driving and expenses with.'

'Where?' he asked. 'Where did you advertise?'

259

'I pinned cards to notice boards,' I said. 'You know – at the YMCA and the Automobile Association.' Now that I was back with the truth I could afford to elaborate.

'Yes?'

'Yes, and I didn't find a co-driver but a few people got in contact because they wanted things delivered. There was a French woman sending a crate of wine to one of the road camps . . .'

'What about the man with the letter?' he cut in.

'I met him one night at the Y and he said his girlfriend had taken off with another fellow. There'd been a misunderstanding. He wanted her back, so would I take a letter.'

'This was . . . er . . . Josh Rollins?' He said it as if he couldn't quite remember the name.

'That's what he said. I didn't ask for his passport. It was only a letter.'

'Only a letter,' he repeated flatly. 'And what did the letter say?'

'It was sealed.'

'But you must have looked – I mean, after Moyale.'

'I don't read other people's letters,' I said, sounding offended. 'Everything that belonged to Nastasia has gone to her parents via the Embassy.'

'That'll be a nice surprise for them,' he murmured. 'Depending what's in the letter, they might find out what an opportunistic little thief their daughter was.'

'Well, how was I to know?' I said. 'I thought *you* were the thief. After all, you stole the pineapple and you took all my clothes.'

'Shut up about the pineapple!' he snarled. He stubbed his cigarette violently in the ashtray. 'I'm sorry about your clothes,' he added more calmly. 'I didn't know that's what I was taking.'

'Well, you did,' I said, aggrieved. 'Flat broke with nothing to wear – that's how you left me.'

'Why didn't you to go the police?'

'In Moyale? Would you?'

'I suppose not,' he admitted, tapping the envelope with

260

his pencil. After all, he'd been there. He was one of the few people who knew what it was like. 'And that's all you remember,' he went on, 'about how you got the letter?'

'Yes.'

'It'll have to do.' He sighed. Now that I was calm enough to look at him properly I noticed several more things about him. It wasn't only the sweat: his collar was too loose, there was a tremor in his hands, and the whites of his eyes looked yellow.

'I'm going now,' I said suddenly. I was amazed at my decisiveness. 'Where are my rose petals?'

'Your what?' he asked, startled.

'Rose petals. You make an infusion and it helps with the fever. Where are they?'

He opened the glove compartment again and handed me Mr Singh's package. 'Rose petals,' he muttered. 'Pineapple chunks. What did I do to deserve a dip-head like you?'

I opened the car door and a wave of hot air rolled in. 'Go and see a doctor,' I said. 'You aren't at all well.' I walked away. I didn't look back, and I didn't run. If you don't run, they won't chase you.

58

A woman worked in the allotment behind the Quaker House. She moved slowly along, bent double over a short hoe. A baby slept peacefully on her back and beside her a seven-year-old boy carried a toddler on his hip. She straightened and flicked the sweat off her chin with the back of her fingers.

I sat in the shade on the kitchen doorstep and watched. There is nothing special about a woman working in a garden but I felt I was seeing it for the first time. The colours were suddenly brilliant: her bright green scarf, the dark red earth, the yellow of the maize stalks the goat was munching. I felt as if I had removed a pair of dark glasses. I had left my shadowy room and was sitting freely in the open air. It didn't matter who saw me now. I could watch as I had watched my mother when she planted out her seedlings in late spring, and with less risk. 'Don't just sit there gawping,' she would say. 'Go and fill the watering can.'

I was always reluctant to help Mum in the garden: it was her place and in it I could only obey orders. I told her I didn't like gardening, but I could imagine how different it might be if I had a garden of my own. I wondered what the boy was thinking. Did he resent following his mother around when the world outside her allotment was so big?

A door banged in the house behind me, and a few moments later Rajib came into the kitchen.

'Come inside, Fay,' he said when he saw me. 'Aren't you afraid someone will come snooping?'

'Not any more.' But I got up and went in to make tea. Rajib had a look of frowning concentration on his face.

'Wait,' he said as I began to fill the kettle. 'We have

business to discuss. You must leave tomorrow. I spoke to my uncle, and with his help I have arranged it. It has cost a lot of money but my uncle agrees – the matter is very urgent.'

I stared at him. 'Why?' I asked. I had expected Rajib to withdraw, or force me to leave the Quaker House, but not to arrange my flight home for me.

He looked extremely serious. 'It is Twiga Tours,' he said. 'My uncle knows something about them, and they are to us like the Mafia is to the Italians. You go to them for help if you wish to leave Kenya, but afterwards they own you. They have an import-export licence: they will help you move your family and, most especially, your goods. It is very expensive, it is most illegal, and it is very dangerous. My uncle says on no account must we become involved.'

'It's too late,' I said. 'I saw Graham this morning.'

'You saw?' he cried, shocked. 'Did he see you?'

'We spoke,' I said, almost with pride. 'And he thinks I am so stupid and ignorant that I am not worth his attention any more.' I finished filling the kettle and lit the gas.

'You are safe?' Rajib asked. 'You believe this? You know, Fay, you cannot trust these people.'

'I know. But I think maybe Graham trusts me. Or rather he thinks I'm too insignificant to bother him.'

'And are you?' Rajib watched me narrowly. 'Will you now make trouble?'

'No,' I said. 'I just want to go home.'

'Good.' Rajib sat down at the kitchen table. 'Because this is best for me and my family too. Trouble is like disease. It spreads.'

I agreed. Nastasia's trouble had spread to me, and I wanted simply to be rid of it.

'A person who disturbs a wasps' nest will be stung,' Rajib went on, reinforcing my natural inclinations. 'But as for me, I would not like to abandon a friend in trouble.' He grinned suddenly with embarrassment. 'Shanti and

Gita had some harsh words to say about leaving you behind last night.'

'Family first,' I said. 'What else could you do?'

'I told them you understood.' He still looked doubtful. 'You are not one of us, but sometimes it seems you are not very different either.'

I made the tea, and Rajib carried a tray through to my room where we would not be interrupted. There he showed me the ticket that had taken him so much time and money to buy. 'What a palaver,' he said. 'We had to pay a man not to go, and immediately his trip became essential.' I paid him in cash with the money I had from Mr Dar and Mr Singh. I counted out more for the rent and what I owed Dr Kekri. Finally, after a furtive glance at the door, he showed me the small packet Mr Dar had asked him to bring.

Mr Singh's parcel was hidden under the pillow. I took it out and started to unpick the sticky tape.

'You are going to open it?' Rajib asked, biting his lip.

'Yes,' I said. 'I want to know what I'm carrying from now on. If I'm taking a risk I want to know what for.'

'But perhaps when you know – the risk will be too great.'

'Maybe. But I'm fed up with being ignorant.'

I unrolled a layer of brown paper. 'You open Mr Dar's Rajib. He's your uncle.'

The glass jar contained faded pink petals which gave off only a whisper of scent. It also contained white tissue paper to which the petals adhered. Wrapped in the tissue paper was a heavy, solid gold necklace.

'My God!' Rajib breathed. He held out his hand and showed me twenty or so cut diamonds. They caught a stray shaft of light from the window and winked at me. I gulped.

'A fortune,' Rajib murmured. 'What will you do? If you are caught taking these out of Kenya the penalty will be severe.'

'Yes,' I agreed, unable to take my eyes off the jewels. 'Oh dear.'

'What will you do?'

'I think I'd better wear them,' I said, swallowing painfully.

'You can't wear loose diamonds.' Rajib stirred them with his forefinger.

'Yes, I can,' I told him.

And I did. I walked out of Nairobi Airport's immigration building, across the gasoline-smelling runway, and on to the plane wearing thousands of pounds' worth of gold and precious stones. No one gave me a second glance.

After all, as I told Rajib, I spend most of my working life making worthless things look valuable. Why shouldn't I do the opposite for a change? If I can make glass look like diamonds it should be easy enough to make diamonds look like glass. I set them in a rubber-based glue and fixed them to a denim strip with the cheap brass eyelets you find in shoes or leather belts. I wore the strip as a headband disguised still further by my woolly mop of hair.

The exquisite heavy necklace was transformed, with plastic beads, fuse wire, and scarlet nailpolish, into dross.

'It looks awful,' Rajib said, shocked.

'Yes,' I agreed proudly.

'If you are not in jail,' he said, when he shook my hand, 'write to me and tell me how you got on.'

I left Kenya like an ex-convict. The few things I possessed were in a brown paper bag. No one asked to look in it. If they had they would have found two T-shirts, a pair of jeans with a strip missing from one leg, a jar of rose petals, and a packet of brewer's yeast. I wore my wealth the way a gipsy does. But no one noticed and anyway it wasn't mine. Heat shimmered on the runway and the sky was almost white with sunlight.

It was a cool grey April morning. The green of England was balm to tired eyes. It's as if all the muscles round the eye and in the eye itself clench against the glare of the

African sun, and only relax again when the eye sees green. Perhaps, if you are from Africa, it works in reverse: you strain your eyes to peer through the gloom and only relax in the glare. But to me, grey and green were the colours of home.

Even so, I could not count the trip over and done with until I had made the two deliveries, so I did not phone my mother or Tony. I went instead to my room in Notting Hill Gate.

I lit the gas and pulled a sweater out of the chest of drawers. The sweater smelled of lavender – an old-fashioned smell. My shirt smelled of pepper and sweat. I took it off and my skin rose in goose bumps.

Just as when I returned from Ethiopia, I found I couldn't rest. The world seemed to turn under my feet. I did not want to stay in one place, so I moved on.

It was only when I returned from Wolverhampton that I put an end to it by going home to my parents' house in Gerrards Cross. It might have taken longer still, but, stupidly, I fainted in the Euston Road and ended up in the casualty unit at University College Hospital where I was berated soundly by an intern with fair curly hair and official-looking horn-rimmed spectacles.

'Why on earth didn't you go to your GP?' she scolded. 'You're really very foolish to run around with glandular fever, if indeed that's what it is.' She took a blood sample from my arm and started to change the dressing on my shoulder.

I said, 'Doctor, if a man has been so badly beaten up that his head looks like a shapeless lump, and you give him water and he immediately throws up blood, have you harmed him?'

'How much water?' she asked, squinting at the healing wound. 'Half a pint?'

'Much less.' I could see a dribble of Ambo washing the bloody teeth.

'That shouldn't hurt him. Of course if he's beaten up

266

he could be suffering from a ruptured oesophagus. That might cause him to cough blood.'

'And what should you do for him? – supposing there's no medical help?'

'Well, without expert advice there's not much you can do. Of course you would put him in the recovery position. You know what that is, don't you? – One leg bent towards the stomach, head and thorax at a forty-five degree angle towards the earth. You would cover him up and keep him warm and comfortable, and, naturally, you would go immediately for help.'

'But if none of that was done . . . if he was rolled out into the rain . . .'

'You wouldn't do that.' The doctor smiled as she taped the new dressing in place. 'No decent human being, however ignorant, would do that.'

59

It was very quiet at my mother's house. Dad went to work every day. John and Bill had a flat in town and only came home at weekends. From my window I watched the new green leaves unfurl. The tiny rogue violets, which should never be in the lawn but grew there unchecked, peeped out of the grass, and starlings fluttered by with straw stalks in their beaks.

The kitchen smelled of chicken broth and garlic. As I had supposed, Mum approved wholeheartedly of Dr Kekri's advice, and to the high-protein soups and concoctions she made for me she added liberal amounts of garlic.

'It purifies the blood, dear,' she explained, throwing a handful of cloves into the simmering pot. 'And you look as if purification is just what you need.'

'Putrefaction is just what you need.' I mimicked her tone of voice. She cocked an eyebrow at me but made no comment. I was irritable. She was always right and in her house I would always be a child.

I needed her fluffy clean towels, her warm blankets, her soups and potions. I wanted her cool hand and good advice, but she annoyed me. This was her little world and it was strangled by rambling roses, strings of onions, and lost library tickets. Mine was an uglier, more dangerous place which contained ragged little boys with running sores on their faces, pregnant bar-girls, men with bloody teeth, and the sound of gunfire in the night.

She was a reproach to me: she cared for me so completely, and I, the only time I had been tested, had neglected to do what any decent human being would have done. I could not imagine circumstances which would come between her and her humanity. Not even fear. I saw her as a T. E. Lawrence of the humane world. Her moral seemed to be: if it's alive, care for it.

It was more comfortable to be with my father. But because I had been there he insisted on reading out loud the few snippets of news about Ethiopia which appeared in the paper. He thought I would be interested, and you couldn't blame him because I never told him about the incidents I wanted to forget. I was too ashamed.

'Listen to this,' he'd say, rustling the paper and letting his egg go cold. ' "Student unrest returned to Addis following a statement by the Defence Minister that a plot by dissident armed forces had been foiled." '

Or: 'You'll be interested in this, Fay. "Riot police dispersed students demonstrating against the newly formed Government. They were pressing Prime Minister Endelkachew for land reform . . ." Odd, isn't it, there seem to be parallels with the way Mr Heath's government was brought down here. You missed all that, Fay. But I don't suppose you mind.'

Another time he said, ' "In an Addis paper, three members of Parliament claimed that 250,000 people died in the famine in the northern province of Wollo last year. They lay the blame on the former Government." '

'What about the southern provinces of Gemu-Gofa and Sidamo?' I said. 'That's this year.'

'No wonder there's civil unrest,' Dad went on. 'It's easily understood.'

'Not when you're there,' I said. 'You don't understand a single thing and it just looks frightening.'

The past was best forgotten and the present seemed irrelevant.

Dear Rajib [I wrote], I'm not in jail. Tell Mr Dar his delivery was made safely and I paid the money I owed him into his bank. But your aunt, or whoever the lady of the house is, spends all day, everyday, indoors. She is frightened of everything. She cannot speak English.

If she could understand what is going on around her I'm sure she wouldn't be so scared.

Mr Singh's brother is the opposite. He has a finger in every pie and one day soon he's sure to make it in a big way. If you have time, will you visit Mr Singh too? He's a nice man and a very good mechanic. Tell Gita and Shanti that the record they wanted, *Goodbye, Yellow Brick Road*, is on its way. Please give them my love.

'Who's Rajib?' Tony asked, fingering the envelope on the hall table. Tony was back from Edinburgh where he had been overseeing a new production of *Lear*. He thought he could get me a job if the play transferred to London.

We had become engaged in a quiet, unspectacular fashion, and he had bought me a Georgian pearl and coral ring. He was looking for another locket.

'Is he in any of the photographs?' Tony was responsible for the one roll of film being developed.

'No,' I said. 'By the time I got to know him properly I'd lost the camera.'

'How properly?' He smiled. 'Should I be jealous?' He wasn't at all jealous. It was just something he mentioned now and again to make me realize how much he had worried while I was away. The locket's disappearance was the thing he took most hard.

'You gave it to her?' he asked with a puzzled frown as he pored over a picture of Abbavich. It was a close-up, and she was giving me one of her teasing, coquettish looks. 'You weren't even supposed to take it off.'

'She's pregnant,' I explained. 'I was worried about her.'

'How can you worry about her? You didn't even speak the same language. It's her country and she'll manage.'

'You don't just *manage* if you've got a baby and there's no food or a revolution going on.' I spoke sharply: he hadn't been there and he didn't understand.

He changed the subject. 'I wonder where she got that

270

awful scarf,' he mused. 'It looks like hell with the traditional costume.'

'She loved that scarf,' I remembered. 'She gave it to me as a goodbye present. But I lost it.' Graham stole it, I should have said. But I didn't.

'You seem to have lost a lot on that trip of yours,' he said lightly. 'Your mother says you still haven't put enough weight back on, and you're always waking up with nightmares.'

Tony treated my mother like some sort of guru. I think he thought she was the perfect woman and was hoping I would turn out like her. She liked him too. She thought I was in safe hands when I was with him.

He thought I was in safe hands when I was with her, and in spite of the inconvenience of driving out to Buckinghamshire two or three times a week he thought I should give up my room in London permanently.

'You can't really afford it now that you're not working,' he pointed out sensibly. 'And if you do go back to work you could always stay with me. We're going to be together after the summer anyway. Don't you agree, Mrs Jassahn?' He pronounced it 'Jason', of course, and it was odd that nowadays it was this pronunciation that seemed unfamiliar. It's because she's Mrs Jason, but I am Fay Yas*sahn*, I thought. That was the way Rajib had spelled it when he arranged for the ticket.

Mum turned to look at me. Her auburn hair swung across her cheek making her look young and vibrant. 'Yes,' she said. 'It's only till the wedding. I'd like Fay to stay here. She still needs building up.'

That was the night my father went to answer the phone at about nine o'clock and came back with a puzzled frown on his face. He said, 'It's a Mrs Beyer calling from America, Fay. She sounds very drunk and she says . . .'

I leapt to my feet and a teacup spilled on to the coffee table.

'Sit down, Fay,' Tony said. 'If it's nasty, I'll handle it.'

He got up too, and I had to run to get to the phone first. But when I picked up the receiver the line had gone dead.

'She's gone,' I told them when I went back to the drawing-room.

'If it's important she'll ring back.' Dad picked up his cup again and Mum soaked up spilled tea with a cloth. 'Extraordinary woman,' he added. 'Forty dollars, I think she said, "Don't worry about the forty dollars." '

'Must've been a wrong number.' Tony put his arm round me and squeezed reassuringly. But Dad looked at me with a puzzled frown. He expected me to explain, but I didn't want to and after a while, with Mum and Tony talking about the theatre, the moment passed.

60

One Saturday in May Tony and I came back from a walk
in the woods to find Mel having tea in the kitchen with
Mother and the twins.

'You've got a visitor,' Mum said brightly.

'Surprised?' Mel asked, his mouth full of toast and
honey. I was so surprised I dropped the bunch of bluebells
I'd been carrying.

'I looked you up,' he said. 'There aren't that many
Jassahns in the phone book.'

'Christ!' I burst out. 'If you're an Ethiopian you can
live and die without anyone knowing you've existed. But
you can just pick up the phone book, and there we are on
a list.'

'This is Fay's fiancé,' Mum said, hurriedly introducing
Tony.

'G'day.' Mel waved his toast. 'I was just telling your
brothers some of our trials up-country.'

'He said you and he drove down from the border in a
single night,' John said. 'You never told us that.'

'I thought it was an African who stole your luggage,'
Mum put in reproachfully. 'You didn't tell us it was
someone you knew.'

'How did you get here?' I sat down beside Mel. Crushed
bluebells stuck to my shoe.

'Green Line bus,' he said. 'Oh . . . see what you mean.
Took a boat from Mombasa up the coast, changed at
Suez, and on to Marseilles. Easy once you know how.'

'Easier than overland,' I said.

'You're telling me!' It was something we both understood without explanation. I relaxed.

'Tell me one thing,' I asked. 'Did you know Graham
before you met in Moyale?'

'Why? That Pommy bastard given you any more hassle?'

'What "Pommy bastard"?' Tony asked stiffly.

'Nothing personal, mate. I was just telling Fay's old lady about how the bugger jumped us and ripped Fay off in Moyale. She did all right.'

'I didn't do anything,' I said. 'I just gave him the keys.'

'Never stand between the dog and the lamp-post,' Mel snorted. 'You didn't do nothing foolish neither. Did you ever find out what he wanted?'

'Yes . . . no . . . well, sort of.'

'What *is* going on?' Tony looked bewildered. 'Fay, you haven't said a single thing about your holiday except famine and riots.'

'Some holiday!' Mel said airily. 'Dropped you in it, have I?'

'Want a drink?' I suggested. 'The pubs are open.'

'You're not going out now!' Tony protested.

'Suits me,' Mel said, getting to his feet. 'We'll be back for supper.'

'Has he been invited?' Tony asked. Mum shrugged. I could see the twins trying to hide their laughter.

'Of course he's invited,' I said crossly. 'He's a friend of mine.' Mum could always be relied upon to be nice to my friends even if Tony couldn't.

We walked briskly along the leafy lane towards the Saracen's Head.

'I didn't think you liked me,' Mel said. 'How come the invitation?'

'You'd've stayed anyway.' I sighed. 'I'm pleased to see you. I don't have to like you too.'

'The way you dumped me in Nairobi and buggered off without a word, I thought you hated my guts.'

'I thought Graham had left you to spy on me.'

'No kidding! What did he want, anyway?'

'Nastasia's things. I don't know exactly, but he and she were working for a travel firm which I think was a front for couriers taking Asian money out of Kenya.'

274

'No kidding,' he said again, looking genuinely astonished. 'I'd never've thought the bugger had it in him.'

'And I think Nastasia took off with a delivery. Graham said he was sent to get it back. But she died and I ended up with her stuff.'

'But he did take it back.'

'No,' I said, laughter suddenly welling up in my throat. 'What he took was my dirty laundry. Nastasia's things were stashed in the spare petrol tank to avoid a hoo-hah at immigration.'

'So Pom-face winds up with your dirty drawers – ' Mel doubled over with laughter – 'and you got the goodies. Hats off!'

'Don't be an idiot.' I stopped outside the pub door. 'I told you – I don't even know what the goodies were. Someone else must've taken them in Ethiopia. All I had was her personal things. And I sent them back to her family.'

Mel pushed the door open and we went in.

'It's an improvement on those bloody *talla-bites*, I'll say.' He glanced round the comfortable interior.

'But aren't you claustrophobic?' I asked. 'Isn't the sky awfully small in England?'

'Bugger the sky,' he said, and ordered a pint of best bitter. I paid. Mel, as he put it, hadn't quite cracked it yet. At the moment he was washing up in a restaurant in Fulham, which was about the best job he could find at short notice. He had done his best for a social occasion. I could tell by the spots of dried blood on his cheek that he had recently shaved. But his shirt, though clean, was unironed and there were no creases in his trousers. The rhino-hide boots made way for a pair of tennis shoes.

After the second pint I asked him what he really wanted. It wasn't much. He was making the rounds of anyone with whom he had the slightest acquaintance in order to find a better job. He wouldn't turn down a free meal either. I promised to get the twins to ask at the engineering firm they worked for.

After the third pint he explained that he was taking a year off before settling down and going to college.

'Agricultural college,' he told me. 'My dad has some land in Queensland. There's a lot can be done with it. It's mostly cane at the moment.'

'Land use, soil improvement – is that what you'd learn about?' I asked, interested. 'They need people like you in Ethiopia.'

'Bugger Ethiopia,' he said, and ordered another pint.

When his glass was half empty he said, 'How come you're engaged to that piss-brain?'

'He isn't a piss-brain,' I replied, offended. 'He's a designer. He's very talented and very nice.

'Nice! You're reverting to type, Fay. I might've guessed I'd find you shacked up with some po-faced Pom.'

'I'm not shacked up!'

'Only because you're living at home with Mummy.' He paused. 'She's not a bad sort, your old lady, but I thought you'd have a place of your own.'

'I have.'

'Well, why ain't you in it? You showed more spunk in the Black Hole.'

I bought him another pint and a vodka and orange for myself.

'Spunk?' I asked after a while.

'For a sheila,' he said. 'You pulled your weight. Those were a couple of good rides you got us out of the Black Hole. And you gave that Pommy bastard a creaming in Conso.'

'I gave you one too,' I said.

'I mean when the slimy bugger tried to leave me behind.'

'You heard?'

''Course I did. Mrs Poole didn't bring no suckers into the world. He was supposed to smooth-talk you, being a Pom as well. I always thought he'd rat on me so I listened. Never let a rat out of the cage unless you've got a cast iron meat safe, I always say.'

'That's because you think everyone's as shitty as you are.'

'Wasn't wrong, was I?' He showed me his yellow teeth. I grinned back at him. I found the conversation oddly liberating. And that was because I didn't have to be nice to him. He didn't think I was nice. Nice had no value for him. He could not judge me for my failure in Arba Mintch because he had acted the same way. Of course he might not judge it as a failure at all: simply an exercise in self-preservation.

We rolled home for dinner rather the worse for wear. It was not a particularly relaxed meal, because although John and Bill seemed to take Mel with a pinch of salt, Tony obviously did not, and became, as time wore on, more stiff and formal. I was annoyed with him: he was acting, as if for Mel's benefit, like a po-faced Pom.

'Don't ask me to give him a lift back to London,' he said, in the kitchen where I was helping Mum to clear up. 'He's a bloody barbarian and a scrounger. In fact, if he's going to London I think I'll go to Cardiff.'

'He does seem an odd sort of companion for you,' Mum said. She was stacking dishes in the sink and had her back to us. She sensed conflict in the air, and though she hadn't been much offended by Mel, she was prepared to side with Tony as a matter of loyalty.

'Odd!' Tony said, 'I don't know how you put up with him for a minute.'

'It wasn't easy,' I admitted. 'But he's a good driver.'

61

The bedroom window was open a crack allowing the cool
night air to stir the curtains. It smelled of grass and
mushrooms. I sat at the table where years ago I had
revised for my O and A-levels. In front of me was a slim
block of cream-coloured stone with a fossil fish etched
into it. It looked like the delicate remains of a sardine.
'*Leptolepis*,' I said out loud, and realized with a shock that
I had got the word from a book, and since I had never
talked to anyone about it, I didn't know how to pronounce
it.

I scratched the stone with my fingernails. 'Jurassic sediment,' I whispered. As far as practical recognition went,
I didn't know sediment from cement.

'How are you going to find out?' I set my jaw and
caught sight of my reflection in the window – a little doll's
face with its teeth clenched. The trilobite, in its bed of
shale, was on the shelf above my bed: I looked at it too.
It still reminded me of a woodlouse. I thought, it's all
very well for a woodlouse to curl up in a ball and do no
harm, but it's not enough for a human. I turned off the
light and went to bed.

There was kedgeree for breakfast – Mum's Sunday
special. Dad looked at me over the top of the *Observer*
and said, 'Why didn't you tell us how bad things were?
We shouldn't have to find out from a stranger. We could
have helped, you know.'

'Yes,' I said. 'I mean, no.' I set my cup down. They
were both waiting.

'I can't explain,' I said.

'Try.'

'There are some places you shouldn't go to,' I began.

'And there are some things you shouldn't see. Because if you go and see them and you don't help, you're guilty.'

'I don't understand,' Mum said, and I nearly told them about the man who might have been Mr Latybalu. I stopped myself because they are kind people who think well of me and they would have tried to comfort me and make excuses when I knew there were none.

'Do you remember, Mum, once when I was little and we were walking back from the shops one day, and there had been a car crash. There was a fire engine, and an ambulance, and there was blood on the road. I wanted to go and look. But you said then there were some things you shouldn't just look at.'

'That's right,' she said. 'Imagine you remembering that. You couldn't have been older than four at the time. But, darling, it was you I was trying to protect. You were always a sensitive little thing and I didn't want you to have bad dreams.'

'Thank you,' I said sincerely. 'But I'm having bad dreams now.'

'That's because you've been ill.'

'No,' I told them both. 'It's because of what I didn't do.'

Dad folded his paper and put it down beside his plate. 'That wasn't really what I was talking about,' he said. 'I'm talking about you in Nairobi with no money, no clothes, and no ticket home. I'm talking about you mixing with thieves and moneylenders rather than asking your own family for help.'

'I wasn't thinking very clearly,' I said apologetically. 'The only way out seemed to be on my own hands and knees. I thought I had to do everything myself. I didn't mean to reject your help, but in a way I'm glad I did. There are a lot of things I'd've never found out if I'd come straight home.'

Mum poured some more coffee for all of us. 'You're depressed,' she decided suddenly. 'You've quarrelled with Tony. I knew he was upset about your Australian friend.'

I smiled. Mum's instincts about me were rarely ever wrong. Usually I felt I was an open book to her. But not today.

'No,' I said. 'I haven't quarrelled with Tony. Not yet. And, as a matter of fact, I'm not depressed.' This came as a surprise to me. That morning I felt cheerful for the first time in months, and it made me realize how unhappy I had been.

'I think I'd like to go back to school,' I said slowly. 'I want to learn something useful – like the difference between cement and sediment. I'm tired of not understanding things.'

They both looked up sharply. They both had something to say. Maybe Dad was wondering if I was bright enough and maybe Mum had it on the tip of her tongue to ask if it would make any difference to the wedding. But they didn't discuss it. Something had changed.